THE DUST THAT DANCED

THE DUST THAT DANCED

A. CAVUTO

NEW DEGREE PRESS

THE DUST THAT DANCED

ISBN   978-1-63676-727-7   *Paperback*
          978-1-63730-040-4   *Kindle Ebook*
          978-1-63730-142-5   *Ebook*

This is a work of fiction. All the characters, organizations, and events portrayed in this novel are either products of the author's imagination or are used fictitiously.

*To those who see life cinematically, may
you realize what a gift that is.*

SCENE SELECTION

THE ESTABLISHING SHOT   **11**
THE ESTABLISHING SHOT   13

THE WIDE SHOT   **21**
SCENE 1   23
SCENE 2   27
SCENE 3   35
SCENE 4   41
SCENE 5   47
SCENE 6   49
SCENE 7   57
SCENE 8   63
SCENE 9   69
SCENE 10   75
SCENE 11   81

THE MEDIUM SHOT   **87**
SCENE 12   89
SCENE 13   97
SCENE 14   103
SCENE 15   111
SCENE 16   119
SCENE 17   127
SCENE 18   137
SCENE 19   147

SCENE 20   151
SCENE 21   163
SCENE 22   171
SCENE 23   177
SCENE 24   189
SCENE 25   193
SCENE 26   199
SCENE 27   207
SCENE 28   215

THE CLOSE-UP   **219**
SCENE 29   221
SCENE 30   227
SCENE 31   233
SCENE 32   241
SCENE 33   249
SCENE 34   257
SCENE 35   263
SCENE 36   269
SCENE 37   273
SCENE 38   279
SCENE 39   287
SCENE 40   293
SCENE 41   303
SCENE 42   313

THE DELETED SCENES   **321**
THE DELETED SCENES   323
SCENE 43   329
CREDITS   333
DIRECTOR'S STATEMENT   337

"It is a serious thing just to be alive on this fresh morning in the broken world..."

— MARY OLIVER

"...but poetry, beauty, romance, love, these are the things we stay alive for."

— DEAD POETS SOCIETY

THE ESTABLISHING SHOT

THE
ESTABLISHING SHOT

———

I had often wondered if the Minotaur grew lonely inside the Labyrinth. Sentenced to darkness, wandering the maze and awaiting company that couldn't be kept for long, I'd imagine it was something to tire of quickly. How could you remain trapped with yourself for all that time? Not that it had a choice. But do we ever really have a choice?

I've always been fascinated by myths. Their ability to withstand years of the world moving on without them. Their ability to plant a seed of doubt in your mind when you assure yourself they aren't real. Theseus slaying the Minotaur is but one example, and I've often said that the moment I grew up was the moment I realized that these legends don't simply exist in the past, and they don't always keep their distance. Some myths, I've come to learn, stay very close.

And some are, indeed, very real.

Take, for example, our university. A campus so riddled with ghost stories (as is any school with a significant history), it was a wonder fresh faces continued to appear each fall. You hear tales of the ghosts of university priests seen wandering the quad at night, of a campus theater haunted by the musician who was never able to take center stage. The foundations of these anecdotes were laid countless years prior, providing them the necessary time to sink in and solidify within the minds of students past, present, and future.

A relatively new myth, however, appeared to have struck a chord with the student body, ironically, the year I was born. No one knew how or why the rumor started, only that it persisted, and there we were, twenty years later, hearing the story recited with passion on whichever campus tour happened to cross our path. It was always thought to be possible that the source of what became ever so dark (and what truthfully should have been concerning to the average prospective student) was in fact something much less ominous, much more innocent, and that it had become twisted to the point where there was no untangling the knot. It had already rendered itself legend.

Truth be told, I used to think that as well.

But look at me, rattling along about pure speculation when I haven't even shared the story in question.

It was said that our school boasted an intricate pattern of tunnels that ran hidden beneath the campus grounds. It was also said that, during the fall semester of 1972, the first year that women were admitted to our fine university, the body of a female student was found in those tunnels.

Now I, a veteran film major myself, am admittedly a fan of stories.

That is, I'm a fan of fiction. I don't much enjoy when a conflict-ridden tale decides to sprout legs, leap off the page, and remain hellbent on sabotaging my sophomore year of college.

But I digress.

My years studying film taught me that there are many ways to tell a good story. You can provide an audience with the whole picture and allow them to pick and choose what's important to extract greater meaning. You can also narrow the frame, limit their perspective, point them in the right direction, indicating *This! This right here is what you should be looking at! This is the answer! Have I made that clear? This!*

In my (the director) efforts to tell you (the audience) the story of our sophomore fall (we being the protagonists...the leading ladies...with some deserving of more agency than others), I'm going to provide a little bit of everything. I'll start wide, then narrow the scope. I'm curious to see if you can figure it all out before it's time for the close-up. And, rest assured, the answers will all be there.

You just have to know where in the frame to look.

And yes, yes, I know this literary medium of storytelling is better suited to the psychological rather than the visual and *why don't I just write a screenplay?* and all that, but I happen to believe a story such as this one requires both. There is, after all, a great deal of the psychological hidden within the visual, is there not? Perhaps I feel I need to show you just how much. And trust me, this will be fun.

Well, "fun" is a relative term, but believe me, that's exactly how it started for the five of us.

Speaking of the five of us, I think I'll briefly introduce you to the central cast: myself and the girls I befriended during my collegiate years. It was actually somewhat of a miracle that we became friends at all, given how unaligned our paths were at the time, and how much physical distance kept it that way.

If you've attended college, you know how those first few weeks typically unfold. Proximity is your ally when securing a companion to the Dining Hall or your first campus party or your first trip to the library. Residents in the same dorm section cling to each other like a balloon to hair and suddenly that heart-pounding fear of having to navigate the vast grounds on your own is silenced. If you're lucky, these relationships last and you're awarded a *Congratulations! You've met the one(s)!* notification that exists in your head and your head alone. But many times, those microwaveable instant-friendships are left to boil a minute too long, and what could have been a mouth-watering, long-awaited cup of noodles turns to mush.

Moral of the story: cheat meals are hit or miss.

Thankfully, our group of friends took the time to marinate before forging our *unbreakable* bond. (Because it's always that simple, right?)

There's STELLA (19, Film Major, Analytical)—That's me. You've already met me. As for what else I can share, I suppose I've been told I'm observant, that I can read people, their body language, their facial expressions. (This talent pairs particularly well with social anxiety, in case you were wondering, but once you learn to overcome *that*, it actually becomes a very useful tool.)

There's JOSIE (19, English Major, Simple)—She was my sophomore-year roommate. We met about midway through our first fall semester, having run into one another in the dorm bathroom one comfortably crisp Friday night in October. She'd complimented me on my sweater as she washed her hands (she'd apparently had one just like it) and next thing I knew, she dove headfirst into chat without hesitation. Truth be told, I'd welcomed her interrogation and wondered why we hadn't run into each other sooner. She listened to you as if you were the only person of importance, her head nodding quickly anytime your speech faltered, encouraging you to continue. I found it surprising and mildly disappointing that it was my first time meeting her. As it turned out, she didn't actually live there, but was hanging out with some friends before going out for the night. The words leaving her mouth sparked some realization. I watched it flash across her honey-brown eyes.

"You have to come with us!" she'd said, grabbing hold of my shoulders.

When I'd gone to the bathroom that evening, I'd done so with the intention of heading back to my room to read myself to sleep. But something drew me to her proposal. Perhaps it was her confidence, or the way the redness of her hair highlighted the freckles that were splattered across her face (as though someone took a paint brush and ran their finger over the bristles).

Whatever it happened to be, I felt myself nodding eagerly, telling her that I just had to quickly change out of my Jack Russell Terrier–patterned pajama bottoms and into something more fitting for a night out. And almost a year later, there we were, living together.

We also have MEG (19, Music Major, Gentle)—I'd met her first, seeing as she lived down the hall from me. This was an instant-friendship that seemed to work well. After we'd happened to sit next to each other during Mass one evening, we quickly realized how much we simply enjoyed each other's company. She was the type of person who, in everything she did, aimed to make you smile. It helped that her own smile was positively contagious—the way the corners of her eyelids would crinkle shut and her plump cheeks she had yet to outgrow would shift upward.

Affectionately nicknamed "Megara," she was quiet in a serene way, and her status as a skilled violinist meant that the scent of fresh rosin accompanied her everywhere. Finally, MONICA (19, History Major, Chaotic)—Monica was the type of girl who could take over the world if she wanted to. When her hair was a mess and her hands were covered in ink, you knew she was at her best. One would think winning the highly coveted position of editor in chief of the University newspaper as a sophomore would earn you some enemies around campus, but excluding her competitors, relatively all her peers respected the girl who would receive perfect scores on her essays she'd started mere hours before they were due (and mere minutes after she'd returned from whichever off-campus party she'd graced with her presence). Essays which, I might add, she would only craft using her trusty typewriter. Josie had once made the mistake of informing her that the campus had a computer lab, to which she'd replied, "Do I look like someone who needs anything other than a blank sheet of paper?"

Now, if you've mastered mathematics at the first-grade level, you'll notice that there is, in fact, one more of us. I'll get to her, don't worry. Besides, I think you have a pretty clear picture already.

We were simply five soon-to-be twenty-year-olds hoping to excel on our mythology presentation, make dean's list, and occasionally meet in a secret, beautiful, dust-ridden attic library.

We never could have been prepared for what that fall semester had in store for us.

How *could* you be prepared for a dead body being found in the tunnels underneath your school?

It all made me wonder—would we have dug deeper, had we realized we had no one to pull us out? Would we have continued on, had we known that history was preparing to repeat itself?

Would we have entered the Labyrinth, had we known the Minotaur was there, waiting for us?

Alfred Hitchcock once famously said, "The only way to get rid of my fears is to make films about them."

So, in a sense, that's what I'm going to do. For you, and for myself.

As for my other questions, perhaps you can develop your own opinion, as I deliver the details more clearly.

(Cinematically, of course.)

THE WIDE SHOT

SCENE 1

I'll begin with the moment that, to this day, refuses to be forgotten. The first time I saw her.

I made a trip to the campus bookstore the weekend before classes began, which was only about a five-minute walk from my dorm—five minutes that went by slowly when the pathways were flooded with new and returning students rushing this way and that to prepare for the year ahead. There was nothing about the sight that made me think the year was going to be any different from the last. Well, apart from three things:

1. We no longer needed to try and make new friends.
2. We'd be making far fewer calls home to Mom and Dad.
3. Our "Freshman" status would no longer paint a target on our backs.

The invisibility that came with this rise in the academic ranks was something I was, without a doubt, looking forward to. I'd be able to walk to class without feeling like I had a giant "ROOKIE" sign flashing above my head or like at every social gathering, my entrance was announced regally:

Ladies and Gentlemen, The Child has arrived!

These feelings were ones I happily abandoned as I made my way through campus that day, only brought down by one uncomfortable factor. The August heat was no friend to Move-In Weekend.

Actually, let's CUT there. Take Two:

The August heat was no friend to me.

Shots of the typical college students this time of year would illustrate activities including but not limited to stretching out on the quad, grass fresh and soft from the months spent in our absence, music pouring out of open windows, friends reuniting, and parents following closely on the heels of their departing children.

"Mark!" one mom might say. "Mark, honey, look at the church. Stand there so I can take a picture!"

Then there was me, attempting to weave through the chaos as quickly as possible before the beating of the late summer sun could do too much damage. As someone who always has and always will opt for pants no matter the season, it's no secret I'm more partial to the fall and wintertime. There is no worse feeling than a bead of sweat silently trickling through my mud-blond hair and down the nape of my neck. It's a feeling that's significant in its insignificance. A profoundly uncomfortable experience brought on by a tiny source that is often only visible to the eye of a camera.

How ironic, then, that I would soon learn it's often the things you can't see that do the most damage.

But let's return to the more pressing matter, introducing you to the last of our leading ladies. The girl in the bookstore.

Eyes glossed and legs operating almost entirely on memory, I was making my way past the basic utilities area, which stood between me and the alphabetized rows of bookshelves

I'd been aiming for. By the time I noticed the blur of movement, someone stepping out from the aisle ahead of me, it had been too late, and my aforementioned glossed-over eyes were met with a sharp burning sensation as though someone had stuck my head in an incubator full of the kindergarten class chicks.

I jerked back as fireworks danced behind my eyelids and listened to an unfamiliar voice spew out a string of apologies. "I can't believe I did that," "I just wanted to make sure it worked," and "Why won't it turn off?" were the few sentiments I'd managed to process while my mind was preoccupied with blinking rapidly and pulling the lens back into focus. A few slight twists of the ring and the image was clear again.

She had lowered what I then realized had been a flashlight (a large one at that) so that it no longer beamed *directly at my eyes*, but at my stomach. I watched as she finally figured out the correct number of clicks necessary for the Ultra-Mega-Super 500-Watt PowerLight 3000 (self-proclaimed, but you can trust me on this one) to cease its attempts to burn me alive.

She was around my height and wore a silver "D" necklace that gleamed against her skin. A black, oddly shaped bag hung around her shoulder.

"Is it totally cliché to be afraid of the dark these days?" she'd asked me.

I'm not sure why I was so surprised to hear that her voice didn't sound anything like what I'd imagined it would. How could I have possibly imagined what her voice would sound like at all? It was my first time meeting her. But perhaps in the few seconds I'd studied her, the striking raven hair that sliced straight across her shoulders, the hollow cheeks, the brown eyes burdened with questions, perhaps in those few seconds I'd subconsciously decided that her voice would be low and strong, yet detached, closed like her smile after she told me her name.

ALICE (19, Major Not Yet Known, Inquisitive).

But I'd been all wrong. When Alice spoke I heard honey, mildly watered down to flow freely to my ears. And exchanging brief introductions only allowed me to notice her finger tapping the side of her leg, or the way she'd repeatedly move her hair behind her ear before pulling it forward again. It only offered me one useful piece of information: she was new.

Then the camera stopped rolling and we each moved on with our days.

I'd see her many times before we would eventually become friends. In fact, once I became aware of her existence, it was as if I couldn't *not* see her. She was everywhere. Even though it was a big school, it wasn't *that* big, and people talk when there's a new face in town. Flying under the radar, it appeared, was simply not in Alice the Transfer Student's future. And as much as I'd hoped leaving behind that "freshman" title would guarantee anonymity, it wasn't in mine, either.

It wasn't in any of our futures.

SCENE 2

———

We were running late.

And by "late," I mean we were thirty-five minutes early.

"If we don't get there at least half an hour beforehand, we'll be in the back and I won't be able to see," said Meg, who was struggling to find her second loafer.

"You know, there's a reason you bought glasses, Meg," said Josie.

"Yes, but they give me headaches."

"Squinting *also* gives you headaches."

Finally locating her shoe's twin, Meg hopped around on one leg, her left arm flailing in the direction of her desk in an attempt to steady herself.

She was famously known for needing glasses but never wearing them, claiming they gave her "headaches." I'd noticed, however, the way she'd pause in the mirror when she wore them, a disappointed scrunch of her nose followed by her decision to take them off. I always thought they looked nice on her, the circular, brown-wire frames drawing wonderful attention to her light green eyes. On one occasion, I remember her mentioning that they were "too round" for her face, which was "already too round," and therefore she didn't find them flattering. As a result, she would subject herself to fuzzy vision and the panic-ridden need to arrive at all events absurdly early, such as the Opening Mass we were headed to that morning.

We had met at Meg and Monica's room before heading to the section stairwell, the clicks of our short Mary Jane heels echoing with each step.

Lucky for Meg, we were early to the event and able to grab seats close to the altar, only about five pews back. Other students slowly filled in the space around us, while faculty settled into their reserved seats in the rows ahead of ours. The echoing chorus of murmurs was relaxing, floating through the air as if stirring the campus awake out of a long nap.

While it was only my second time attending an Opening Mass, it had already begun to feel ritualistic, a privilege of sorts as if to indicate that you were home, you were wanted, you were meant to be there. I guess there were many facets of the school that reeked of tradition and exclusivity, and, truth be told, some of them were comforting. But I shouldn't be the first to tell you that the term "exclusivity" all but shoves another word aggressively in your face.

Secrets.

The Basilica definitely looked like a secretive place. Who knew what could have been going on when mass wasn't being held? *Probably nothing,* is what any reasonable person would assume, but another fabulous lesson you learn with age is that there are many things you'll come across in life that defy all preconceived notions of reason, especially when it comes to that which has been around for a very long time.

I'll add, however, that the place of worship wasn't actually the oldest building on campus. That honor belonged to the Main Hall, the first piece of architecture to grace the grounds all those years ago, and it was located directly next to the Basilica. Functioning as your standard administrative building, it was home to the offices of those who mattered, and while students could be found meandering in and out each day, and even taking certain classes inside, there was only one part of the building, of the entire campus, really, that was off limits.

You see, along with the myths and ghost stories that had become engrained in the image of the school, there were also superstitions, one of which was that using the back entrance to the Main Hall would guarantee that you wouldn't graduate after four hard years of work.

Silly, right? I mean, who would prefer to travel all the way around to the back of the building when you could just go in the front?

But the legend stuck, and students avoided that side of the building like they did the sweaty, fever-ridden kid who shows up to their final exam despite having come down with the flu.

The continuous hum of voices that vibrated along the wooden benches we sat on had practically lulled me to sleep on so early a morning, but I was snapped out of my daze when our conversation shifted from mundane back-to-school gossip to an interesting wager.

"So, how much do we want to bet his speech is word-for-word the same as last year's?" Monica asked.

The speech in reference was President Gallagher's opening address that he delivered prior to the service.

"Ooh, tough call" I said. "Can we define 'word-for-word'?"

"Eighty percent?"

Josie jumped in. "Eighty percent of what, exactly? Word choice? Themes?"

"Themes are implied since the speech serves the same purpose. I think key phrases and word choice are the way to go."

Meg leaned over from her seat on the far left. "How about key phrases and word choice, as well as same opening and closing remarks."

"That sounds like eighty percent to me," Monica said.

"Lovely. We all agree, 'word-for-word' has been defined. Now, who's— *Oh my God.*"

We all turned toward Josie, who was looking over her shoulder, eyes frozen wide like a deer in the headlights.

"What?" Monica looked around. "Who is it?"

Josie sank lower into her seat, peering briefly toward the back of the room again and then quickly ducking down. I knew who it was before she told us.

Josie's freshman year boyfriend (now ex), SCOTTIE (20, Finance Major, Delicate Subject), was making his way up the center aisle toward the pew across from ours. It appeared his older brother had saved him a seat.

Josie and Scottie Morgan had become an item fairly early on in the year, and we'd all thought they were going to make it. He was the "eats lunch with your friends" type of boyfriend who, no matter how hard we tried, we couldn't seem to find a bad thing to say about. Josie didn't tell us why they broke up, only that it happened around a month before the start of the semester when she'd gone on vacation with their family and that she "couldn't wait to be free again." Not that she'd ever complained about being tied down, but I supposed everyone worked through those things differently.

"Oh my God, oh my God," she whispered, eyes glued to the altar.

Meg's eyes widened when she realized who we were looking at. "Oh my God!"

Unfortunately, *her* exclamation came out louder than was probably intended. A professor seated ahead of us turned around abruptly to glare at her, and she muttered a soft apology only to find the three of us grinning. Monica, who I had always been convinced was the doppelgänger to one Anna Karina, mouthed playfully, *In church, Meg?* And despite her acknowledgment of the joke, I could feel the heat prickling against poor Megara's rosy cheeks for her.

With a few minutes remaining before the opening address, I let my eyes wander around the building, inspecting the faces that fell under my gaze. There was Mary O'Sullivan, the girl I sat next to in my freshman seminar, who casually informed me of the existence of her family's private plane that would be taking them to the Caribbean for their winter vacation amidst a rant about how much studying she had to get done *prior* to boarding said private plane. There was also Anthony With the Bowl Cut from Intermediate Spanish, whom I'd overheard whispering to Kevin With the Frosted Tips that the girl who sat across the room wasn't "hot enough to offer to hold her drink at a party." (And he didn't even say it in *Spanish*.)

I was about to return my attention to the front of the room when I heard, above the gradual dimming of voices, the tapping of footsteps against the floor, growing louder. I listened closer.

SHOT: the profile of heels as they make their way past rows of students' casual footwear.

They didn't slow. The steps remained steady, confident, traveling past latecomers. Past open seats. Past us. All the way to the second row.

She appeared to be young, likely in her late thirties or early forties, with Hitchcock Blonde hair that wrapped around one shoulder and waved along the length of her arm. After she sat down and the professor to her left whispered something in her ear, she turned, granting me a better look at the sharp features of her face—her protruding cheek bones, her straight nose. She wore an expression blank as an empty sheet of paper. When music filled the air, the hushing of all voices was just as audible. The spotlight on her faded. The Hitchcockian Glow was interrupted. The narrative resumed.

I did my absolute best to remain engaged. Ironically enough, my desperate attempt to pay attention occupied my mind more than that which I had tried to focus on. When the service concluded, I was informed by Monica that the word-for-word standard of eighty percent similarity had in fact been met. We'd both picked the winning side. (Our individual prizes would be a small sum of cash and one activity of our choosing for which attendance was mandatory. Monica had already decided on dragging us to an open lecture on Medicine in Antiquity.)

We shuffled out of the building, met with the muggy August morning and the bright haze that accompanied the sudden burst of sunlight.

Weaving through the intermingling crowd of students and faculty proved difficult, but when we finally made it through the worst of it, I turned to Josie and held my hand out with a grin.

"Pay up."

But when she draped her arm over my shoulder, I saw the woman again, not far from us, under the shade of a tree. She was approached by Sister Catherine, one of the oldest nuns at the school and a campus gem who would often reintroduce herself every time she saw you. (Yet, her enthusiasm for meeting you in that moment never dimmed.)

She smiled, lovely as ever as she gingerly extended a shaking hand toward the tall, unidentified faculty member, and asked, "Rebecca?" to which she replied, "No, I'm sorry. I'm Madeleine Shaw. The new classics professor." She accepted her hand delicately.

PROFESSOR SHAW (40s, Classics, Mystifying).

She looked like a Madeleine.

SCENE 3

——

I suppose one area in which the old black and white films fell short was the ability to deliver a compelling sunrise.

In the earlier hours of the morning when I was no longer capable of sleeping, I'd often make my way across campus to the lake, where a solitary bench sat comfortably between twin trees.

I wasn't usually the only soul up and about at that hour. Every so often during the visits I paid to the sunrise, I'd hear the rhythmic compression of rubber into concrete as joggers pursued their early doses of endorphins, or feel my hair shift as a passing biker sought the same.

That Tuesday morning, the first day of classes, I was alone.

It took minutes for the light to glide over the water and reach land, even longer for it to timidly inch toward my toes. It felt like an eternity, the time it spent approaching me, until finally the sun's gentle pinks and oranges dared to meet my face, submerging me in a warm bath of silence.

Quick SHOT-REVERSE-SHOT between me and the rising sun.

The sight of a duck persisting toward the shallow edge of the lake occupied my attention until a hand brushed past my ear and presented a small, paper cup of coffee.

"For you," said the gravelly voice to which the hand belonged.

I accepted the offering. CLAY (20, English Major, Harmless) crossed in front of me to join me on the bench. A brief, cold moment in his shadow.

"I was the first one in line again," he said. "I've become a familiar face to Eleanor. She remembered my name even after a whole summer apart."

"Eleanor?"

"Yes, Eleanor. The lovely old woman who checks everyone into the Dining Hall. We're friends now."

"Are you really?"

"Oh yeah." Clay blew on his coffee. "I believe you're up to owing me roughly fourteen cups at this point?"

"I'll pay you back," I said.

"I'm sure you will." He grinned and elbowed me. (Lightly, so I didn't spill my drink.)

Clay Calloway and I had met in our freshman science course, a topical elective detailing the ins and outs and origins of various diseases. I found it fascinating. Clay, on the other hand, was rather squeamish, as I quickly learned, and also suffered from undiagnosed anxious tendencies of the health variety. I struggled to watch as each new case study sent him into a fit of heavy breathing and pencil tapping, muttering his belief that he had developed or would soon develop whatever affliction we'd be studying that week. Whether he'd signed up for the course in an attempt to face his fears, or he simply lacked any other options to fulfill his science requirement, my expert advice would have been that he not take it, if only so that he could sleep soundly at night. I did feel a little selfish, however, for being grateful that he did.

Because that lanky, dark-haired boy with round glasses that slid down his nose too easily, that poster child for hypochondria, would eventually become one of my best friends. The kind of best friend I decided was worthy of hearing information no one else knew.

He'd become aware of my frequent trips to the lake early last spring when he'd made the decision to develop a workout regimen consisting of early morning walks and the occasional jog. One morning, he passed by and took it as an opportunity for a well-deserved break from his light aerobic activity. He eventually gave up on his fitness goals entirely, deciding that he would no longer run (walk) in the mornings, but he would bring me coffee every so often and offer some company.

"What class do you have first?" I asked. I winced as the liquid wake-up call scalded my tongue.

"Narrative in Fiction. How about you?"

Clay was an English major, as was his father and *his* father. Despite the obvious familial pattern, he was passionate about stories all on his own. I think that's why we'd always gotten along so easily; we both believed that those who possessed that love, within any medium, maintained a different view of the world. Having that in common with someone was a simple, yet impactful, luxury.

"Critical Film Theory. The professor is supposedly tough."

"You love those types of professors, though."

I did. They pushed me, and that's when I excelled the most.

"How are Jamie and Leo? Sick of them yet?" I asked.

Clay's triple was made up of three of the most interestingly different people I'd ever met. Clay was without a doubt the most academically driven (but otherwise incredibly unmotivated), JAMIE (19, Accounting Major, Organized) and his Type-A nature compensated for Clay's laziness, but he often fell behind on classwork, and LEO (19, Marketing Major, Wild Card) was lacking in both areas (although he did find success among the lovely women at our school, likely because he resembled what a child of either River Phoenix or Johnny Depp may have looked like). The three of them together were, without a doubt, a sight to behold.

"I still find them tolerable, although Jamie did already ask me to make my bed this morning."

"How thoughtless of him."

"What's the point of making a bed if you're just going to unmake it later?"

"Sorry, I don't go near the philosophical before seven in the morning."

He made a face. One that said, *Very funny*. He then looked out at the lake.

The duck I'd been watching had made it ashore sometime in the twenty minutes we'd sat there, and was now waddling around the bank, inspecting the ground, likely for any semblance of sustenance.

"How are the girls?" Clay asked. The question was entirely transparent, as was the way he avoided my gaze by studying the water in front of us. I played along for his sake.

"Motivated as ever. Monica holds her first staff meeting for the newspaper later this week, so she's busy preparing her 'I'm in charge now' speech. Living with Josie has been fun so far, but she did keep me up last night questioning me about who she should pursue first as a newly single woman. And Meg," I said finally, taking note of how he tried to mask the fact that he was now invested. He studied his coffee as though he saw a gnat floating around the rim. I grinned. "Meg is aiming for second chair this semester. She's trying not to get her hopes up, since she's only a sophomore, but—"

"Yeah, but this is Meg we're talking about. She has it in the bag."

"You think so?" I smiled. It was clear to anyone, except maybe Meg herself, that Clay had developed a classic schoolboy crush. I still remember the night I first introduced them the previous spring, when I invited Clay to come along with us to a party. Introverted as he was, Clay usually held up relatively well socializing in small numbers.

Watching him meet Meg, however, truly was painful. He'd spent the entire evening attempting to steer clear of her while simultaneously remaining near her, and any time she tried to start up a conversation it looked like he was concentrating on something far more fascinating that he'd noticed across the room. "I don't think he likes me very much," she'd mentioned one time when he came up in conversation. "She's really pretty," was all he managed to say when I asked what he thought of her after that evening. Any time I broached the subject of his feelings for her, he'd initiate what I'd determined to be his tell. I found that, whenever he lied, he would remove his glasses, inspect the lenses, then wipe them with a cloth and return them to their original position. It was a clever stall, really, but not one that slipped past me, unfortunately for him.

I enjoyed watching him secretly pine over her, and I found it difficult to restrain myself from meddling in the situation. Clay was wonderful and would've been great for Meg, who was just as wonderful. They had a lot in common, like the fact that both their dads were alumni. And Clay thought the world of her, even when she didn't think so herself. (Meg, who was top of her class in high school, occasionally felt her decision to study music would make others see her as academically inferior, but Clay recognized each and every one of her strengths, and often made sure she knew it.) Yet, despite all these reasons why I thought they should be together, I'd decided I'd rather let things play out as they were meant to be. So, I always went along with what he perceived to be sly approaches to talking about her. It was the least I could do.

When voices began to waft toward us from up the hill, we made our way back to the center of campus.

Walking along the bend that led past Clay's dorm and toward a row of academic buildings, I couldn't help but notice a girl a hundred or so feet away, her dark hair being picked up left and right by the soft winds that blew around her.

Now, zoom in. A little closer. There.

It was Alice. She walked slowly alongside the buildings, glancing up every so often and studying the walls, the windows. Eventually, she'd move on, slowing down when she reached the next one.

She came to the Dining Hall, pausing and looking up again, but this time, she didn't turn away. Instead, she reached into that oddly shaped black bag she wore around her shoulder, removed a Polaroid camera, and took a picture.

Now, let's pull back out.

Our paths diverged when we reached the home of the English Department, but Clay stopped before he went inside. "By the way, I may need to consult your expertise this semester. A junior said the syllabus for my Narrative class had a unit on films."

"Really? Did he say which ones?"

"He mentioned, *Rear Window.* That's up your alley, isn't it?"

I laughed and turned, calling back over my shoulder, "You could say that."

SCENE 4

——

"I mean, seriously, how many times do you get to take a class on murder?"

"I'd guess about every semester it's offered. Which is all of them."

"You know what I mean."

We'd barely arrived at our meeting spot outside the building when Monica jumped in to gush about her new history elective. Even the most superficial of character studies would tell you that history was the only subject she could possibly pursue, as it allowed her to learn about practically anything. Monica had maintained a vested interest in everything from ancient Greece to the nuclear revolution to, yes, all historical applications of murder from a young age, so if you were ever in need of a fun fact (or your standard seventy-five-minute lecture) about nearly any topic, she was your leading lady.

"You can think about it as the history of murder," she said. "Covering everything from the different systems of law across the Atlantic Empires, to manslaughter, to infanticide." She said that last one with a particular display of enthusiasm.

"I'm sorry, infanticide?" Josie looked at her with a grimace.

"Oh yeah. Super popular in England actually—*early modern* England, that is. Standard reasons—overpopulation, financial hardship, reputation. There was this story on the syllabus about a man killing his young nephews for their inheritance, *Snow White* style. You know? Send them into the woods with a hitman—"

"Okay," said Meg. "That's enough for me."

We turned into the stairwell, heading for the top floor. The third floor. (It was an old building.) It was the first class we were going to be taking together, a foundational mythology course within the Classics Department that, surprisingly, let four nonmajors join. I assumed that they had extra seats free up when it was announced that the long-time professor of the course, who'd been there for nearly forty years, finally retired. It was likely that some didn't want to take a chance on whoever was going to attempt to fill his shoes. The name of the new instructor hadn't been released, but I had a sneaking suspicion as to who it might have been. (Or maybe hindsight really is twenty-twenty.)

Three flights and a couple more murder-related factoids later, we'd reached the room. The *only* room.

It turned out that the entire third floor only housed one lecture hall. And it was gorgeous.

The mahogany-paneled walls reflected the light pouring in through tall, narrow windows. Our shadows floated across them. Rows of long wooden tables cut across navy carpeting, candle-decorated chandeliers (unlit, unfortunately) hung above the seats. I couldn't imagine being able to fill the multiple chalkboards that spanned the length of the front wall, and their pristine condition told me others hadn't, either.

Despite having shown up a full ten minutes early, the first few rows were already taken, and we had no choice but to travel further back. I flashed an apologetic smile to Meg, who sighed, and reluctantly reached into her backpack for her glasses.

We used the remaining minutes before class started to continue filling each other in on the electives we'd already had.

"The first unit in my Narrative class is on the marriage plot. Guess what book is listed at the top of the syllabus." Josie pulled out her notepad with a grin.

"Something by Austen," I said, venturing.

Her eyes lit up as she nodded. "*Persuasion*. I could write this paper tomorrow."

"Did you say narrative, as in Narrative in Fiction?" I asked. "Is Clay in your section?"

"I honestly couldn't tell you," she said, lining up her pencils. "I don't remember seeing him."

She continued on about how her professor was Australian and attempted to mimic his pronunciation of *fabula* and *syuzhet* from when he went over the Sherlock unit. With only three minutes left before class was set to begin, the professor hadn't yet arrived, and the procession of students entering the classroom was dwindling.

I'd also been happy with my first classes from the day before. My film professor wasted no time in diving right into the material, beginning with a lecture on technological reproducibility and the inherent inauthenticity of film. Five students were cold-called within the first thirty minutes, and only two of them had done the assigned reading. A sobering start to the semester.

My Adolescent Psychology class proved interesting, Dr. Howard likely shooting for forward-thinking when she asked each of us to share what we thought was a defining, potentially traumatic, event from each of our childhoods along with our names, class years, and hometowns. I quickly realized that course would either turn out to be highly unproductive or the mirror image of intensive group therapy.

I was looking forward to taking the mythology class with my friends, despite the fact that all our knowledge on the subject was rooted in nothing more than independent reading.

The murmuring that filled the room quickly dissipated, and all eyes shot toward the door as it was pulled closed, the noise echoing against the silence. Her back was turned to us, but I instantly recognized the Hitchcock Blonde I'd seen earlier that week, now donning a black pencil dress that fell just below her knee.

TRACKING SHOT: she strides toward the front of the room the same way she did in the Basilica.

After she passed our row, Monica turned to me, her eyebrows raised. *Damn*, she mouthed.

Professor Madeleine Shaw. (Did you see that one coming as well?)

She stood at the podium and surveyed the room.

"This will be more than your average foundational course," she said. "Regardless of what the class description implies."

There were a few murmurs, a few sideways glances.

"Yes, we will cover many myths. Some more well-known, others more obscure. But you will not just be required to know the material." She leaned on the podium. "You will be challenged to think about the implications, especially the contemporary ones, of such texts. Are these just stories? Or are they indicative of something more?"

Her eyes swept over the students. Though they passed over me only briefly, I felt myself sit up straighter. She began to move around the room, taking more detailed notes of each of our faces. She was a lioness, pacing back and forth, already well aware she had her prey cornered and defenseless.

"You will app—" the lioness stopped, her gaze frozen on one unlucky gazelle.

She stood there, unwavering, as I tried to read the expression on her face. Recognition? Surprise?

Fear?

After a few seconds passed, I peered over to try and see just what it was that had her so visibly flustered. Low and behold, I caught a glimpse of short, raven hair a row or two ahead on the left side of the room, the girl beneath it staring back at her.

There was a beat. Someone coughed.

Professor Shaw snapped awake, recognizing the confusion that had set in around the room, and blinked, trying to relocate her train of thought.

"You will apply this way of thinking to a final group project," she said, though less self-assured than before. The pace of her delivery increased. "Groups of five. Your myth of choice is due to me by the end of midterms, but you must have the names of the members in your group on the podium before class on Monday."

The four of us looked at each other, nodding. We still needed one more.

"The point is to think critically about these myths, apply them to the world around you. We speak of heroes and their roles within society often. But I think that we as humans have this innate instinct to be drawn toward, or rather, fascinated by, the monsters we meet every day."

Monica leaned in and looked at Meg, shooting her a wink.

I smiled at the sight, but my eyes were slowly drawn back to Alice, who looked down at her desk, evidently perplexed.

(I assumed from her stare-down with our new professor.) Whether or not she could actually feel me staring, she turned to look back at me, and that same closed smile appeared on her face. Walking with Clay wasn't the first time I'd noticed her after our initial encounter, but this was, as far as I knew, the first time she had seen me again. Looking at her, I couldn't help but feel like something was missing. A light in her eyes, perhaps. One that used to be there, but had since been dimmed to a subtle, empty glow.

Professor Shaw's voice continues off-screen, in voice-over.

"And most of these monsters are those we don't recognize for who they really are."

SCENE 5

———

I'd now like to recall, if only briefly, one moment that took place only two mornings later.

I was on my way to grab breakfast with an acquaintance from my Critical Film Theory class. We had been assigned to lead a class discussion the next week on psychoanalysis in cinema, Metz and all that, and discussing over food seemed like the most productive option.

We ran into each other down the quad from the building, and walked the rest of the way together, shooting ideas back and forth to get warmed up.

"We could start with Lacan? And the Mirror Phase?" she asked, dragging her feet subtly with each step.

"We could," I said. "Do you think we could tie in Mulvey, too?"

She shook her head. "Mulvey is reserved for the next pair. We're just supposed to focus on *The Imaginary Signifier.*"

I was about to suggest comparing cinema to a one-way mirror rather than simply a mirror when I saw Alice turn around the corner of the Dining Hall and walk up the steps.

She looked to be in a hurry, her head bowed low, and even though she hadn't been that far ahead of us, the speed with which she ran inside made it seem like she was never there in the first place.

I had to apologize to my classmate, who was confused by my sudden silence.

When we opened the doors and went inside, I expected to find her on the other end, waiting to be checked in like the rest of the students in line. But she was nowhere to be found. I looked up and down the hall that functioned as a lobby. I glanced around at the different food stations while I searched for my own meal. I even eyed the various tables I passed on my way to sit down.

It was as if Alice had simply disappeared.

I tried not to let the odd occurrence distract me from our work as we ate there that morning, and each time I remembered the incident that day, I told myself that nothing strange had taken place. I told myself that I would see her again, soon. And as it turned out, I would.

Later that night, to be precise.

SCENE 6

———

The thick stench of sour beer and body odor that floated out onto the porch was enough to make me regret letting Josie drag me to Charlie Morgan's house party that Friday night.

I had been all set to microwave some popcorn and watch *Shadow of a Doubt* again, but my roommate didn't seem to see the merit. "It's the first big night out of the semester," and "What if the love of your life is there and you'd never meet him?" and "You *know* once work picks up you're never going to go out," were among the many pleas that didn't manage to sway me. I only relented when she stopped applying her makeup and looked directly at me, her voice dropping to a sincere tone, "I just really wanted to have fun with my girls tonight." Yet, there we were, forging ahead through the threshold and into the dark pit of humidity, blood, sweat, and tears, when she turned around and yelled, "I'm going to go find Robby!"

And with that, I leapt headfirst into the abyss and welcomed certain death.

I'd often too harshly exaggerated my distaste for the college party scene. But can you blame me? They were fickle things, house parties. You might have gotten lucky and

witnessed the shy boy from your medieval lit class performing karaoke atop a less-than-sturdy side table, serenading the
nearest lucky lady with a mesmerizing rendition of Boyz II
Men's "I'll Make Love To You." And ideally, she'd sing right
back to him in a moment of glorious, authentic connection,
interrupted only by the sound of wood splitting as the boy
did, in fact, break his makeshift stage and come crashing
down, right into her open arms. Unfortunately, more often
than not you'd find yourself being shoved this way and that
as you tried to squeeze through the mass of six-foot-two
bodies, the damp backs of their shirts making more contact
with your arms and face than was preferable. And if you
were really in for a rough night, you'd try to escape to the
periphery, only to be bumped into the wall, cursed with the
phantom presence of an unidentifiable sticky substance on
your arm for the following hours. There was a time I could
ignore all these pitfalls, but it was a time that had been long
gone once I reached my sophomore year.

With Josie, our main connection to the party, quickly disappearing into the crowd at her ex-boyfriend's older brother's
house in search of another boy, the night was already off to
a rocky start. I felt a tap on my shoulder. Clay leaned in and
pointed to the far side of the room.

"Drinks."

I nodded and grabbed Meg, pulling her behind me as I
followed him and his roommates. We lost Monica when a
girl I didn't recognize hooked her with an invisible fishing
rod and reeled her in across the room, and what started as
a lively conversation between Meg, Clay, and me eventually
turned into the two of them speaking at a very close distance, leaning toward each other's ears and then away to
laugh loudly. I surveyed the room for any signs of a familiar

face, and despite having no luck, I figured that venturing in search of someone would be better than watching Clay and Meg fall in love without the courage to do anything about it. I made my way through the crowd, careful to avoid spilling my drink or bumping into anyone. It was one of my more adventurous moments, journeying deeper into the belly of the beast, the cigarette smoke finding its way into my lungs despite my best efforts to hold my breath. A tall drink of club soda (bland and altogether unenjoyable) approached me from the left, and, upon noticing my obvious discomfort, proceeded to blow a hefty cloud in my face. When he followed up by offering me what was left of the substance, I accepted it graciously before swiftly submerging it in his drink.

But now for the interesting part.

I'd made it halfway to the kitchen when I saw Alice in conversation with Ron Davis, whom I'd not-so-affectionately nicknamed "Scottie" (not to be confused with *Josie's* Scottie) for his *Vertigo* Complex (after word spread that he practically forced his ex-girlfriend Angela Myers to dye her hair platinum blonde). Poor Alice looked cornered, glancing around every few seconds and straining to lean backward when he bent down to yell something in her ear. For a brief moment we made eye contact, and whether or not I imagined the pleading in her eyes for some form of intervention, I found myself striding toward her with a sense of purpose and inebriation.

Putting on my most convincing smile, I reached out and hugged her. "Alice! I'm so sorry," I said, acknowledging the lurker. "I need to borrow her real quick."

Without waiting for a response, I dragged her toward the kitchen, then out onto the back porch.

For a moment I worried that my reading of the situation had been wrong. Maybe I'd taken this girl away from a conversation that she'd actually been enjoying. And for that matter, maybe she didn't even *recognize* me. Sure, she had smiled at me in class, but that may have simply been a polite gesture, one to ease my mind after having been caught staring. It suddenly occurred to me that my awareness of Alice's existence could very well have been entirely one-sided, and that I would have to confront that just momentarily because of my impulse decision that relied solely on the possibility that I knew what was going on in her head. That talking to Ron "Scottie" Davis was less thrilling than it was claustrophobic, and that she had been experiencing that all too familiar feeling of being trapped, but too afraid to yell "cut." It was always a nauseating prospect, bowing out of the narrative. Leaving it in his control alone.

Or maybe I actually brought her out to the porch because she had piqued my interest. Because she had made Professor Shaw's stony facade crack momentarily, and because she would wander aimlessly. Because she always appeared to be in search of something, yet she never knew exactly what. I'd be lying if I said I wasn't curious about her.

My thoughts ran wild for the duration of our journey, only silenced by the fresh air that chilled my skin as we finally made it outside.

There it was. The moment of truth.

"Thank you, *Stella*," Alice said, emphasizing that she remembered my name.

I let out a sigh of relief. (And tried my best to hide it.) "*You* are welcome."

I squinted beneath the fluorescent lights, the one drink (yes, one) I'd downed inside numbing me to the mosquitoes that tickled my neck. It was uncomfortably quiet for a moment.

"So, you're a classics major," I said, scrambling.

She raised an eyebrow. "Actually no, I'm not."

Shoot. "You're not?"

She shook her head. "Just interested in the subject. I'm studying architecture."

ALICE (19, *Architecture Major*, Inquisitive).

"Oh, I just figured since you're in our class..."

"So, you're a classics major, then?" She leaned against the porch railing.

The logic had caught up to me too late, unfortunately. "Nope. Just interested in the subject. Film." I gestured to myself with my thumbs.

Her eyes widened for a moment. Just a flash. Then it was gone. Anyone else would have missed it, but the *camera* would not.

"Why did you choose architecture?" I leaned on the railing, too, mimicking her movement. Her mouth smiled even when her eyes didn't, just like in class. "I guess because it was the most interdisciplinary thing I could find, you know?"

I nodded, though I didn't actually "know."

It appeared she could sense that.

She continued. "It's art and drawing, which I love. But it's also math and history. It makes it so that I don't have to be confined to just one subject."

That, I realized, I did actually get. "Funny enough, that's why I love film. You get to study so many different topics, but through that consistent...lens." I cringed. The pun had left my mouth before I had time to realize what I was saying. I was grateful when she laughed.

"Yeah, that's a good point," she said. "It actually sounds similar to this project we have, right? Studying the myths within a contemporary context?"

I don't remember what my exact thought process was in the moments that followed. But it was somehow both chilly and humid out, and as I mentioned, I was unreasonably tipsy off of a singular drink, so when I heard the word "project," it was like an alarm bell went off in my head. What better way, after all, to figure someone out, than by forcing them to spend time with you?

I blurted the question out impulsively. "Do you want to be in our group?"

She was taken aback, and in the moments before her response, my mind reminded me of all the possible reasons why I shouldn't have done that. Such as:

1. She already had a group.
2. I answered her question with a question.
3. She simply had no des—

"Yes, I would love to," she said.

Oh. Then. Perfect.

"You would?" I asked, just to be sure.

"Yeah, I mean, I don't know anyone else in the class."

"Great!" I exclaimed, wrapping her in a tight hug.

It appeared *boundaries* were not my strong suit that evening.

Before I had time to let my lack of regard for personal space really marinate, we were approached by none other than the host of the party, CHARLIE (22, Finance Major, Golden Boy). Straight-A student, model for the admissions pamphlet, nice person (at least superficially). These were the things that made Charlie Morgan the kid that everyone knew at a school this big.

That and the fact that his family name was on almost half of the buildings on campus. (But it was the *other* stuff that really sealed the deal, I'm sure.)

He strode over to the two of us, an extra red solo cup in hand.

"Ladies," he greeted. Turning to me, he said, "You look like you're in need of this." He handed me the cup.

Ouch. "Oh, thanks," I said, raising the cup to my nose and sniffing it.

He was about to say something else when Clay came over. "Stella, there you are," he said. "You're needed inside."

Clay glanced at Charlie twice, as though he just noticed he was there. An uncomfortable half smile on his face, Clay signaled a "hello" with a quick nod. He was always awkward around guys he didn't know well.

"What's up, Clay," Charlie said, glancing around as though he'd suddenly lost interest.

Clay nearly stepped back, winded, as though Charlie had punched him. As though he'd insulted his favorite tweed blazer. (Yes, Clay wore blazers every day, even to house parties. Did I forget to mention that?)

Clearing his throat, he turned back to me. "Josie needs you."

"Josie?"

"Yeah, she said it was urgent, so I came to find you." He reached out, offering to take my drink.

"Huh, I can't imagine why. Did she lose track of Robby already?"

"You're snippy when you're drunk," he teased, forcibly removing the cup from my hand this time.

I sighed with an exaggerated frown. "I *know.*"

I shrugged and said my goodbyes to Alice before turning and making my way inside. I located Josie quickly, as she was just in the kitchen, looking rather occupied in Robby's arms. Still, it seemed safe to approach, so I tapped her on the shoulder.

She turned toward me, her expression blank, if not mildly annoyed. "What?"

Before I could answer, blue and red lights flashed through the window, followed by the sound of sirens.

SCENE 7

—

I'd mentioned our university was one steeped in tradition, like the Opening Mass service, or the fact that the first snowfall of every year was celebrated with a school-wide snowball fight. But we had other, less *school-sanctioned* traditions that somehow took place repeatedly without fail.

Such as how, every Monday of the second week of the fall semester, a male student ran across the Main Quad wearing nothing but a ski mask. To preserve his identity, as one might.

It had become so popular that students would actually line up on either side of the route that remained identical year in and year out. And as we walked to class that morning, we could already see the crowd of people forming near the Main Hall, restless with anticipation.

(Don't worry, I won't keep the cameras rolling during this one.)

How these students got away with it was beyond me, along with many other details of the operation. The long list of questions I'd asked myself had included but not been limited to: How long was their route, and where did it end? How did they figure out which male student in particular would be taking one for the team? Was there any coordination at all? And what if there wasn't? What if *multiple* candidates volunteered for the esteemed position? Did they have tryouts? Or did they all run into each other at the designated starting line and realize, rather embarrassed, that at least one of them was going to have to change?

Eventually, I'd accepted the fact that I would likely never know the answers.

"I just don't understand what could possibly motivate someone to do something like that." Josie was peering over Meg's shoulder, observing the crowd. "Or why people would want to watch that."

"For the glory, probably," Monica said. "The notoriety. That stuff matters to boys. If you're the one who streaks across campus, that's worthy of, I don't know, immortality or something. That's one possible answer."

"But no one knows who it is. So, what's the point of doing it if you don't get recognition?"

"Well, therein lies my second answer. Boys are idiots."

Cheers erupted from the distance. We turned back to see the lines of jumping bodies melting into a mob. They chased after the runner.

Monica gasped and covered Meg's eyes with her hand. "Meg! Don't look," she said, earning an elbow in response.

"I just feel like that would hurt," she said.

I grimaced. "Like running without a bra."

"Exactly."

"*Speaking* of guys being idiots," said Josie. "Did you all see Ron Davis yack all over that girl Natalie on Friday night?"

(And to think, that could have been Alice!)

We lowered our voices at the sight of oncoming professors.

"What was with that party?" whispered Monica. "Three girls got taken to the hospital after the cops showed up. *Three.* All passed out."

Josie pulled half her hair up and clipped it to the back of her head. "Probably freshmen who don't understand their tolerance yet."

"And yet, no one in that house gets in trouble. Cops show up, cops go home." Monica let out an exasperated sigh. "They also busted two other parties, and the hosts at each one got fined and are now on academic probation. But Charlie Morgan?"

"*Never,*" Josie said. "It pays to be Legacy."

Monica was also on our university's Judiciary Council, and if that tells you anything about the judicial process here, it's that calling it "rigorous" would be an understatement. Yet, every school has their favorites. And I think you'll understand when I say that any punishment of the son of one of our top living donors is not something for which I'd waste precious air holding my breath.

Climbing to our third-floor lecture hall once again, I unfolded the sheet of paper I had been holding in my hands and looked it over.

I'd told the others about my conversation with Alice at the party on Friday, and no one had any objections to her being our fifth team member. Considering that we didn't know anyone else in the class, I don't think they were in any position to be picky, and frankly, we were lucky we even got Alice. The whole thing actually felt more than lucky. Running into her so abruptly in the bookstore one of my first days back, seeing her everywhere, it could have just been a coincidence, a trick of the mind, as I'd mentioned. But then, she was in our class. A class that fell outside her major, as it did ours.

And there was the party, and my own lack of self-restraint the moment she mentioned our project.

If I'm being perfectly honest, there was something a little too sequential about these coincidences, something that made me feel less like it was a matter of luck, and more like it was a matter of—forgive me—*fate.*

It was a thought that made me shudder, both because it was a cliché and because there was something relatively discomforting about the trajectory of your life being in the hands of anyone but yourself. As though the Moirai really were somewhere out there, spinning their thread until it was time to snip, laughing at your naïveté as you went along believing that you had any say in the matter at all.

But if this thing with Alice really was their doing, if our meeting, our becoming friends, our…well, let's just say that if it *was* their intention, then, there we were, indulging in the thread they'd spun for us.

We even saved her a seat over with us, which she'd accepted without hesitation.

"Happy to see you made it out of that party in one piece," I said after she put her stuff down.

"Just barely." Alice twirled her pen in the air, her left index finger tapping the table. "It was practically a stampede. I saw one girl getting trampled, but I couldn't do anything about it."

Monica leaned over from my other side, her face mere inches from mine. "Jackie Moore, right? I heard she went to the hospital, too. *Concussed.*"

"Alice," I said, motioning toward my eager friend. "This is Monica. Monica, Alice."

"Pleasure," Monica said, extending her hand across me toward our new group member.

Alice took it, smiling. "Nice to meet you."

"I'm Meg!" called Meg from the end of the table.

"Josie." She hardly looked up from her book and did so only to lean forward and smile briefly.

"Tell me, Alice," Monica said, resting her head on her hand. "What inspired you to transfer here?"

"The school I went to didn't have an architecture program, so, I decided to make the switch."

"From where?" asked Meg.

"Just a small school on the East Coast. Massachusetts, near home."

Josie peered over again. "That's a pretty long trip. Couldn't you have chosen a closer program?"

"Sure," said Alice. "But it wouldn't have been the right program. Some things make the distance worth it, I guess."

Alice was calm and wearing a smile despite the obvious interrogation. I knew she'd fit in well with us if she could handle the fact that we were a curious bunch. Given her own curious tendencies that I'd witnessed, I was sure it wouldn't be a problem.

Already she looked more comfortable than I'd ever seen her, and I wondered if maybe what she'd really been looking for all those times I saw her, was a friend. The thought made my stomach squeeze.

"Well, I for one am happy you're here, Alice," Meg said. "I think you're going to like us, too."

When Professor Shaw arrived, I was sent to the front of the room to hand in our team list. The four of our names, plus one more:

Alice Demetria Helena Dayholt

It was a mouthful, to say the least, but there was also something admirable about the way she insisted upon using her full name. Even on something as insignificant as a scrap of paper ready to be thrown out by the day's end.

I approached the podium, slowly shuffling in line until I was next. The student in front of me peeled away, and I was left staring at her, watching as she wrote down the names of the team ahead of ours. She then crumpled up the sheet of paper and tossed it to the side, her eyes never leaving the list of names in front of her.

Finally, she looked up. At me. Her eyes cold and questioning, she looked as if she were about to speak, but was biting her tongue. I realized I'd completely forgotten why I was standing in front of her in the first place when she held her hand out toward me. Internally kicking myself, I quickly placed the paper in her hand and turned to leave.

I only looked back once more to see her watching me as she crumpled the team list into a ball and dropped it into the small trash bin at her side.

Walking back up the aisle, I paused momentarily when I saw the four of them, talking, laughing. Somehow it already felt natural, the five of us. Together.

And I wondered if the Fates could see us. I wondered if they'd be smiling.

All these years later, I'd say they were laughing.

SCENE 8

———

"It needs to be revolutionary. We need to change the game. She thinks she's throwing us off by coming in here and deviating from the traditional syllabus? Just wait until she hears our idea. Time is of the essence people, let's get moving."

Monica was pacing in the aisle beside our table, oblivious to the passersby who needed to swing their trays out of the way in order to avoid her gesturing arms. Nearby students stared. People looked up from their food. Monica didn't care.

"You do realize that the *topic* isn't even due for another seven weeks, right?"

Monica stopped in her tracks.

"And?"

"*And*," Josie emphasized. "That's more than enough time to come up with a solid idea. Besides, you don't start assignments until the night before they're due."

"Typically, yes." Monica took her seat at the table. "But this is a group project. I'm not just relying on myself here, so I need to take some precautions. No offense."

"Offense taken," Meg said, frowning into her chicken fingers.

"Look, the topics are first come first serve. What if we think of something great but, whoops! It's already taken. I simply will not have that."

"Monica," I said, blowing on my soup. "Eat your lunch, strategizing can wait."

She sat down with a sigh and reluctantly picked through her salad. The Dining Hall was just beginning to wake up with the noon buzz as people slowly trickled in from class, and the five of us had booked it over there to try and beat the midday traffic.

Yes, the *five* of us. We'd invited Alice to come along, hoping to get to know her better, and, while it was only the second week of classes, I had taken that possibility that she was in need of a few friends to heart.

So, there we were, occupying a quarter of one of the long wooden tables in the Hall, enjoying the spoils that day's menu had to offer.

The building had always been one of my favorites on campus. Looking up and feeling dizzy at the sight of the impossibly high ceilings, like you could fall up into them. Studying the person sitting across from you as they were painted with the colors that shone through the stained-glass windows. It all carried this feeling of warmth, of safety.

Of being home.

And what is a home, after all, without a few rowdy siblings to playfully bicker with?

I noticed that Monica had been chewing on the same piece of lettuce for at least thirty seconds, her teeth nibbling on the corners, her eyes flitting around to the rest of us. She desperately wanted to speak, I could tell, but she was searching for the right way to do it.

"Could we at least..." she ventured finally. "Could we at least discuss some options? If not for the project, then for fun?"

Josie shot me a look and I shrugged. Alice looked unable to hide the grin appearing on her face. Monica's eyes widened at the prospect of us warming to the idea.

Alice placed her fork down abruptly. "I would really like to, for *fun*, bring up the story of Pandora's Box."

Monica beamed, shooting out of her chair. The sound of wood scraping against the floor sent a shiver down my spine. She pointed at Alice. "Interesting! And its application?"

Alice's eyes scanned the table as Monica leaned toward her, arms outstretched and fingers beckoning. She chewed her lip until, *bing!* A lightbulb went off.

"We could talk about how it depicts woman created as punishment for man? In essence, the patriarchy—"

"Oh *God*," Josie muttered, rolling her eyes.

"Shh! Keep going." Monica held her hand in front of Josie's face. She slapped it away in response.

"It's in essence a story about the creation of women being the source of all that's horrible in the world. Hatred, war, death, disaster…" she trailed off.

"Look, if you're searching for even a whiff of feminism, you won't find it in *Greek Mythology*—"

"It has potential. Meg! You looked like you wanted to say something." Monica pointed at her quickly, causing her to drop her chicken finger.

"Umm," she looked around, her cheeks warming up. "Daedalus and Icarus? I feel like that applies to a lot."

"Sure, sure." Monica was back to pacing now, her hands clasped behind her back, her eyes studying her shoes. "Stella, go!"

"Perseus and Medusa!" I shouted louder than I'd intended, and it seemed to only rev her up more.

"Why!" she exclaimed.

CUTAWAY TO: the guy at the table next to ours chokes on his drink.

"I don't know. You put me on the spot. It was the first thing that popped into my head."

"Fair enough!" She clapped giddily. "See you guys? We can definitely have fun with this."

"And what about your contribution, ringleader?" Josie asked.

"Oh, I've got plenty of ideas brewing up here," she said, tapping her temple. "Don't you worry. This was just rapid fire, to warm us up."

"I enjoyed it," Alice said.

"Thank you, *Alice*." Monica shot a smug look to Josie. Her breathing was heavy, as if she'd just run a mile. She picked up a carrot to examine it closer.

"Well, I am going to have to excuse myself because my professors felt the need to assign an absurd amount of work during the *second* week of classes. I doubt I'll even get a seat at the library. It's weirdly always packed at this hour." Josie stood to collect her things.

"I'll go with you," Meg said.

I was planning on heading out myself, but I paused when I saw Alice's face. She looked torn, like she was debating whether or not she should say whatever she was thinking. Her brow furrowed, she looked up and saw me staring, quickly softening her expression. She definitely had something on her mind, but I couldn't have begun to hazard a guess at what it was.

"You know," she said, possibly feeling pressured by my, I don't know, direct eye contact, maybe, "if you don't want to try and secure a seat at the library, I actually found a pretty cool study spot."

The four of us glanced around at each other. I wasn't sure what spot she could be talking about that we weren't already aware of. I also wasn't sure why she was approaching the matter so delicately.

I spoke first. "That sounds good to me."

The others followed my lead and nodded. She looked relieved.

"Okay, but before we go, you have to promise me one thing," Alice said.

We looked around at each other again. When I realized she would wait for our answer, I nodded.

"You can't tell another soul about it."

SCENE 9

―――

None of us knew how Alice managed to find her "study spot."

After we put our trays away and made a beeline for the doors, we stopped at the sudden feeling of an absence.

Alice had disappeared. The entrance area was empty, as though she'd vanished into thin air.

"Alice," Meg said.

She turned around. Glancing over my shoulder, her eyes widened. She pointed.

SHOT: *down the hall and past the main exit, Alice peeks her head around a corner.*

Until that very moment, it was a corner that I'm not sure anyone, including myself, knew existed.

"Hurry," she yelled with the strength of a whisper, motioning us forward.

The four of us complied and walked quickly toward her, eventually reaching a path that had been hidden behind a long curtain. I realized I had seen it before, but up until then I had assumed it was a storage area or some other entirely mundane hallway.

The sneaking. The shushing. The delicateness of it all. It was odd how walking up the flight of stairs hidden down the hall could suddenly feel so...illegal.

CUT. Take Two:

There were *multiple* flights of stairs.

And what was waiting for us at the top looked like something dreamt up by C. S. Lewis.

We were met with a short, wooden door that came to a point at the top. A door that looked like it could have had a whole other world waiting behind it. In a sense, I'd say that it did.

Alice looked at us and held a finger to her lips, then delicately turned the brass doorknob and led us inside.

It was a small room, but big enough to fit a couch and a large armchair, with bookshelves lining one wall and a large window occupying the second. The third wall formed a semicircle with a stone bench, and one tall and narrow window that looked out over the Main Quad stood above. There was a dark, ornately patterned rug that filled the floor.

I realized in that moment that I'd have known exactly where to look for us if I were outside the building. In fact, I'd noticed the tall window many times before, never once stopping to think about what might be behind it. But something told me Alice had.

Because I also remembered that I'd seen Alice looking at that very window when she was wandering around the previous week. I remembered her removing a camera from her bag and taking a picture of it.

It was relatively clear that the room hadn't had visitors in years, besides Alice, of course. You could tell from the resistance she'd found in turning the doorknob and the way we could see the dust floating through the air.

It could have been that very dust that had made Alice's eyes mist over as she looked around the room. That's what I remember telling myself, at least.

We made ourselves at home almost instantly, Josie claiming the stone bench under the far window, Meg plopping down on the red velvet chair, legs draped over one arm. Alice took the floor, basking in the sun shining through the large window on the left wall, and Monica and I reclined comfortably along the green velvet couch. For a little while, we just sat there, breathing in the light and the aura and the time that had been held captive there for all those years.

I thought about why such a mesmerizing place would have been buried for so long.

Why did it exist in the first place? Who had been there, before we had?

Slowly, each of us began to pull out bits of homework or reading, finding peace in simply working away in each other's company. At one point, Alice stood up to look around, her eyes roaming over the stone walls and wooden floors. Curious, yet again. She moved to peruse the bookshelves, eventually focusing in on one small, black hardcover. She reached for it, but something stopped her. I watched the internal tug of war she'd been playing—longing against caution—and I tried to see if I could make out the title.

Zoom in. The Shadow in the Veil *by George Everett.*

She didn't even let her fingers graze the spine. Instead, she turned to a dark green hardcover with gold detailing. She picked it up and examined it, flipping through a few pages.

The minutes ticked away, although none of us were keeping count, and the room grew hot as the sun seemed to move around it. It wasn't an unpleasant hot, however, but a comforting warmth. A hug you didn't know you needed.

Sitting with her back against the windowsill, her knees meeting to form an upside down V with the floor, Alice frowned into her book. After a minute or two of chewing on her bottom lip and repeatedly dragging her eyes across what appeared from my point of view to be the same paragraph she began on, she let out a huff and loudly shut the book closed.

The air propelled upward by the pages sent a herd of dust stampeding around through the beam of sun that shot through the glass behind her.

Her eyes followed the dancing particles, as did mine. And it seemed I wasn't the only one observing the scene, as Meg rose from her spot on the chair and joined Alice by the window.

The two of them peered into the tunnel of light, Alice attempting to play God to the dust by violently whirling her hand through the air and bringing about chaos once more.

Meg's open mouth bent at the corners as she watched.

CLOSE-UP: *Meg's hand slowly reaches upward into the light.*

The particles of dust gravitated toward her hand, seeking refuge and clinging to her skin. Her palm was the ground upon which they landed like ash, Alice the raging fire that sent them to her.

"We're lucky none of us have allergies," said Josie, who peered over as well.

"Even if I did, I don't think I'd be able to stay away," said Meg, comfortable on the floor.

I silently agreed, staring up at the ceiling. Just looking.

Of course, we'd all promised Alice that we would tell no one about the little haven. It would be our place of refuge, a space to clear our minds or work or simply stay hidden from the world. To escape time for just a little while.

How Alice had found that room, why she thought to bring us there, none of it mattered to me. I wanted to stay there and bask in its history, in its secrecy, both of them fresh for our enjoyment after years of slumber.

In that moment, it had never occurred to me what we might have been stirring awake.

SCENE 10

———

Three weeks later, the four of us were on our way to pay a visit to Alice in the Architecture Studio.

It was mainly Josie's idea to show up unannounced ("with a chocolate muffin to be gracious guests"), and the whole thing had actually started with a Polaroid photo.

You see, in our weeks spent getting to know Alice, I began to form a pretty clear picture of who I believed her to be.

There were the basics, such as how she'd developed a love of mythology at an early age. Born Alice Dayholt to a pair of strict, Catholic parents, she gave in to her mother's insistence that she use her confirmation name, Helena, on the condition that she would be able to self-assign a second middle name of her choosing. She said that, to her, the choice was obvious. A name that meant something to her. And from that moment on, the name Alice Demetria Helena Dayholt appeared at the top of each assignment and on every form of identification.

While these facts helped me gain a better understanding of Alice, I'd decided that to truly know her was to know the subtler expressions of her mind, such as the way her knee never stopped bouncing in class, or the way I'd catch her walking back and forth across a room, continuing to do so until I verbally made myself known. There was also the way her dark eyes would occasionally glaze over while you talked, her mind detaching from the words spoken to her. It wasn't that she meant to not listen, it was that her head was filled with so many thoughts and ideas that she found it difficult to latch on to just one. While having to repeat yourself often with her could become frustrating, there was something fascinating about looking into her eyes and knowing just how much was taking place behind them.

One thing that she liked to do to be able to reel in her fleeting thoughts was take an instant picture of anything she found notable. She'd then label it with a sharpie and put it away for safekeeping until she needed to refer back to it.

"It helps me remember things," she said. "Small things I don't have the time to put clearly into words and write down."

FLASHBACK:

The topic had come up one afternoon when we were doing homework in our hidden library and Alice took a picture of the bookshelf. She'd gone to put the photo in her bag when Meg asked to see some of the pictures she'd taken. There was one of a bird perched on a bench, one of a door on the side of a building, one of the narrow window connecting that very room to the outside world, taken from the ground below. She moved to put them away, but one in particular caught Josie's eye, and she snatched it to get a better look.

"Who is this?" she asked, her smile widening. She flipped the picture around to show us a man in an office grinning with his thumbs up.

He looked mature, but he dressed young. He'd rolled the sleeves of his white button-down shirt to sit just below his elbows, and he'd propped his loafer-clad feet up on his desk, a wall decorated with certificates, pictures, and other miscellaneous memorabilia serving as a backdrop.

"That," Alice said, taking the pictures and putting them back in her bag. "That is one of my architecture professors."

Hence, the label: PROFESSOR ALDRIDGE

FLASHFORWARD:

We were practically jogging to keep up with Josie as she led us to the studio, claiming, "As much fun as it is to hang out in a musty old attic, it would be cool to learn more about Alice's world."

"You know," Monica said, "you can say Alice's professor, Josie. We're only judging you because of your feeble attempt to be sly in all of this."

"Who said anything about attempting to be sly?"

We reached the building that housed the studio, a large, white marble structure with tall columns and a flight of long steps leading up to the door. The studio itself had a low ceiling and stretched on for roughly fifty feet, slanted desks lined in rows.

I was admittedly impressed when Alice first told me she was in the architecture program, seeing how ours was famously one of the top in the country—certainly the top where the classical style was concerned. I'd never actually met any architecture students before Alice, but it was a well-known fact that each of them received multiple job offers prior to graduation, putting them in the unique position to actually *turn down* employers.

Alice had been hunched over her desk, her nose practically brushing the surface, when we'd arrived. It's likely she heard our collective footsteps advancing because she glanced up, her eyes widening with surprise. Just when she'd lit up at the sight of us, she noticed Josie beaming at the front of the group, leading the way. Her smile morphed into an all-knowing grin.

"Hello!" Josie said cheerily.

"He's not here," Alice said.

Josie tried hard to mask her deflation, and she nearly succeeded. Nonetheless, she recovered quickly. "We're here to see *you*, silly. Muffin?" She plopped it on the desk, Alice lunging to catch it as it rolled down the incline.

"Thanks," she said, eyeing the treat. "What can I do for you guys?"

"We just figured we'd switch up the hangout spot for once," Monica said with a hint of sarcasm, playing along for Josie's sake.

"Well hey, pull up some chairs." Alice motioned around her.

So, we sat and talked while Alice sketched, her eyes sweeping over the page.

That reminds me of another thing I'd learned. While she sometimes found it difficult to ground her thoughts in a simple conversation, it was ironically easier for her to hear you when her mind was otherwise occupied by some mechanical task, like drawing.

"How are things at the paper, Monica?" she asked, flipping her pencil to erase an error.

"Just peachy. I received yet another joke submission today."

"I don't know why you guys even allow those," I said.

"There's nothing we can do to stop people from sending in anonymous tips or pieces. I'm just tired of getting excited that we have mail only to find out it's another gag article about famous women who have slept their way to the top, or 'Five Signs Your New Position is Out of Your League.' Do you mind?" She pointed to the chocolate muffin Alice had yet to dig into.

"By all means."

Monica had devoured the entire thing within the minute. "Someone please share some good news," she managed, her mouth full and her cheeks puffed like a chipmunk.

"I actually have some," Meg said, her voice small and hesitant. We looked at her expectantly. She took a deep breath before smiling. "I made second chair."

Time stopped. A full three seconds went by in silence. I don't remember who yelled first, but suddenly we were all jumping, cheering, hugging Meg. Making the orchestra's second chair as a sophomore was practically unheard of, but Clay was right. That wouldn't stop her.

I heard a faint voice growing louder beneath our celebration. "Whoa whoa whoa," it said.

I turned and saw the man from the Polaroid himself approaching, sleeves still rolled, sandy hair lighter in person, wearing a brown leather bag slung over his shoulder.

"We should be aware of the others trying to get work done in here." He motioned around the room. A boy in a Pearl Jam hoodie glared in our direction.

"Sorry, Professor," Alice said.

"Max, remember? No 'Professor.'" He looked at us and blinked, as if just realizing that we weren't supposed to be there.

Alice caught on quickly. "These are my friends. I don't know if we're allowed visitors—"

"No, no, I don't mind. I was just worried that I wasn't recognizing my own students. I'll be in my office if you need anything. Feel free to stay, just remember," he motioned again, mouthing just below a whisper, *Be cognizant*. "Oh, and assuming I heard correctly, congratulations to you." He bowed his head to Meg, whose cheeks were now bright pink.

Josie waited until he was in his office to let out a dramatic sigh. Later, while we stayed with Alice and talked quietly, she wandered over to his door as nonchalantly as possible, earning an eye roll from Monica.

"How old is he anyway?" she whispered to Alice.

Alice furrowed her eyebrows without looking away from her work. "Not sure, I know he went here actually. A long time ago, I think. He seems like he'd be, what…" She looked at the ceiling behind closed eyelids, mouthing her mental math.

"Too old for Josie?" I asked.

"Well, that wasn't even in question," Monica said.

Josie made her way back over to us, practically skipping. "I vote we hang out here more often."

"I vote we don't," Monica said. "All those against Josie's proposal?"

The rest of us raised our hands in agreement. Even Alice.

SCENE 11

───

More weeks sped by with the help of a somewhat constant routine.

MONTAGE: *going to class, studying in our secret room, eating meals, studying in our secret room, the occasional night out, studying in our secret room.*

You get the idea.

I've always been a fan of routine. Routine is comfortable. Routine is safe. *Routine* means no surprises.

And I would have been perfectly happy to remain in that routine for the duration of the year, no matter how mundane it may have appeared to an outsider. Mundane often goes unappreciated until it has disappeared. Often, without warning.

Often, not by choice.

In the years following that fall semester, I'd go on to wonder a number of things, one of which was whether I'd taken the simplicity of our existence in those earlier weeks for granted. Of course, the answer is, without a doubt, "yes, I had," but I don't think appreciating it more would have resulted in the semester going any other way. It seemed that all paths we could have taken would have led us to the same destination, regardless.

As I'd said, the Fates had made their decision. The thread had already been cut.

And I've repeatedly had to remind myself that altering the events of the following months may not have necessarily been a good thing. Who knows what outcome would have been reached, had we not followed Alice up to that hidden library? Had we not had the means of putting the pieces of the puzzle back together?

The same goes for the decisions that weren't ours. Who knows what would have happened, had no one painted that door on that last Friday in September 1992?

We happened to be on our way to the Dining Hall that morning, hoping to beat the brunch crowd and sneak upstairs undetected. We took the pathway that would cut across the Main Quad. The fastest route.

"It doesn't matter what form of art it is," Monica said. "It could be a photograph, a painting, a film, it could even be a poem. It's all unreliable."

She and Josie had entered into a debate about art as truth, about whether it ever could be.

"I just don't agree with the term 'unreliable,' though," Josie said. "If something is 'true' to one person but not another, why does that *have* to be unreliable?"

"I guess it depends on your definition of truth, but I know that mine is muddled by one thing: perspective. The story-teller, even unintentionally, brings certain biases to the narrative. The photographer chooses a certain angle for a reason."

"Like this," Alice said. She snapped a photo of the four of us, the picture sliding out into her hand.

"And the filmmaker makes edits. Right, Stella?"

I nodded. "Yeah, I agree. Even if you're dealing with something that's supposedly 'real,' like documentary film, the director makes choices with a message in mind. Chooses certain shots, asks certain questions, tells the story in a certain structure. It's all to convey a message. And their message is informed by their perspective."

I could tell Josie didn't want to concede, but she was outnumbered in the matter, and she tended to side with the majority, if only to have been "right."

"Fine," she said. "I guess I get it. But I'd still rather use a different word."

"Inauthentic?" I asked.

"Manipulative?" Alice asked.

"A complete and utter pile of garbage?" Monica asked with a wink. "Oh, that was like...seven words."

Josie laughed and nudged her with her hip. Monica felt this warranted a response, so she elbowed her. Back and forth they went, lightly sparring until Monica ran and jumped onto a bench to escape her attacks.

After a moment, her smile dropped into a frown, a look of confusion taking over her face. The sound of a mob of voices grew louder as we neared the bend in the pathway. The one that would take us to the Main Quad.

"That doesn't sound good," Josie said.

"I'm sure it's nothing," Monica said, although even she sounded doubtful.

"Could it be another streak?" Meg asked.

"They never do it twice a year. This is something else."

We followed the bend, my confusion growing as we saw the large crowd situated outside the Main Hall, just below the steps that led up to the front door. The closer we got, the more chaotic it all became. Friends yelling to each other over the noise. Shorter students jumping to try and get a good view of what all the commotion was about.

We walked along the outer edge of the crowd, looking for an opening. I turned when a voice called my name.

It was Clay, pushing his way through bodies. He made it out to me, breathing heavy. His glasses were fogged.

"Did you see it?" he asked.

"No, we haven't been able to get a good look—"

"Stella!"

PAN TO: Josie waves me over.

They were all near the very back, climbing onto a bench. One that stood directly across from the center of the building.

I ran over, noticing the shock written across their faces. I stepped up to join them.

"What?" I asked. "What is it?"

And then I turned.

There is an element in a film called "identification." *Primary* being the spectator's identification with the camera, *secondary* being the spectator's identification with a specific character. When the two collapse, it does so in the form of a "point of view" (POV) shot.

Here was my POV:

There were more people there than I'd realized, gathering on all sides of the Main steps. They were all trying to get a good look at the doors of the Main Hall, and it looked like we had the best seats in the house.

An unobstructed view of those doors showed us that there were letters painted in a red substance. Paint, I assumed. I remember praying that it was paint. Because regardless, the sight was nauseating enough.

It looked like blood.

It had dried, but in a way that showed that it had dripped down the door as it was painted. The sight of it, however, wouldn't have been nearly as effective, had the letters not spelled out what they did.

Had the message said, *PARTY ON MAIN QUAD TONIGHT!* it wouldn't have been as disturbing. Had it said, *SCHOOL-WIDE EMERGENCY!* it *still* wouldn't have been as disturbing.

It felt in that moment like the only possible statement that could have made me feel as confused and unsteady as it did, was, in fact, written right there for all of us to see.

The message read:

YOU KILLED
THE GIRL
IN THE TUNNELS

Monica cleared her throat. "Well, that's certainly new material for the tour guides."

The flash of Alice's camera went off.

THE MEDIUM SHOT

SCENE 12

——

Now, let's zoom in a bit closer, shall we?

The incident that took place on that Friday morning had somewhat of a lasting effect on the campus community, remaining the subject of discussion for longer than the average mishap. If that's what you could call it.

People started clearing out about half an hour after we got there. A probably harmless yet admittedly eerie PDA (Public Display of Accusation) didn't warrant an excused absence from class, so many found themselves reluctantly abandoning the show until the only onlookers left were those who had hurried over once the news had traveled.

And it traveled.

Each of my classes later that day began the same way. Students filing in next to their friends, whispering to their neighbors, trying to figure out just what had happened. The boys who sat behind me in my morning lecture were particularly invested, gossiping excitedly until our professor felt compelled to cut in.

Boy 1: Did you see it?

Boy 2: No! I was in Calc A!

Boy 1: It was crazy. It was like blood oozing through the doors.
Boy 2: Are you serious?
Boy 1: Oh yeah. Unreal.
Professor: As "unreal," as your attendance record, Mr. Hutton? I find that doubtful.

"Mr. Hutton," discussed the morning incident no further.

There was also some debate amongst students as to what exactly the statement meant, and who it was meant for. Who was this "you"?

"You," as in a specific member of the community, killed The Girl in the Tunnels?

"You," as in whoever sat behind that door, killed The Girl in the Tunnels?

"You," as in "we the spectators," killed The Girl in the Tunnels?

"Why on earth would they be talking about the entire student body, Jessica?" I'd heard someone ask in Adolescent Psychology.

The word had spread through campus like wildfire, and the few who didn't sprint to see it in person made sure they were completely up to date before the weekend festivities. The buzz was understandable, as it had been the most out of the ordinary thing to take place at our school since, well, I would have to assume the inception of the old myth itself. Despite all the hearsay, and no matter how entertaining it may have been, the general consensus that had been reached was that the "message" on the doors of the Main Hall had simply been a prank. A ruse, to stir things up on campus.

But that didn't mean that all the theorizing simply came to a halt. No. The hypotheses, no matter how ill-informed, would continue to weave throughout campus, flames continuously stoked by even those who claimed to be disinterested.

Because as much as people wanted to believe that the message was simply the product of some jokester trying to pull one over on all of us, there was also a part of them that wanted to believe the worst.

But don't we all?

The headline's already long shelf life was only aided by the fact that it took them so long to clean the mess up.

Three hours after I'd left the bench upon which I'd stood gawking, they were still there, scrubbing. In that time, I'd taken two classes, grabbed a snack from the Dining Hall, and held a fairly in-depth conversation with Katie From World Cinema (as I'd known her) about neorealism in postwar Italy. And, despite what I'm sure were their best efforts, I have to admit that the whole thing looked...*worse*.

Gone were the letters, that's for sure. But in their place was a dark, runny blob that had melted onto the stone and somehow migrated to the Main Hall steps. Certain drier areas appeared to be stained, the red paint fused with the ground, as if it were a canvas, for what could've been an eternity. It ultimately took a few days of scrubbing to fully remove any remaining signs of the "prank," and even then, that morning wasn't forgotten. It was as though the message refused to be erased. It had been burned into our minds and our architecture, and it intended to stay there.

The following Wednesday, we'd just sat down with our food when a group of girls passed our table, whispering about whether or not the school would figure out who it was that started it all in the first place. (That was what the administration had promised us, at least, in the letters everyone found in their mailboxes that weekend.)

"Why are people still talking about this? I thought we'd collectively decided to believe that it was just a prank," said

Josie, who was struggling to cut into her chicken entrée, a campus dining dish often described by many as "rubbery."

"Prank or not," Monica said, her mouth full of pasta with marinara, "I'd want to know who painted it. And why, of course."

"Because it was a *prank*," Josie emphasized.

Meg jumped in. "My first move would be to figure out whose paint it was."

"How would they—"

"Oh, they already figured that out. It was Mindy Cohen's."

We all stopped eating and looked at Monica. She eyed us suspiciously, as though she was confused as to how we weren't already in the know.

"*Mindy Cohen?*"

"Yeah, you know, the art major. Blonde? Wears clogs?"

She sighed heavily when none of us responded, adding, "She's the one who paints nude self-portraits."

Josie clarified. "We know who Mindy Cohen is, but I'm having trouble seeing how she'd be connected to any of this. Also, how do you always hear this stuff?"

"You just have to be perceptive enough to know where to listen." She winked.

A beat.

Two beats.

The skeptical looks on our faces.

Monica piecing together the fact that we, collectively, simply did not buy it.

With another sigh, she conceded, "Fine. I heard through the judiciary channels and may or may not have asked her nicely to elaborate on her morning route to class."

CUT TO: Monica corners Mindy outside of the Art Studio at eight in the morning and "nicely" insists that she tell her what she knows.

"So that's the answer then?" I asked. "Mindy Cohen painted the message on the Main Hall doors?"

Chugging her water, Monica waved her hand, shooing me away from the thought.

She gulped and inhaled deeply. "Oh no. Mindy's not the *culprit*, but it was her paint. And that's where it gets interesting." She scanned our surroundings before leaning into the center of the table. "She was on record at the campus shop as having bought the paint *Wednesday*, but when she got into the studio on Thursday, it was *gone*."

Her face was frozen, her eyes wide and her smile knowing as she awaited a reaction that she wasn't going to get.

"So, let me get this straight," I said. "Assuming that the paint used on that door Friday morning is the same paint that Mindy Cohen purchased Wednesday, and not, say, paint purchased literally anywhere else on any other day, then whoever took that paint *might* have done it?"

Monica nodded slowly, eyes surveying the ceiling while working through the logic. "Yes."

I sat back in my seat with my arms crossed. "Well then, Sherlock, I think it's time to hang up the old deerstalker. You've solved the case!"

"To Sherlock," Meg said, raising her water. The others followed suit.

Monica rolled her eyes. "Laugh all you want, but when the administration proves it, you'll all owe me, I don't know...I'll think of something."

"Trust me, I don't think the administration is going to be doing anything about this," Alice said.

It was the first time she had spoken that evening.

"And why is that?"

Alice looked up from her plate, her dark eyes widening only slightly, as though she hadn't meant to say that out loud. Josie's question seemed to wake her from her introspection, and as she sat there, glancing at each of us, I realized just how long she was taking to produce an answer. It was like she was off-book for the first time, and she'd drawn a blank. I watched as she visibly searched her mind for what came next in the script. A race against time. I was about to yell *CUT*—

At last, someone fed her the line, and she tilted her head. "Isn't it obvious? If they answer the question of 'who' they'd also have to answer the question of 'why'."

Okay, keep the cameras rolling.

"The 'why,' as I've said time and time again, is that *it's a prank*," Josie said, stabbing her chicken with her knife on each of the last three words.

Alice shrugged. "Believe that, if you really want to, but this feels like something more." She took a long sip of her drink, then continued. "I mean, why go through all that, and risk getting caught, just for some prank? And, why the tunnels, of all things? It's so...specific. So pointed."

"Alice, darling, no offense, but you haven't been here for all that long." Monica patted her hand. "People have been talking about those tunnels for years, okay? It's just a myth."

"But you've never thought that it might be true?"

The table was silent. I'd never admitted this out loud, but there always had been a part of me that wondered about the rumor. Perhaps it was because of how fresh it was. Had it stemmed from some arbitrary year too far back to remember, I likely would have found it easier to distance myself from my own speculation.

But this was a mere twenty years later (and an *anniversary*, no less), and a story about a woman entering a new environment, only to never leave, well, it wasn't one I could simply stop watching and forget altogether. Besides, if I'm being honest, I think the other girls felt the same way.

As if sensing our mixture of apprehension, discomfort, and Josie's unyielding resolve, Alice laughed. "Look, it may be morbid, but I think it would be pretty interesting if the story had an element of truth to it."

Interesting. I wasn't quite sure that was the word I would've used.

"Well, to be fair," Meg said. "I'm pretty sure there technically are tunnels down there, but they're unnavigable and serve no real purpose, at least not to people, anyway. Someone wrote an article about it a year or two ago."

"That's all the more reason to believe it."

"How?" Josie asked. "Why would they admit that the tunnels exist if they don't want people looking into them?"

"Because, admitting that there is something down there, just nothing nearly as mysterious as people think, provides closure. It allows them to move on without needing to ask more questions."

And yet, there she was, asking more questions.

"You know, Alice, it sounds like you already have your mind pretty made up about this. So why ask?" Josie leaned forward in anticipation of her answer.

Before she could respond, the hollow sound of a cup bouncing across the ground echoed throughout the room, prompting loud applause from everyone present. We watched as the responsible party scrambled around to catch the runaway.

It was another one of our beloved (humiliation-inducing) traditions.

Monica groaned. "I seriously hate that."

SCENE 13

———

"What is it, exactly, that warrants our fear of death?"

A weighted question, to say the least.

But the lecture had already been a rather dark one on that Monday afternoon, so the question didn't necessarily come out of left field.

Still, eyes studied hands, notebooks, even the bare tables beneath them. Any hints of whispers or the shuffling of papers vanished before Professor Shaw had time to glance up from the podium in front of her.

What felt like minutes passed, the weight of the silence pressing down on my chest. I'm not sure why I always felt burdened with those uncomfortable moments when everyone seemed perfectly content to wait for someone else to come up with an answer. Though, maybe I'm being dramatic. I'm sure everyone felt just as desperate for some generous volunteer to step up and enter the arena. To fight the battle for the rest of us.

Unfortunately, the clock kept ticking, and we approached that dreaded time limit after which she'd inevitably select the unlucky student of the day to share whatever they could possibly come up with before it was revealed that they really had no clue what they were saying.

CUT TO: a shot of my "pensive" face, meant to convince her that I was thoroughly searching my mind for an appropriate answer.

"Perhaps I should rephrase," she said. "What if, instead, I ask how mythology appears to add to our understanding of death? Are there any stories, in particular, that shed light on what takes place *after* death?"

The bait remained where it was. Untouched. Unwanted.

At that point in time, and in any other class, I'd typically surrender, and take one for the team. But our mythology lectures weren't like my other courses. The stakes felt higher. And her usual blank stare that she gave in response to any contribution made it nearly impossible to gauge whether or not you were on the right track. (But you *could* often tell soon afterward when she either chose to run with your answer, or simply repeat the question. In *that* case, it was clear as day that your thought or mind or reputation, even, was essentially worthless.)

I mean, even Monica opted on the side of staying silent during those debates, and she would normally jump at the chance to be heard. Although, she had mentioned to me in passing that she was concerned that her frequent participation was too heavily feeding into her God complex.

So, that was another possible explanation.

Professor Shaw's shoulders lifted and fell with a sigh as she moved from behind the podium and strutted toward the front row, her movements slow and deliberate. The lioness had come back for more.

As if it couldn't get any worse, her wandering eyes somehow managed to land on me, the heat rising up my neck toward my face. But then, in a moment of sheer luck, they moved. One seat to the right. To Alice.

And this time, she didn't freeze.

This time, she planned to go in for the kill.

Turning to see if Alice had become aware of her impending downfall, I was instead met with a girl who looked like she was waiting to be called on. I was sure that, if I'd had x-ray vision, I would have been able to see her biting her tongue behind her slightly upturned mouth.

"Ms. Dayholt," Professor Shaw said. "You might be able to see where I'm heading with this question."

She walked up the aisle to confront her prey.

"Of course, I'd be disappointed if you didn't. Alice *Demetria*, isn't it?"

The emphasis she placed on Alice's middle name made my skin crawl. There was a certain edge to her voice in that moment, sharp as the distinction between the dark blouse she'd worn that day and her fair skin. To me, her tone stuck out like a sore thumb. But Alice appeared unscathed.

In fact, she gave in to her smile. "Yes, it is."

Our professor continued to wait patiently.

"And if I had to guess, I'd say you were leading toward a discussion of The Rape of Persephone."

"Ah yes, The Abduction of Persephone."

Alice shrugged. "To each her own."

"I think," Professor Shaw continued, "that I was looking for something a bit more specific. I mean, we all have a basic understanding of the relationship between Hades and Persephone, right?"

She motioned around the room, but was met with silence. "Anyone?"

"The Rape of Persephone," Monica offered monotonously, her God complex alive and well. "Hades falls in love, brings her to the Underworld—*sans consent*—Demeter strikes a deal with Zeus to get her back, but Hades feeds her these *pomegranate* seeds and long story short, she can only spend part of the year up with her mother. Hence, the seasons."

She really had a way with words, didn't she?

"In the simplest of forms, yes, that's correct. But I'd like to look a little closer at Demeter, which is why I initially called on Alice. The goddess of the harvest and fertility, her story is one of the most significant to Ancient Greek culture, is it not? At least, from what we understand, Demeter had her own dedicated, albeit discreet, following. A group that had endured for nearly two thousand years, thriving in the shadows, basking in knowledge only those deemed worthy had access to. Those like Socrates and Plato. There was something about Demeter that they believed would lead them on their path toward spiritual enlightenment. So I ask about death, and I ask about Demeter and Persephone, because I hope to bring us to," she extended her arm toward Alice again.

"Eleusis," she said.

"Specifically..."

"The Eleusinian Mysteries."

"*The Eleusinian Mysteries.*"

Professor Shaw turned and walked back to the front of the room, grabbing a piece of chalk and scribbling the phrase on the board in front of her. She turned back to the class. "A set of rituals for a secret society in Ancient Greece that worshipped Demeter and Persephone, seeking to accomplish what, exactly, Ms. Dayholt?"

"Essentially, by revealing the afterlife, initiates realize that death is not to be feared, since life continues on regardless."

"Through three phases that parallel the story of the mother and daughter goddesses." She turned again to the board. "The descent." *Scribble.* "The search." *Scribble.* "And the ascent."

Scribble. "The concepts of life and death would be altered in one's mind. No longer did death, as Ms. Dayholt explained, mark the end of life. Now, could one argue, I wonder, that fearing death is a good thing?"

Ancient cults, schools of mystery, it was all very captivating. I'd read about the rituals once before, but learning about them in that context, it all felt much more lifelike. It felt as if I were looking into the past, like I could reach out and grab it, become enveloped in it.

I raced to get all the information down on paper, our professor's voice fading as I concentrated on retaining the previous information.

I did hear, however, when she asked, "Stella?"

My pen stopped dead in its tracks. As I glanced around quickly, I noticed Meg resting her head in her hands, her glasses fogging up with each nervous breath she took. I hoped desperately that my efforts to think, to scramble, weren't half as noticeable as I thought they were. "Maybe," I said slowly, buying time. "Maybe fearing death could be considered a good thing in that it keeps people in check. If you don't fear death, then what *do* you fear? It could imply a lack of consequences, which could be dangerous."

"Interesting. Now, the rituals were eventually banned, the society supposedly dissolved, but for a group that believes that death is not the end of life, it makes you wonder. Does a society ever really die? Or does it, like the Eleusinian members upon initiation, simply transform? Does it just become something else?"

She placed the chalk down and walked back over to our table.

"Stella pointed out that not fearing death may imply a feeling of invulnerability. That the comprehension of your own immortality could prove dangerous, maybe not to you, but to others, certainly. Would you care to counter?" She looked to Alice, as did I. She stared at the table in front of her.

"Not on the logic, no," she said. "But I will say that the practice itself creates an interesting paradox."

"And what might that be?"

"Well, to reveal the nature of the rituals, to share the secret *of* the society, that is, was punishable by death."

"Ah," she replied, "And you take issue with that idea?"

"It's just ironic, really. To attempt to control someone with that which they do not fear, but to succeed nonetheless."

Professor Shaw leaned forward slightly, as if drawn toward the girl who had originally stumped her.

"Ironic?" she asked, raising an eyebrow. "Or poetic?"

Alice looked up and met her gaze.

"Tragic."

SCENE 14

———

If you happen to be thinking, *that class simply screamed,
"Happy Birthday, Stella!"* then you'll be happy to know that I
wholeheartedly agree.

Although it was an uncomfortably tense lecture, and
although it was a Monday, it was also, in fact, my birthday.
And we intended to celebrate. Clay had graciously offered
to host a small gathering for our closer friends, so there we
were, walking over that night.

We traveled at a quick pace, occasionally breaking into
a playful jog while Monica tried to keep the bottle of wine
stuffed in her jacket hidden from anyone we passed.

The mission was a success as we arrived at Clay's third-
story room, alcohol undetected. Each of us proceeded to
knock rapidly, all five sets of knuckles rattling the wooden
door until it swung open to reveal an already overwhelmed
Jamie on the other side.

Clay, Jamie, and Leo boasted your typical boys dorm
room, with any seating pushed to the periphery, a plastic
table set up in the center, and the inescapable stench of dirty
laundry radiating from the hidden corners where one would
undoubtedly find abandoned articles of clothing. The student

radio station played at a low level, prompting Meg to go over and turn the dial before climbing up onto one of the couches and pointing in my direction.

"Friends," she said, her voice large with the help of the shot of tequila she'd taken back at her room. "Let's all wish our dear Stella a happy birthday." She raised her cup. "Carpe diem, isn't that right, Alice?"

Alice, our resident Latin expert, raised her own cup. "Carpe *noctum*," she corrected.

"Actually, I think you all mean…" Monica said, pulling the bottle of wine up and out of her brown, oversized jacket. "Carpe *vinum*."

This prompted cheers from the rest of us. Cheers that were interrupted by the sound of a heavy door slamming. Clay turned around and started toward the drinks. "Right, ladies, how about we check the Latin at the door, shall we?"

Monica booed. Meg shook her head. Alice jerked her thumb toward the host, as if to say, *This guy!*

"Looks like you're outnumbered, Calloway," I said, making my way over for a hug.

"I'm never not outnumbered when it comes to the five of you," he said, grinning.

FLASHFORWARD:

I did my best to ignore the stains on the couch beneath me, and did better than my best to avoid trying to identify their origins. I often found it wisest to steer clear of taking in my surroundings in a boy's dorm room. But sitting on that couch, the red tweed scraping against my exposed legs, I certainly felt more at ease than at the house party we'd attended at the start of the term.

What didn't make me feel at ease, in that particular moment, was Josie loudly proclaiming to the room how incredibly disappointing my apparent social inadequacy had been in that first month and a half of the semester.

"She used to be so much fun," she said, referring to me in the third person despite my immediate presence within the conversation. "You should have seen her last fall. The life of the party."

She gingerly placed her hand on my head and laughed, evidently unaware of the connotative weight that the subsequent silence held. Monica was suddenly parched, downing her drink in one swift gulp. Meg looked up from the ground to offer me a quick, sympathetic smile, and Jamie and Leo were altogether disinterested, which was more than I could say for myself.

It was no secret that my habits had changed drastically since the previous year, but that didn't make the situation any less uncomfortable. And, to tell you the truth, if it hadn't been for Josie, I wouldn't have been the "life of the party," she so affectionately titled me in the first place.

When I first met her, that night in the bathroom during our freshman fall, I couldn't have realized that her entrance was my inciting incident. I looked at her, up on the big screen, and I thought I saw what I wanted to be. Glowing with confidence, capable of convincing someone like me that I belonged next to someone like her.

I reveled in it. I told myself that she was right.

And somewhere amidst the late, blurry nights and hazy, head-throbbing mornings, reality caught up with me. (But to be fair, I'd never been an excellent runner.)

Regardless, I had never considered that the glamour of Hollywood might dim when the cameras stopped rolling.

Before Josie could bring up any particularly mortifying anecdotes, I felt a hand graze my shoulder.

Clay leaned down and whispered near my ear. "Before I forget, I have your birthday present."

I was thankful for the intervention, and wasted no time in following him over to the side room, a tiny space cluttered with three beds lofted above desks. I immediately decided that it was not the hidden corners, but rather this room, that was the source of the dirty laundry smell. I felt guilty for being the reason the door was opened to allow an unfortunate source of airflow.

Clay opened and closed desk drawers, rummaging through in search of whatever gift he seemed so giddy to give me.

"I know it's here somewhere. One second."

While he continued to look, I took a step back to glance around his side of the room, realizing I'd never actually been inside it. His desk was a mess of notebooks, loose sheets of paper, and old coffee cups. It was the exact opposite of Jamie's, which sat on the other end and was bare save for a stack of books and two cups of pens organized by color. Clay's wall was also much more cluttered than his roommates', lined with photos of family and childhood friends, various certificates, a small flag in the corner with a crest that I assumed belonged to his high school, and one movie poster, actually. (*Star Wars Episode VI: The Return of the Jedi.*)

"Okay, ready?"

I turned back to Clay, who was hiding something behind his back, fighting away a grin. I had no idea what to expect in the first place, but when he handed me what he did, it took a minute to process what I was looking at.

He brought his hands around and into view, clasping a vinyl record. When he gave it to me and I turned it over, it was like the floor dropped from beneath me. My mind went numb. Words no longer formed.

It wasn't just a record.

It was an autographed record, that read, *All my love—*
And, here's where I had trouble comprehending.

It was signed, *Frank Sinatra.*

Despite the logic of it all, like the fact that it *was,* after all,
Frank Sinatra's hit album, *Songs for Swingin' Lovers!,* or that
I happened to be aware that Clay's dad *knew* Frank Sinatra
(they'd become drinking buddies during his Comeback Era,
post-*From Here to Eternity*), it was simply impossible to me
that an object held by—

The Voice

The Chairman of the Board

Ol' Blue Eyes

—was being held by none other than yours truly, in that
very moment.

My mother loved "Frankie," as she'd call him, and she
made sure I loved him too. As something small we shared, I
had only mentioned this love to Clay in passing. It was during
one of our case studies the previous year. I don't remember
exactly how it came up, but somehow, in the midst of discussing the implications of various blood types, I'd learned
of his dad's friendship with the heartthrob, and momentarily
lost my cool.

(Perhaps that was why I decided to become friends
with him.)

I had actually made the mistake of bringing him up in
front of the girls, once, and was met with complete and utter
disapproval. Frankie's comeback didn't matter to them. In
their eyes, he was simply a crooner, and anyone who liked
him was simply a "bobby soxer."

I'd always thought of that moment as only a distraction
for Clay, an anecdote he welcomed to keep his mind off of

the anxiety-producing assignment. It was so brief and insignificant that even I had forgotten he knew this tidbit of mine. But, of course, he had remembered. It was like I said, there were just certain things that only Clay knew and understood about me.

And I wouldn't typically do what I did next.

No, I didn't scream or jump around or faint. I looked at Clay before my vision went blurry, holding my breath so that I didn't melt into a puddle of tears before him. He seemed to notice this internal struggle of mine, his smile dropping to a concerned, *Oh no,* look. No matter how wonderful Clay was, he (like many men) was utterly incapable of handling a woman's tears. I covered my mouth to suppress a sob, then did my best to put on a convincing smile and assure him that everything was all right. That I was only behaving like that because of the overwhelming realization that someone might have actually known me better than I knew myself.

Through a combination dose of "there there's" and hesitant pats on the back, Clay succeeded in subduing me, my erratic breathing reduced to a steady flow of air.

"Back to the fun?" he asked, a hint of sarcasm laced in his voice.

"Back to the reminiscing, you mean?"

"Same thing."

I gave him a light shove. "I'll have you know, my friends are plenty fun."

"Oh, trust me, I like *almost* all your friends."

"Almost all? All except Meg, you mean?"

A light shade of pink grew along his cheeks. "Meg *is* the worst," he said with a smile.

I gave him a knowing, "Mhm," and was about to open the door when something stopped me.

I don't know exactly what it was that made me think of asking him about her, but one second, the thought popped into my head, and the next, it was leaving my mouth.

"What about Alice?"

Clay tilted his head. His eyes scanned my face. "What about her?"

Truthfully, I didn't know, but after all the time I'd spent analyzing her, I felt like I needed a second opinion. "What do you think about her?"

He looked above my head, at the door behind me, then shrugged. "She seems nice enough. Kind of lost, sometimes, or, curious, maybe."

I nodded, able to confirm his observations against my own. But the look on my face gave away that I wasn't quite satisfied with his answer, so he leaned back on his desk and crossed his arms.

"I mean, I get the sense that she's pretty closed off," he continued. "She doesn't reveal much about herself, so, how much do you really know about her?"

I tried to mask the fact that I had asked myself the same exact thing many times over the previous weeks, with a corny rebuttal. "How much do we ever really know about *anyone*?"

"Valid point," he said. "We all have our secrets, I suppose."

He wiggled his fingers in my face like a child portraying a ghost for Halloween, and I rolled my eyes.

Reentering the common room, I attempted to erase any remnants of our conversation from my expression.

The party had continued on without us, it seemed, with Alice and Meg deep in conversation near the drinks, Monica following Jamie around as he scooped up trash, and Josie talking Leo's ear off on the couch. (Not that he was in any condition to listen at that moment.)

"But that's exactly the point," she was saying, leaning over. "Memory is inherently sporadic. It doesn't operate chronologically, it's not like you remember your life from start to finish. You jump around at random, correct?"

From the looks of it, she'd lost him. He just sat there, eyes half-shut, nodding his head. Or he was bobbing it along to "Janie's Got A Gun." Either way, it was clear his mind was elsewhere.

"Can we change the channel please?" Meg asked, when she saw that Clay and I had rejoined the group. "We can't dance to this."

"How disappointing, Meg, Ms. Music Major," Clay said, grabbing my hand. "You can dance to anything if you really want to."

He pulled me into the center of the room, leading me in a tango arguably unfit for Aerosmith. Alice grabbed Meg, twirling her about. When Monica saw the commotion, she dragged Jamie over, unfortunately causing him to drop the cups he'd been collecting. Clay insisted on dipping me on each eight-count, despite my protests out of fear that he might not catch me, and I'd plummet down onto the sticky tiled floor, unable to pick myself up. Josie ditched Leo, who had been fist-bumping lethargically, and ran over, weaving through the rest of us. At one point we'd become a band, Meg on guitar, Alice on the drums, and I as lead singer as we performed with gusto and passion, Clay our one-man audience.

That concept that Professor Shaw described in class, of believing that you're immortal? That you're truly invincible? Dancing there, that night, was one of the last times I remember feeling that way.

SCENE 15

———

"If I live to see the day we use a robot as a witness in a murder trial, I'll write the four of you into my will."

The sun appeared to be in hiding on that October afternoon. Although it often would be around that time of year.

There came a point in our town where the days turned gray, not rainy or snowy, just cold and dark. And sad. It was nearly impossible to have energy on a day such as that one, where the lack of sunlight feeding our little haven meant we'd sit in the shadows, our minds cloudy like the sky we'd see each time we glanced out the window.

We couldn't even bring ourselves to do homework. We just lounged around, staring at the ceiling and pretending we were unaware that midterms were approaching.

Josie had been reading Asimov in one of her classes, which interested us at least to the point of a relaxed discussion of the "shortcomings" of the Three Laws, as Monica had called them. I didn't pretend to know a ton about Asimov or his fictional laws of robotics, but Monica could always be counted on to suddenly make things engaging.

"Okay, so we up the stakes," Alice had said in response to Monica's claim that a murder suspect facing the death penalty wasn't enough to force a robot to break one of the laws. "Let's say that *two* men are on trial, and one of them is the murderer. If the robot testifies against one, that man dies. But if the robot refuses, and they have enough of a case against the other man without the robot's testimony, then through inaction it would allow the other man to die. Therefore, it causes harm to a human either way."

A few rebuttals later, I decided to pull the plug before things got too heated. "I guess we'll just have to wait for the real thing."

And that's how we arrived at Monica pledging to leave all her assets to be split between the four of us if it turned out that we did in fact get to see the day a robot was used as a witness in a murder trial.

"You'll get it all," she said. "Sorry, little Johnny, Mom lost the entirety of your financial safety net because she's a pessimist about scientific innovation."

I continued to study the ceiling from my position on the couch while Meg added, "I still think Alice's answer sounded like the one to go with."

"It sounded utterly ridiculous to me," Josie said, her head buried in her copy of *Great Expectations*.

I looked over to Meg, who scrunched her nose. Monica suddenly looked very interested in the floor, and Alice, well, as per usual, she didn't seem too bothered.

I already touched on the increasing number of snippy and unwarranted comments we'd started to see from Josie. Whether it was a transparent attempt to appear superior in the company of those outside of our immediate group or a different transparent attempt to appear superior in the company of no one other than herself, one thing was clear: the gradual dimming of her spotlight was only reaffirmed by her fear of standing in the dark.

And she had no clue that she was the one turning the dial. It had seemed that the majority of her remarks were targeted toward Alice. Meg had filled me in on what I'd missed at my party the week before when Clay was giving me what I still consider to be the best gift of all time. Apparently, Leo and Alice had struck up a conversation (whilst he was still lucid), and Josie took notice. She asked Meg why Leo would be flirting with *Alice,* and when Meg said it didn't look like they were flirting, Josie essentially told her how naïve she was. Meg insisted she wasn't paraphrasing when she recalled how Josie had later added, "Well I've been into Leo since last fall, so I should probably tell her he's off limits."

"Since last fall? You mean when you didn't know him and also had a boyfriend?" Meg mocked the next morning as we walked to the performing arts building.

Unfortunately, however, each of us would have our turn standing at the center of this unwanted negative attention. Like Meg, herself, that very afternoon, when Josie started to recount her recent escapades with Robby.

"No boys, please. Anything else," Monica said.

"Agreed," Meg said, closing her eyes

"You're one to talk, Meg," Josie said, rolling over onto her stomach. "I mean, you are aware that Clay is essentially in love with you, right?"

Alice gasped, and Monica looked over with a grin.

But Meg cringed. "No, can we please not talk about this—"

Josie leaned over, persisting. "He can be the Hercules to your Megara!" She followed with sarcastic oohing and aahing, and Meg hid her face in her hands.

"Seriously, if we talk about it, I'm just going to get weird. It's the truth. Let's stop now."

And despite the fact that Monica and Alice had taken the hint, Josie felt the need to press further. To milk Meg's discomfort.

"Don't worry, Meg, what is there to lose? He doesn't seem like the boy to lose interest in you if you admit you feel the same way. And if you're leading him on because you like the attention, I certainly won't tell him—"

"Josie," I said. "She doesn't want to talk about it."

She raised her hands in surrender, and I saw Meg let out the breath she'd been holding in, the tension slowly seeping out of the room as we tried to turn our attention to other things.

By then, our minds had been sufficiently warmed up, the world outside our windows seeming brighter by the minute. Monica stood, shaking out her arms and legs and joining Alice in her daily pacing.

I had just picked up my Critical Film Theory textbook when a soft melody began to vibrate through the air. I glanced down to Meg, who was sitting on the floor with her back against the couch, her head resting by my feet. Her eyes were closed as she quietly hummed the opening notes to Tchaikovsky's *Swan Lake*, her left fingers imitating the movements along the board of her invisible violin.

She opened her eyes to find all of us staring at her.

"Play for us, Meg," Monica said.

She hesitated, but eventually reached over and pulled her violin case toward her, carefully removing the instrument. I inhaled deeply as that familiar rosin scent traveled. The room, the couch, the books, they all seemed to breathe it in as well.

Watching Meg play the violin was unlike any other experience. In all the times I'd seen her smile, or laugh, or emote in any fashion for that matter, none compared to the emotion she communicated each time she picked up her instrument. It was the same even when she'd simply glide up and down scales in her room, failing to notice when we'd open the door or put down our pens and listen. She would be so entranced by the melody that, when she did finally realize we were there, she'd jump back, her bow sliding off the strings and producing a spine-tingling sound, like nails tearing at a chalkboard.

My favorite part was watching her begin, the way both she and the violin would inhale sharply and come alive together.

As she did, I sat up, pulling my knees to my chest. Her fingers gradually climbed higher, the melody gaining strength. At the first crash of the phantom symbols, Monica took off, pirouetting around the room with little grace and a lot of passion.

"I always wished my parents made me do ballet," she said.

Another crash. She leaped. Another. She kicked as high as she could.

The climax of the song approached as Monica moved next to the couch, daintily stepping onto the rug. Shooting for one last, dramatic spin, she used her leg to propel her, and it went well.

Until the rug slipped beneath her weight and she plummeted to the bare wooden floor.

The music stopped abruptly. The four of us gawked at her, each afraid to be the first one to speak.

"I'm fine," she said, slowly picking herself up. "In case you were wondering."

"We weren't," Meg said, helping her to her feet.

Monica dusted herself off with a grin. "I thought I was pretty good. And I was sure that rug had to have, like, grown into the floor by now." She kicked it lightly, watching it slide again.

CLOSE-UP: Alice's smile slowly disappears. Her eyes narrow at the floor by Monica's foot.

"Alice?" I asked.

She didn't answer. Instead, she moved forward, crossing in front of the red chair and reaching down for the rug. She pushed it further to the side, grazing her fingers over the wood.

"What is it, Alice?" Monica asked, peering down.

"There's something written here," she said, motioning for us to move out of the way.

From my POV, I could make out a few letters that looked like they'd been carved into the wood.

"Are those...names?" Meg asked, peeking over Alice's shoulder.

Moving closer, I saw that they *were* names. But they weren't ordinary ones. And the more rug Alice rolled out of the way, the more of them were revealed.

The five of us gathered around the center of the floor, crouching down to get a good look.

"That's not something you come across every day," Josie said.

"Yeah, well, neither is a hidden library," Monica said.

"Valid point."

There were seven names in total, placed to form a large circle, with a date carved in the center: 1972. The names, as I said, were not ones you'd typically find carved into a floor. Not that you'd expect to find names carved into a floor at all, but there seemed to be a significant pattern to the ones we read that day.

Aphrodite
Athena

Artemis

Demeter

Hera

Hestia

Tyche

They were the names of Greek goddesses.

"Who do you think did this?" Meg asked, running her hand over the etchings.

Alice studied the discovery in a daze. She had a strange look on her face, an unusual mixture of longing and familiarity for someone who was happening upon it for the first time.

She had yet to look away from the floor. I had yet to look away from her.

"Whoever left this room behind."

SCENE 16

———

I think it's a simple yet overlooked fact that going to a "football school" would have been much more enjoyable if any of us had actually liked football.

Although, to be fair, Josie *loved* football.

She loved it so much, in fact, that she insisted on being at every game and pre-game event. Which meant we had to do the same. Then, about roughly ten to fifteen minutes into the game, she would take off in one direction or another to say hello to this friend or that friend and the four of us would be left to sit in a mostly empty area (so we didn't have to stand to see) and wait until she was ready to leave.

That particular Saturday was worse than usual, as it was forty degrees and raining. It was too warm for the precipitation to be snow but too cold to be even remotely comfortable. And had Meg not packed extra ponchos for us, I don't know what we would've done.

So, there we sat, huddled together on the damp wooden bench staring numbly at a game most of us didn't really understand, while the rain made our pants stick to our legs and our hair curl up at unfortunate angles.

Oh, and while there wasn't much we were able to take away from the display of aggression in front of us, we were perceptive enough to notice that we were losing.

Meg, who had grown up going to those games, would explain certain calls and plays every once in a while if they piqued someone's interest. Why that player could *hit* that player like that but couldn't *grab* that player like that, or why *this* counted as a catch but *that* didn't.

I watched as raindrops rolled down her glasses, the bridge of which she had to continuously slide back up her then-slippery nose. I had grabbed them off her desk before we left, paying attention to the way she glanced at them before running out the door empty-handed.

"It doesn't really matter if I see the game or not," she said when I pulled them out a few minutes into the first quarter.

"But then how would you answer our questions?" I replied.

Flash forward to just before halftime, she was resting her head on my shoulder, kicking the bench in front of us. I found myself entranced by the rhythmic beat of her shoe against the wood, and I studied it. I studied the cracks that ran along the surface, their patterns, their intentions, and I remembered doing the same that other day in the attic.

I remembered tracing the names with my pointer finger, feeling the way the surface dipped in and out, the way years of solitude hardened the edges.

"So, what are we thinking, some kind of cult?" I remember Josie asking before we left.

"What makes you think that?" Monica had asked.

"What normal group of people carves the names of Greek goddesses into the floor?"

"I assumed they were code names. If you're hanging out in a secret room, doing who knows what, I'd think you'd want your identities to be a secret, too."

"Then why leave their mark at all?"

Monica frowned, brushing over the "1972" with her thumb. "I don't know. Yet."

I think each of us had taken special note of the year placed in the center of it all: 1972. The first year that women were admitted to our university. But at the time, none of us had all the pieces we needed to put together a clear picture.

I remembered the way Alice looked at it all, like she had seen it somewhere before. Or perhaps I'd imagined the light film of moisture that coated her eyes, threatening to spill over if she refused to look away. Eventually she did, and she didn't look back for the rest of our time there that afternoon.

That is, until we started to head out, and I turned around to see her remove the rug once more, take a photo with her camera, and bury our discovery all over again.

I tore my eyes away from Meg's shoe to look to my left, at Alice, who stared down at the field with what I perceived to be sheer concentration. Her hair somehow looked darker, no doubt thanks to the water that had an easy time seeping past the flimsy hood of her poncho.

I realized my gaze had been obvious when she turned toward me, quickly, so that I didn't have time to look away. And of the millions of thoughts I knew she had racing around her mind, I swore I saw one of them flash across her eyes, addressing me.

Asking, *What is it that you think you know, Stella?*

If she'd posed the question in a live conversation, I'd likely respond, "Nothing, Alice. Absolutely nothing. To this day, I have yet to figure you out."

As if she had read my mind, she smiled weakly, bumping my shoulder with her own. And I returned the gesture, eager to get back to pretending I was enjoying sitting there in that moment.

It was possible, I thought, that Alice could have just been one of those people who would always remain a bit of a mystery.

My thoughts of attics and engravings and Alice were interrupted by a loud collection of cheers erupting throughout the stadium. Meg jumped to her feet to join the spirited audience, clapping her hands and offering them around for high fives. We were still losing, but we were losing by *less*, which was cause for celebration.

Monica leaned over from the other side of Meg. "Bathroom? Before the rush?"

We had three minutes until halftime (meaning anywhere from five to ten minutes until halftime, if you factored in "stoppage of play," as Meg had called it), so we left our home base and started for the stairs, gripping the railing on the way down.

The path to the bathroom was empty with everyone still in the stands, our voices echoing throughout the concourse as we made our way. We had just passed the food vendors when Alice stopped, looking to her left.

"Hold on a second, guys," she said, heading in that direction.

The three of us slowed, glancing over at her.

"Where is she going?" Meg asked.

"Looks like informal office hours to me," Monica said with a grin.

I peered over to see who she was approaching, my eyes focusing in on the familiar sandy hair and khaki pants. They greeted each other out of earshot, and we stood watching until Professor Aldridge glanced over the top of Alice's head and noticed us waiting for her. He smiled and waved, likely recognizing us from the studio earlier that year. Monica took it as an invitation, and tilted her head toward the pair, beckoning us to go with her.

"Hello, ladies," he said when we were within range. He was brushing beads of salt off of his fresh soft pretzel. "Lovely to see you again."

"You, too," Monica said with a prize-winning smile. "I was just talking to Professor Aldridge—"

"Max."

"—*Max*, about our term project," Alice said. "It's cool, actually. We have to design a new structure for the campus."

"What were you thinking of doing?" I asked.

"I'm not sure yet, that's actually why I was hoping to ask you something," she said, turning back to Profess—I mean, Max.

He motioned to her and smiled. "Go right ahead."

"I was wondering if it might be possible for me to get some of the plans for the campus buildings."

He thought for a moment. "I think that should be doable. Do you know what you had in mind? To help me narrow it down?"

She shook her head. "Not really, I was just hoping something might inspire me." She paused and looked at the ground. "*But* I think it would be helpful to look at the older buildings on campus, even the original ones. I was hoping to play off the older designs as opposed to the new ones. More classic."

Zoom in. Alice's hand is clenched into a tight fist behind her back. She appears to be digging her nails into her palm.

What are you up to, Alice?

Pull back out.

Max sucked air in through his teeth, grimacing. "*That* might be a little trickier. I could almost definitely get you the plans for some of the newer stuff, but most of the original prints are probably archived pretty deep. I'd definitely have to go through the Department Chair and, well, you know how they are about this stuff. Those older guys rarely budge, I mean, the Chair was *my* professor when I was here, and he has a very specific way of doing things. You know, tradition and all."

Alice nodded. "I understand. Is there any way you could ask? Just in case?"

"Oh, sure. Of course, I just don't want you to get your hopes up. And when you figure out what exactly you're looking for, run it by me. I'll see how I can help."

FADE IN: the all too familiar sound of heels clicking against the concrete.

I turned to see Professor Shaw passing through the concourse, admittedly a little overdressed for a football game. She wore black pants that flowed behind her, and a long black rain slicker that made her hair look almost white in comparison. I don't know if I was simply curious, or looking for some brownie points, but I called out to her.

"Hello, Professor Shaw."

The clicking sound faltered as her head whipped in my direction, her hair sliding back over her shoulder. She surveyed us, her stare cold. Her eyes narrowed further, but, despite the fact that I'd been the one to call her name, she wasn't looking at me.

She was looking, yet again, at Alice.

It was the mirror image of our first day in class. The staring contest between the two of them that made me wonder what was being said within the silence.

If she was going to say anything out *loud*, she decided against it, and kept straight on her original path out into the stands.

It was quiet for a few seconds, her footsteps disappearing as we all stood there.

The silence broke when Professor Aldridge, eyebrows raised, cleared his throat. "*She* seems fun."

After he left to return to the stands, I watched Alice as she fell back into one of her usual trances. Her look that said she had plenty of ideas racing about. She didn't even notice when we started toward the bathrooms. I had to reach over and tap her shoulder to bring her back to reality.

Between her own peculiar behavior and Professor Shaw's failure to present much better, the only reason I didn't get swept up by a tornado of rumination was because the spectators that began to flood the area snapped me out of it.

And, unfortunately, they made it to the bathroom before we could.

"That's great," Monica said as we reluctantly got in line.

I perked up when I noticed Josie's fiery red hair bobbing through the crowd. She ran over when she saw us.

"Where did you guys go?"

"We tried to go to the bathroom," Monica said. "But, unfortunately, Alice's hot architecture professor delayed us."

"You saw Max?" Josie asked, her eyes widening.

I cringed at her natural willingness to use his first name. "Yeah, he actually asked about you. Said he wished you were there."

For such an obviously facetious remark, Josie appeared to be rather annoyed.

"Why didn't you guys come find me?"

SCENE 17

——

"Remind me to never order the salmon at Roy's again."

Monica was curled up in a fetal position on the couch, clutching her stomach and silently mouthing pleas, prayers, promises, anything to keep her from hurling up her lunch at any moment.

"What exactly were you expecting from the fish at a small-town diner," I said, flipping through my psych textbook.

"I was expecting to be cosmically rewarded for purchasing the meal I assumed was a worst-seller. I felt bad, okay?"

"You felt bad for the fish? That wasn't being eaten?"

"Forget it."

Roy's Diner was a staple of the town. One of the longest-standing restaurants and open twenty-four hours, seven days a week, it was especially popular among the students looking for an early morning bite after a late night out. Amidst the stress of work picking up and the increasingly repetitive Dining Hall meals, we had decided to switch things up, Josie borrowing a friend's car to aid in our escape from campus for lunch that day. And apart from Monica's food poisoning, or Josie's ill-disguised contempt for life outside of our school's pronounced bubble ("Excuse me, miss," she'd said to our cigarette-scented waitress while trying to avoid touching the table. "Do you happen to have any disinfectant spray? There's some sort of stain, here."), I happened to think it was a lovely afternoon.

The sun filled the room with a light orange glow emanating from the west side of campus, the trees that peeked in through the window growing barer by the day.

When Alice walked in and slid her backpack off of her shoulder, she froze at the sight of Monica, who was just beginning to sit up, her hand moving to her mouth. She started to speak, but Monica cut her off.

"Don't ask," she said. "If you ask, I'll think about it. And if I think about it, I'll—" she interrupted herself with a gag, followed by a still silence.

No one moved. No one breathed. Eventually she gulped and exhaled shakily, her face pale and her bangs stuck to her forehead.

"Monica, I feel for you, I really do," Josie said, her eyes never leaving the pages in front of her. "But if you throw up in here, I will not be coming back. I just wanted to put that out there."

"Noted," Monica said, curling forward into her original position again.

"How was Studio?" Meg asked Alice as she came over to join us.

"Busy. I'm sad I missed lunch," she replied.

"Next time," Josie said, her irony thinly veiled. She wasn't known to be an expert at concealing her feelings toward another person. But that afternoon, it was clear that she was hardly trying.

TRACK Alice: *she puts her bag down and walks around the couch toward the bookshelf.*

I watched as she looked over the shelves, her eyes scanning from top to bottom, occasionally wandering away to the walls or the floor. I couldn't count the number of times I had seen her do that, even from the first day she took us up there. She had probably covered every square inch of the place. Examining, feeling, searching.

But for what?

She raised her hand, standing up on her tiptoes to reach for the top shelf. She ran her fingers over the row of spines.

The sound of Monica letting out a long groan startled me, and I blinked out of the tight frame, returning to the scene in front of me.

"Alice," she mumbled. "Could you be a doll and pass me one of those books? I need a distraction from this poison *coursing* through my digestive tract."

Josie snorted. "If 'a flair for the dramatic' were a person..."

"Which one?" Alice asked, looking over her shoulder.

"Surprise me," she said, her face buried into a pillow.

"Give her *Jane Eyre*," Meg said as she scribbled something into her notebook.

Without even turning around to look at the shelf, Alice reached down to the left and plucked the maroon hardcover from between two others, tossing it over to the couch, where it missed Monica by only a few inches. There was something so instinctive about her retrieval of the novel. She knew where it was the whole time, probably because she'd spent I don't know how many collective hours studying and likely memorizing everything in the room.

On a whim, I decided to test my theory.

"Alice," I said, glancing over at the others. "Can you grab me...*The Woman in White*, if it's there?"

And before she could move, I quickly added, "With your eyes closed?"

She smiled, the gleam in her eyes only disappearing when she shut them and reached behind her. She felt around the middle-left section of the bookcase, swiping her pointer finger across one, two, three, four, *five* books. She stopped and removed the black hardcover, then opened her eyes and tossed it over to me. I held the book up toward the other girls.

The Woman in White by Wilkie Collins.

Meg sat up. "Can I get, um, *Crime and Punishment*?"

Bottom right, third from the end. Alice threw that one over, too.

Even Josie had grown interested. "*A Study in Scarlet.*"

"*Catch-22*?"

"*Frankenstein!*"

One by one she went, the speed at which she chucked the copies toward us becoming increasingly alarming. (Had we been even a bit athletically gifted, I'm sure the sight of bound pages spiraling toward us wouldn't have been nearly as daunting.)

SHOT: *books flying through the air.*

When Monica muttered weakly, "*1984*," Alice reached up once more for the top shelf, feeling around.

But this time, her hand stopped moving, and she frowned, opening her eyes slowly.

She remained on her tiptoes for a few more seconds, her brow furrowed in concentration as she stretched her arm further. There was something there, just beyond her reach. If only she could *just—*

She got it.

Her face relaxed as she floated down to stand firmly on the ground.

"What is it, Alice?" Meg asked.

All four of us had been watching her, waiting for her to deliver the copy of *1984* that Monica had requested, but what she held in her hand didn't look like a book. (Well, it did. But not that kind of book. This one was smaller, thinner. There was nothing on the front or back cover. It was just, *blue*.)

"It looks like a journal," Alice said, turning it over in her hands.

The way she stared at it, delicately, as though her gaze alone could shatter it to pieces, made me feel intrusive. Like I was witnessing something I wasn't meant to see. But still, I couldn't look away.

And I wanted to know just what it was that had her so mesmerized.

"Can I see it?" I asked.

Her face whipped toward me, as though she'd forgotten I was even there. She hesitated, not too long, but long enough for it to be noticeable.

"I can help you try to figure out what it is," I said, extending my hand toward her.

Whether she handed it to me because she wanted to, or because she felt like she had no other option, the next thing I knew, I was the one examining it.

I ran my hands over the sky-blue exterior, stopping when I felt resistance on the underside. I flipped the book over, spying a rough circular patch in the very center of the cover. It was like someone had scraped away the smooth top layer to reveal the fibers underneath. Opening it to glance at the first page, I confirmed that the defaced side was the front.

I looked up to find Alice, peering over my shoulder and holding her breath. Her cheeks had gone pink from the pressure.

"It's a journal," I said, pointing to the first entry I had found when peering inside. I then closed it again and showed her the rough area. "But it looks like whatever was on the front here was taken off. An initial, likely."

"The rest of it is in perfect condition," Josie said. "The thing obviously hasn't been touched in years."

"Well, what does it say?" Meg asked.

"Here, I can read it," Alice said, reaching for it. She was a little too eager, for my taste.

"Don't worry." I smiled, opening the journal once more. "I got it."

OVER THE SHOULDER SHOT: *the elegant script that lines the first page.*

Zoom in. A date. September 5, 1972.

I read the following out loud:

Well, the day is finally here. The very first day I get to call myself a college student. My mother told me I should keep this diary so that I can look back on everything that I'll experience here. She says I'm making history. I say she's being dramatic. But still, I made her a promise, and I intend to keep it.

So, here goes nothing. They served hamburgers at the Dining Hall today. (That's the first thing that came to mind, I guess.) There was also pizza, and a lot of fried foods. The boys seemed to love it. I myself would have preferred to see a little more variety on the menu, but I don't want to complain just yet. We're changing enough just by being here. I doubt they'll appreciate it if we overstep.

They've put us in the dorm that's right on the central quad. By the Basilica and the Main Hall. One dorm was enough to fit all two hundred of us, thankfully, so we didn't have to displace any more students, but they've assured us no one minds. A boy even helped me carry my bags up to the third floor, but I forget his name. (And I feel awful about it.) But I truly believe that I met more people today than I have over the course of my whole life. It's impossible to get all the names straight.

Our classes officially start tomorrow, and I'm nervous. We were told that, because there are so few of us, there may be a few classes in which we're the only girls. I know I'm meant to be here, so it's not that I'm worried I'm not qualified. It's just, I don't know. I guess I don't know what to expect. But it couldn't be that much worse than high school, right?

A bunch of the girls in my hall were planning on going to eat together tomorrow, and I think I might join them. I certainly don't want to go alone. And they seem nice enough. Perhaps I'll write an update tomorrow, after we all eat together.

Oh, but before I forget, there was one girl I met today who seemed very kind. I think I could consider her my first friend here.

Unfortunately, no matter how hard I try, I just can't seem to remember her name. Gosh, that's frustrating.

I'm sure I'll get the hang of it eventually.

I'd come to the end of the first entry, silent as I processed what I'd just read.

Meg was the first to speak. "So, does anyone else have chills?"

"From a diary entry, Meg?" Josie asked.

"Not just any diary," she said. "That's a first-hand account of the first day women went to school here. That's a *primary* source. I'd say that's pretty cool, wouldn't you agree, Monica?"

Monica grumbled incoherently from the couch, her face smushed into a pillow again.

"I agree with you, Meg," I said, flipping through the pages quickly. "There are more entries here—"

I paused when I recognized an interesting theme.

The first page of that journal hadn't been the one with the September fifth entry at all. Once I looked closely enough, I saw a small tear at the inner seam near the front cover. It was a clean tear, hardly visible, but it was there.

The *very* first page had been removed.

Now, utilizing what I knew about journals, or notebooks, I guessed that the missing page would have held the average contact information. The "Property of" page.

But it was curious that the sheet which, in all likelihood, bore the name of whoever these experiences had belonged to, had been torn out. That what was probably an initial on the front cover, had been scraped away.

It all led me to one conclusion:

Whoever this girl was, she wanted to be invisible.

Why?

With the time passing quicker than we realized, each of us opted to return to our studying. Each of us except Alice, that is. Alice wanted to read more of the entries, so I relinquished the journal and focused on the textbook in front of me, only occasionally glancing up to see if I could gauge whether or not she'd found something of note.

For the most part, her face was blank, her eyes traveling over the pages with little more emotion than pure fascination.

But as evening approached and we prepared to leave, I looked up and saw a different expression entirely. It was a mix between sadness and anger, heartbreak and horror. Her mouth hung open slightly in the form of a frown, her forehead creased with concern. It wasn't until she noticed me staring at her that she regained her composure, and the sentiments written across her face erased themselves, one by one.

She didn't look away, now that she had managed to cover her tracks. Instead, she returned my stare, shutting the book and rising to put it back where she had found it.

"Find anything interesting, Alice?" I heard Meg ask on the way out.

I had been a few steps ahead of them when she replied, "No, not really."

SCENE 18

I used to think that the easiest place to bare one's soul was at a nightclub at two in the morning after getting drunk off of four or so Sea Breezes. The night we found the journal, on October 19, 1992, I learned that I much preferred getting to know someone under the moonlight.

It was around seven when we decided to walk back and finish studying in our dorm. The approaching winter season had made that evening a dark one, and the lack of an artificial light source in the hidden attic meant our time there was dictated by the sun. The five of us traveled home at a quicker pace than we would have on warmer, brighter days, the fallen leaves crunching beneath our feet.

We were within range of midterms, and we hadn't yet thought of our mythology presentation topic. Monica obviously wasn't happy about this, but deep down, I knew she had faith that we'd think of something, even at the last minute, like she often did. Personally, every time I thought about that class I remembered the way Professor Shaw had looked at us during that football game.

At first, I thought she just may not have been used to students addressing her outside of the classroom. I told myself that she was surprised, or confused, or that maybe there was a chance she didn't recognize us in that moment. But I couldn't forget the coldness in her stare. It felt intentional. It felt threatening.

It felt personal.

The other girls had noticed the icy nature of her character, too, and had proposed their own theories. Monica, for example, had taken personal offense when she'd rejected her initial midterm paper proposal for a feminist retelling and analysis of the myth of Perseus and Medusa.

"It's like she's a woman who's sexist against women. How is that even possible?" she had said angrily, pacing back and forth across the room.

"Did you consider the possibility that she just hates you?" Josie asked, examining her fingernails.

Monica stopped and addressed the group. "Okay, *us*. If that is the case, I just think it's important that we clarify. She hates all of us."

Josie looked up, an invisible light bulb flashing above her head. "I actually think she really hates Alice. I mean, you guys heard her. Alice *Demetria*."

And then I remembered the fact that, to me, it looked like her stare had been directed toward Alice. The same way she looked at her during that first class. I observed the way seeing Alice made her pause, and I'll admit, that threw me off guard. She didn't seem like the kind of woman who would often pause.

So, it begged the question, what was it about Alice? What was it about her that affected her so deeply that she'd behave, from what I could tell, so differently from normal?

Then I'd tell myself it was all in my head. That I was turning the mysterious and beautiful Hitchcock Blonde into a character trope rather than a real live human being, with real live intentions. And that would've been unfair of me.

But still, I'd return to those moments, play them over and over in my head, a film on a loop, the reel continuously spinning. And each time I'd think the same thing.

That there was more to both of their stories.

And Alice, all by herself, had exhibited enough odd behavior to fill her own reel. One that kept me up at night, thinking, guessing. Remembering the way she'd looked at the carvings in the floor. And the way she'd been so eager to get her hands on that journal.

And her face when reading it, before she realized I had seen her.

Perhaps that was why I joined Alice on the quad that evening, despite the fact that my teeth were already chattering and that I had, for a reason that is still beyond me, decided to wear a skirt that day.

We'd almost made it to our dorm when Meg looked over my shoulder and asked, "Alice?"

I followed her gaze to find her, about twenty feet from the rest of us, making her way onto the grass. She put her backpack down and waved us over.

"What is she doing?" Josie asked.

Alice proceeded to sit down and get comfortable, lying back onto the ground. "Look at the moon, you guys," she called to us.

We looked up to see the moon in question (the only moon, that is), and I realized what she was talking about. While the moon often looks beautiful, that night it wore a large, diffused glow. A halo that extended far beyond what had to be normal. Suddenly it was brighter than I'd ever remembered it could be.

Josie sighed and rolled her eyes. "I have neither the time nor the energy for this tonight."

Monica (whose nausea had miraculously passed) cupped her hands around her mouth and yelled over to her, "I would love to be all zen and reflective with you right now, Alice, but I do have a paper due tomorrow that I haven't started so I *will* be joining Josie!"

I looked to Meg, who frowned at the ground. "I have a really tough theology midterm," she said quietly.

I don't know exactly what it was that made me decide to join her. It could have been a twinge of guilt that she would've been left alone, or that I really did want to watch the moon with her. But I know that at least part of it had to do with having the opportunity to find out more about her, if she'd let me.

"I'll stay with Alice for a little and catch up with you guys later," I said finally, looking at the girl who was comfortably reclined on the cool grass.

Meg smiled, and I was sure she was comforted by the fact that Alice wouldn't be entirely abandoned. As they continued toward the door, I made my way over to Alice and sat down, cringing as I felt the blades of grass poke and prod my legs through my stockings. Pushing through the discomfort, I put all thoughts of bugs and dirt out of my mind and reclined to her level, observing the night sky from her point of view.

"People ignore the world in the winter," she said after a moment or two of silence.

I waited for her to continue, but she didn't. "In what way?"

"They hurry from building to building, stop walking and start driving. They do everything they can to avoid the outside, to escape it."

She was right, I realized, and I was guilty of it myself. I shivered as a gust of wind burned the few inches of skin that didn't receive the luxury of being shielded by my clothing.

"Can you blame them, though?" I asked. "I like the season, but it's not what I'd consider inviting, especially when it's dark."

"I'll challenge you on the second half of that statement."

I feigned annoyance. "On what grounds?"

Alice smiled up at the moon. "I guess it's typical to view the daytime as safe and the darkness as something more ominous. There's more clarity during the day, and at night you don't really know what's out there, sure. I don't disagree. But I've always questioned why we worship the sun—why we write poems about it and compare its worth to that of the person you love. The one you believe stands at the center of your universe. Personally, I think all the sun has ever done for me is push me away. It's a harsh, unflattering illumination, highlighting what I don't want to see. But the moon," she paused, basking in its glow. "The moon always seems to be shining for me. It's soft and gentle. It wants to be wanted, and in return it lights the way for you while the sun is otherwise occupied..." she trailed off, her eyelids drooping slightly.

For a moment, nothing was heard but the sound of fallen leaves tickled by the evening breeze. I felt that any response I could offer would inevitably fall short of Alice's lyrical observations.

"You're a good listener," she said finally. "You don't trivialize what I have to say. Or, you don't respond with snippy comments. Out loud, that is."

I knew what she was getting at, but I still chose my words carefully.

"Josie is...unsure of herself. And she takes it out on others."

"I know." Alice turned and looked at me. "But it's nice to feel like your thoughts are valued."

It was nice. I realized I'd gotten so used to being on the receiving end of Josie's ramblings and complaints and general negativity that assuming the role of the listener came naturally to me. With Alice, it was different. Yes, she had a lot to say, but her innate curiosity made it so that her ramblings required counter-ramblings. She left room to be challenged, if you were willing to accept the invitation.

"She's usually very nice to people."

The second the words left my mouth, I realized how incredibly terrible they sounded. Alice noticed the horrified expression on my face and burst out laughing, her back arching slightly, threatening to tip her over onto her side.

"I just meant," I said, trying to recover. "I just meant that she has a way with people. They like her a lot, they think she's nice."

"Of course they do," she said, looking up at the sky again. "She's nice to them because she's kept them at enough of a distance to where they can't see past the facade. The four of us, we're close enough to see through it. We know too much, we've witnessed too much of her. So, in the end, we're just reminders of the parts of herself she's trying to keep hidden. Which, more than anything, is the simple fact that she's, truly, very...sad."

Maybe the only thing Alice had been keeping from us was how incredibly perceptive she was.

The wind filled our silence again, but I didn't seem to feel it at that point. It passed over us, as if there were a bubble keeping it at arm's length, hoping we'd stay longer.

I didn't want to overstep, or risk ruining the moment by taking the conversation in another direction, but I still wanted to know more about her. When I thought of a possible way to go about getting some answers, I stayed very still, feeling the only movement in my body to be the steady yet quickening beat of my heart.

"So, what, you're just happy all the time?" I asked. "No skeletons in your closet?"

Her face turned slightly toward mine, and the moonlight seemed to reveal her thoughts like words on a page, its source a tiny reflection in the mirror of her eye. The wind lifted a loose strand of her hair. "I never said that."

"Care to elaborate?" I asked, my tone lighthearted.

She shrugged. "I think we all have parts of ourselves we don't like. Things we'd rather forget." She paused, her eyes moving back and forth like she was reading the sky. "I don't think anyone grows up unscathed, right? I mean, you get hurt, you lose parts of yourself, you lose…"

For the first time since I'd met her, her strong voice seemed to have lost its sturdy foundation.

"You lose someone," she said finally, and I felt my stomach drop.

"I'm sorry," I said, praying I was doing a good enough job masking the feeling of my insides knotting together.

"It's okay," she said. "I don't mind talking about her."

"Her?" I asked, watching her face.

She looked calm, even a little content, to be remembering her, probably.

"My aunt. Daphne. We lost her last year." She paused. "You know, she actually introduced me to mythology. Back when I was younger."

My smile joined hers. "Did she really?"

"Oh yeah. She used to tell me all these stories, these myths." Something flashed across her face, far too quickly for me to analyze it. She was already smiling again, and she rolled onto her side to face me. "Take one guess as to who her favorite goddess was."

I rolled toward her as well, wracking my brain, going over the possibilities. Then it hit me, the small detail of Alice's backstory that I actually knew, that I actually understood. This must have been why, I realized, she felt the name would fit so naturally among her other three.

"Demeter."

And just like that, another piece of the puzzle that was Alice clicked into place. She looked up at the sky again.

"Growing up, I always thought she was so vibrant. So happy. But as I got older, she got worse, and after it all happened..." She struggled for the right words, never losing sight of the moon. She stared, confronted it. She allowed it to hear the questions in her head and she listened to its answers.

SHOT: Alice's profile as she looks up at the sky. The white glow coats her skin, highlighting each strand of her hair.

"Sometimes, when something happens to you, you tell yourself anything to make it, I don't know, make sense to you. To make it hurt less. You rewrite the narrative, you assign yourself more agency, you do anything you can to give yourself control over a situation where you had none. And that's all anybody wants, isn't it? Control? We pick up on the smallest, unnoticeable details of our life as they begin to exit our orbit and try desperately to rein them in again, if only to feel safe for just a little longer."

I swallowed, reminding myself that I was there to listen to her. To learn about her.

I wasn't there to paint myself with her words. I wasn't there to allow her to bring to the surface the things I'd buried. Not before I was ready.

And so I asked her, shifting in the grass, a question to which I believed I already knew the answer.

"Does it work?"

"I don't think it does," she said. "It's one thing to experience that yourself. But to watch someone you love go through it, when there's nothing that you can do about it…I guess it made me see life differently. And for a while, I couldn't really find my way out of that."

I wondered if she ever did find her way out. I wondered if it could be done.

I saw her out of the corner of my eye, taking out her camera and pointing it at me. I made the mistake of turning right as the flash went off, the picture she handed over capturing me with my eyes closed, mid-blink. I grimaced, and she laughed.

I felt her watching me when I looked back at the night sky. "What," I said.

She exhaled, her mouth forming a slight grin. "You're going to fall in love again, Stella."

My reply was hesitant. "I've never been in love."

"Sure you have. When you were younger."

I couldn't tell what she meant, her poetry slipping through my fingers, once more.

But I entertained the thought, nonetheless. "So, tell me. Just who am I going to fall in love with?"

Her answer surprised me, and, to be perfectly honest, I have yet to forget it.

(But for now, I feel I should keep it between the two of us.)

We stayed like that for a little while longer, my gaze lingering on each of our surroundings before eventually finding its way back to her. And as she lay there, continuing her conversation with the moon, I wondered what they could possibly have so much to talk about.

SCENE 19

———

The next night, I was still thinking about the chat I'd had with Alice.

It wasn't the direction I'd foreseen the conversation going in, though I'm not sure I knew what to expect in the first place. All I had been going off of were a few cold stares, a few evasive comments, and a few moments I simply couldn't decipher what was going through her head.

She seemed to be able to figure out a lot more than I could. I thought back to her assessment of Josie, and I wondered if she could tell that much about me from the way I carried myself, from the things I said.

I actually hadn't seen her since we left each other the night before. She felt tired and decided to go back to her own dorm, while I went right to sleep in my own. We didn't have class together the next day, but I was on my way to Clay's room that evening, knowing I'd be seeing her shortly.

Walking through the dark winter air with the collar of my coat raised around my ears by my lifted shoulders, my steps quickened as I spotted the yellow glow peeking through the windows of the door.

The tapping sound made by my shoes was muffled by the carpet as I stepped inside. I took my time going up the stairs, warming my hands by rubbing them together quickly. Reaching Clay's door, I braced myself before turning the handle, aware that I was late and that everyone else would already be there.

That she would be there.

MATCH CUT TO:

I finally opened the door, met by the dark room and the faces of my friends, illuminated by the glow of the TV screen.

But her face, in particular, was missing.

"About time," Monica said, grabbing the bowl of popcorn from Meg.

I put my backpack down by the door and walked over to the couch, squeezing in next to Josie on the end.

"Where's Alice?" I asked, hoping I didn't sound too invested in the impending answer.

Monica shrugged, her eyes never leaving the TV. "We left her a note on her door. Said we'd be here."

Alice always showed up to our little gatherings. I tried to ignore the twisting, nauseous feeling I had thinking that our conversation the night before had anything to do with her absence. She seemed fine when we said good night, but I started to worry that she only felt the need to hide more from us. From me.

Shaking away my nervous thoughts, I turned my attention to the square screen and tried to have a good time. One might think it irresponsible to have a movie night just before midterms, and honestly, we did too, but we did it, anyway.

Funny enough, we watched the film Clay had on his Narrative syllabus, *Rear Window*. Now, I appreciated a night of Hitchcock more than anyone, but I will say that it didn't help to sit there and watch Jeff observe as evil unfolded before him, while he was unable to do anything about it. In a way, we were similar, he and I. All *he* could do, after all, was sit and watch, stuck behind his window. Immobilized. And that feeling of claustrophobia was all too fitting at that point in time.

All that I had wanted to do was enjoy the movie I'd already seen too many times. I wanted to enjoy watching Jeff and Lisa and, yes, Stella, uncover the answers they'd been looking for, but all that did was remind me of how little I knew, myself. I had been trying so hard to pin down the details of something that I didn't even understand in the first place. I didn't even know where to look.

But somewhere between Grace Kelly's big entrance and Jeff watching Thorwald clean the handsaw, I realized that I did have a clue. A place to start.

Alice said she hadn't found anything interesting in those journal entries. But I decided, then and there, that she was lying.

Maybe she had discovered that the woman who left her journal in that room hadn't read a single book on those shelves. Maybe she had stumbled across the true horrors to be witnessed when those women first encountered communal bathrooms.

Or maybe she had found whatever it was that she had been looking for, all that time.

All I knew was that I was going to find out. That, and exactly how I was going to do it.

I was going to read the rest of that journal.

SCENE 20

———

We were supposed to meet in the attic an hour after I got there.

I figured that I—actually, I *knew* that I needed to be alone for what I had planned on doing. If my observations were correct and Alice had been lying about finding nothing in that journal, it was best that she remained unaware of my suspicions.

On my way there, I tried to convince myself that I wouldn't find anything. That the only thing waiting for me in those entries were classic tales of freshman year. Courses, parties, boys. The hardly bearable weather, even. (*Dear diary, the sky was gray again today. It's been a week since I've seen the sun. I've started to get sad when I go outside. I wonder if it will be gray tomorrow, too.*) Yes, I'd decided that my anonymous window to the past would tell me nothing other than, at the worst, how much more defeating it was to be a woman in college twenty years prior.

I peeked my head into the room before entering, checking to make sure none of the others had planned a secret rendezvous with the couch like I had. The coast was clear, the journal right where Alice left it, prepped and ready for dissection. Once I settled in, though, I couldn't stop myself from first examining the missing portion of the cover once more.

The phantom initial, just beyond my grasp.

I knew trying to decipher something that wasn't there would prove to be less than productive, but it was difficult to tear my eyes away. I found myself finally motivated, however, when I remembered that I had limited time to explore the contents of the mysterious diary. Mentally reciting one last reassurance that what I would read would only ease my concerns, I dove in and didn't look back.

September 6, 1972

So, I was right. The girls I went to dinner with are very kind. Though I'm not sure I'll ever get used to the fact that we all come from so many different places. Despite that, though, we actually have a lot in common. I think almost every single one of us loves to read, which is nicer than I would have thought. It's certainly a change from my friends at home. We talked about our favorite books over dinner, an icebreaker of sorts. Everyone loved when I said mine was Crime and Punishment—

I looked over to the copy on the second shelf, where Alice had located it effortlessly.

It felt really good to have everyone agree with me like that. It made me feel like I might have already found a great group of friends here.

Unfortunately, my fear that I'd be the only girl in a class or two turned out to be valid. Like in English this morning. I'll never forget the way they all turned and looked at me when I walked in. I felt like I had shown up naked or something.

Suddenly everything was wrong about me, I kept checking for a stain on my dress or toilet paper stuck to my shoe. But there was nothing. Just this nagging voice telling me that there had to be something embarrassing about the way I looked that they kept staring at. And there was nothing I could do about it, since there was nothing to fix. It was a horribly uncomfortable feeling. While I did my best to ignore it during the actual lecture, it was definitely noticeable when the professor made me stand up and introduce myself.

The only class I have that isn't entirely made up of boys is the one that's entirely made up of girls. They're making us take this seminar as a group to help us transition into our new lives here. And you know what the first "lesson" was? Well, after we'd gone over the basic things we'd already learned in our orientation—the honor code, for example—the instructor (an older nun here, bless her) started to tell us how we should be interacting with the boys here. As though we had never come across boys before. Like I said, though, she was a little older. Her name was, oh gosh, not again...Sister Kate, I think? Yes, I think it was something like that. I don't really know what else we're going to cover during this entire semester, but I'm sure it will be...interesting.

I flipped through the next couple of pages, passing over entries, trying to discern what was mundane and what might be a little more interesting. My eyes skimmed over random sentences.

On September 10:

She said she had never listened to Vivaldi before. Actually, what she really said was that she thought listening to Vivaldi was pretentious.

On September 12:

If I have to do all the work for this project by myself, I might go crazy... Actually, who am I kidding? I don't trust him to cover his portion thoroughly.

On September 16:

But, how was I supposed to know that it smelled like skunk?

I turned more pages, skipping over exactly what I had assured myself would be in there. Nothing out of the ordinary.

But as if on cue, I landed on an entry that caught my eye.

September 23, 1972
    You'll never believe what we found today.
    We stumbled upon it entirely by accident. But what a happy accident it was. You see, we were going to get lunch at the Dining Hall, but we all felt sort of hesitant about it. That feeling that I described in my second entry? About constantly worrying that there's something wrong with your outfit or appearance because those boys just keep looking at you? Well, we had all felt that every time we went to eat. Except it was worse in that giant room, with all those tables. All those eyes. So we figured, why not try to eat somewhere else? We could take our food to go, and find somewhere to sit where we'd be alone. It would be so peaceful. We all agreed.
    Now, we weren't planning on eating our food in the bathroom like we'd just been bullied in the high school cafeteria, but we figured there would have to be some cozy corner for us to simply have the space to ourselves. And when we brought our food out and started looking around, we actually found

one. There was this little hidden corner way down at the end of the hall that you'd never notice unless you were actively looking for it. But the cool part is, when we went behind the curtain that was hiding it, there was a set of stairs!

Of course, being the curious bunch we are, we just had to see where they led.

It was better than we could have imagined. There was this room, like an attic, behind this small door. It looked like it hadn't been used in years and years. There were tarps over all the furniture, and an empty bookshelf that was coated in dust. I sneezed a lot, allergies and all, but it was worth it. Oh, and there was this gorgeous rug in the middle of the room.

So, of course, we ate there. And we eventually came to the decision that we would continue to eat there. We kept coming up with these great ideas. We'll bring our favorite books and fill the shelves. We'll treat it as our space. Our small, hidden spot that we can escape to. A spot that belongs only to us on this campus where we typically feel like we are imposing.

It was the best part of my day. I don't know what else to say other than I can't wait to go back tomorrow.

I took a moment before I could turn to the next entry, instead choosing to look around the room. To picture it as the author of those accounts had described it. I saw the couches covered with tarps, the bookshelf empty and dusty. My awareness of the hiding spot became heightened. What everything around me really meant, such as why these books were here, or the fact that those girls also saw it as an escape, it all came sharply into focus. I had an overwhelmingly clear picture of the significance of the room I inhabited in that very moment.

I then wondered if it was yet another curious parallel that we stumbled upon the room, as well. But almost instantly, I knew that it couldn't have been. Because I remembered that we hadn't simply found it. Alice had. And more than that, she had been looking for it.

FLASHBACK: Alice stops outside the building and takes a picture of the tall, narrow window.

I had to keep reading. I skipped over more sections, taking notice of a few relevant recollections along the way.

On September 30:

We had another idea. We wanted to leave our mark somewhere in the attic, to claim it in some sort of symbolic way. We all love the exclusivity of it—the fact that it belongs only to us. The secrecy inspired us to take this whole thing one step further. Our group, our meetings, it reminded us of the secret societies we've read about, those we've studied. So, we figured, why not become our own?

We made it official, carving our names into the floor and everything. (Not our real names, of course. If this is going to be a secret society, we needed to hide our identities, in case the place is ever discovered.) So, we chose code names. I forget who it was that suggested we each pick a name of a Greek goddess, but being the mythology lovers that we are, it was an easy decision. Mine is ▮▮▮▮▮.

The name was covered in dark ink, impossible to see through. What mattered more, though, was the knowledge that, at one point in time, the author felt comfortable sharing her name. (Or, at least, her code name.) Something must have happened sometime after this entry that made her want to erase all traces of her identity. I forged ahead.

On October 15:

I think the reason she's upset is that she feels like I'm keeping it from her. Which I'm not…entirely. It's more a matter of convenience, and the most convenient thing right now is to simply leave her out of it. That being said, I don't blame her for being upset.

But D was very clear. We can't trust any of them. And I trust D.

I homed in on "D," alarm bells ringing in my head. It was what drew me to the passage in the first place. I thought about the carvings in the floor. The code names. The only one that started with a "D."

Demeter.

FLASHBACK in MONTAGE:

Alice in the bookstore on that late-August afternoon. A silver "D" hanging on a chain around her neck.

Professor Shaw addressing her in class. "Alice Demetria, isn't it?"

Alice and I talking under the moon. "Take one guess as to who her favorite goddess was."

Me, smiling. "Demeter."

Alice taking a picture of the window.

Alice staring at the code names carved into the floor. Staring at "Demeter."

Alice reading the journal.

Alice.

I placed the book down in my lap, my interactions with Alice playing in sequence. In a new light. She had known that the room existed before she'd even taken her first class. Possibly before she'd even enrolled. If her aunt *was* Demeter, Alice had a personal stake in all this. Whatever "this" was.

But why didn't Demeter trust the other girls? What were both she and the anonymous author keeping from them?

The clock was ticking. Realizing that the others would be there soon, I knew I couldn't slow down. The next entry had been written only a few days later.

October 17, 1972

I think things are beginning to fall apart.

D said that it was because we've all been spending so much time together. It's not impossible, after all, that we've started to feel suffocated. All we do is spend time in that tiny, hidden room. It's practically a breeding ground for claustrophobia. I mean, what else could we have possibly expected?

I think part of it is that we've all changed a lot. Can you believe it? Not two months we've been here and some of us already feel like different people. And I suppose it makes sense, what with being thrown into the mix here, on our own for the first time, but I can't help but feel like a lot of us have become polar opposites of what we used to be. Some of them act like people I don't recognize.

Now, I'm not opposed to change, but it doesn't feel like growth. It feels like maybe I misjudged them earlier on...or maybe they were like this the whole time, and I just didn't see it. But that's what happens when you look too closely at something, isn't it? You realize once it's too late that you can't unsee whatever it is that used to be hidden.

It's especially relevant now, knowing what I know, what they've always known. It's more of a burden than I realized, finding out that something everyone else thinks is fiction, is actually right in front of you.

Or below you, in this case.

I have to be discreet about all this, of course. Maybe I'm just paranoid, but I keep worrying that someone is going to read this. No one else can find out about this. I'm already risking

our cover just by writing about it here, even in the vaguest of
terms. I'm already risking everything by simply knowing the
truth. I don't want to know what they'd do to me if someone
found out on my account.

Secret societies aren't meant to be brought to light. Bad
things tend to happen to those who try.

We all heard the stories when we got here. The whis-
pers. But in reality, they're more than that. They exist, hid-
den underground.

I've seen them.

A stinging heat had been making its way up my neck and
toward my face, engulfing me, yet, subtly. It felt like the air
was slowly being sucked out of the room, and whatever would
come next in the story would either save me, or suffocate me.
(In retrospect, it was a lot to digest, no?)

They knew.

The women who met in this room knew that the tunnels
existed. They had been down there.

(Well, assuming that my interpretation of the text had
been correct. Let's be honest, though. It wasn't that hard to
read between the lines...*Below you...Hidden underground...*I
mean, let's not forget, I did get into the school.)

I couldn't quite tell how the author felt about it. She mentioned being paranoid, that someone else might find out. That
it would be her fault. I thought back to our lecture on Eleusis, and the Mysteries. How revealing their secrets came at
a price. I wondered just what price she thought she would
have to pay.

I also wondered what it was that made the tunnels so special. What was down there, that they so desperately needed
to keep from being discovered? What was the secret of their

society, and what lengths would they go to in order to protect it?

There was only one way to find out. I turned to the next page.

November 18, 1972

I haven't written here in a while.

I've been…distracted. A lot has happened since my last entry. Things I couldn't have predicted. To say I've been in over my head would be an understatement. I don't know what made me think any of this was a good idea—maybe I am the one who changed, who has become unrecognizable. But all I know is I can't keep this secret anymore. I have to tell someone. But I don't know if D will understand.

It wasn't supposed to happen like this. None of it was. But now, there's only one thing for me to do. I know what's happening in the tunnels tonight. I know where they'll be.

I'm terrified of doing this, but I don't think I have a choice. I have to go back down there.

Tonight.

I looked up and saw her, whoever she was, staring back at me. As though I had read her story, and awoken her from the pages. Her silhouette.

Her ghost.

When I turned the page, I was met with blank sheets of paper. It wasn't until the last one, right inside the back cover, that I found something. A sequence written upside down. A mere scribble. A quick thought.

3401029B

Other than that, it was empty, refusing me the courtesy of revealing how her story ended.

I have to go back down there. Tonight.

It was the last thing she wrote.

SCENE 21

———

I barely had time to return the journal to its hiding spot before they walked in.

The sound of their footsteps coming up the stairs had jolted me out of my dream-like encounter with the Ghost of Diaries Past, and I'd just stepped away from the bookshelf when Meg opened the door, Josie and Alice following close behind her.

Meg tilted her head when she saw me. "We were wondering where you were. We waited at your room."

"Sorry, you shouldn't have. I just came early to get in more studying," I said, distancing myself from the shelves further.

CLOSE-UP: Alice's eyes flick from me to the books, then back to me.

I cleared my throat and changed the subject. "Where's Monica?"

Josie fell into the red chair, hoisting her legs up over one of the velvet arms. "She's finishing up work down at the paper. Something about being behind schedule and 'publish or perish.' Not that *that* applies to them…at all."

As if on cue, Monica burst through the door, practically falling into the room. (Her entrances were often nothing if not attention grabbing.) The sight had been made only more spectacular by the rhythmic wheezing that interrupted her attempts to start speaking.

She inhaled deeply, waving her hand around as if that could get across what she needed to say. With one more breath, she leaned over, then reached out and presented a piece of paper to the four of us.

Alice took it hesitantly, eyeing Monica as she did so. Noticing her furrowed brow, I walked toward her. It took a lot for me to keep my mind from drifting to the journal entries. The ones Alice had read, and, as I had suspected, lied about. Not only did I feel hurt (and, admittedly, a little betrayed), but I wondered what else she may have lied to me about. Just when I thought I had finally started to understand her, that she had *let* me understand her, I'd had the rug pulled out from beneath me. She hadn't told me the full story about her aunt. That she had gone to our school and had sat in our secret room a mere twenty years prior. And after reading the rest of that journal, I started to form a better picture as to why. But what Alice wanted out of all of this, what she was hoping to gain, *that* was still a mystery to me.

When I reached her across the room, she handed me the piece of paper so I could get a better look, and returned her attention to Monica.

"Where did you get this?" she asked, her voice laced with urgency.

"That," Monica said, still panting. "That is an anonymous submission I received at the paper, not ten minutes ago."

I studied the page. It was a poem, I realized, and it read:

> *On a dark winter's eve*
> *In nineteen seventy-two*

A young woman searched
The tunnels, through and through.

But what she had found
Could never be known
After the monster that lurked there
Claimed her as its own.

Now twenty years later
There is still much to fear
For the monster in the tunnels
Has not left us here.

"Someone sent this to you to be published?" I asked, looking up from the paper.

Reading it within the context of my recent discoveries made it chilling. I could no longer deny the weight that it carried, knowing that there was a girl who had been down in those tunnels. Knowing that those tunnels existed at all.

Monica nodded. "It got here today. It's a good thing I was the one to open it, or I wouldn't have been able to bring it to you guys."

"Why *did* you feel the need to bring it to us?" Josie asked, still seated. "What do we have to do with any of this?"

Monica looked at her like she was crazy. "Are you kidding? This is another message about the tunnels. The paint on the door alone? A prank. But follow that up with an ominous poem? That is a pattern."

"Or another prank."

"Josie, a girl can dream."

"But what are we supposed to do about it?" Meg asked. "Tell someone? Who would we tell?"

Telling someone didn't seem like the route to go, at least, not yet. I hadn't even told the four of them what I'd found. I didn't know how. I had to be smart about it, rather than blurting it out to the room with Alice there, who had told *all* of us that she hadn't found anything in the journal. Things could get messy very easily, I'd decided, so there would be no sudden movements on my end without more information.

"Are you going to publish it?" I asked.

Monica shifted nervously. "I hadn't even thought that far. Should I?"

Alice said, "Yes," at the same time Josie said, "No." They looked at each other.

"Whoever is doing this stuff just wants attention, and you can't give it to them," Josie said.

"Whoever is doing this stuff," Alice countered. "Is obviously trying to send a message. One they think we all need to hear."

Josie returned the shot, their rally laced with tension. "Do what you want with it, but don't come crying to me if you get in trouble for helping the cause. How do you think the administration would take to the newspaper's editor in chief, and a member of *Judiciary*, contributing to campus hysteria? It's clearly just someone trying to get a rise out of us by capitalizing on some silly myth—"

"Oh my God," Monica said, her eyes wide. "That's it."

Josie looked around. "What?"

"You guys," Monica continued. "That's *it*." She laughed and started to pace. "The *myth*. Think about it. An underground network of tunnels, a monster, a girl goes in, she doesn't come out." She stopped in her tracks. "It's the *Labyrinth*."

Meg's eyes widened as she started to catch on. "The Labyrinth...and the Minotaur," she said, a smile forming on her face.

"I still don't follow," Josie said.

I did follow. "Our project topic." I said. "We apply the myth to the one here at our school. The Girl in the Tunnels becomes The Girl in the Labyrinth."

Alice nodded slowly. "We investigate, and we figure out just what happened down there, and that's our application."

I felt my skin crawl as I watched the pieces fall into place around her. The thing I realized she had been searching for during those last few months would now be masqueraded as academic research. I wondered if she would bring up the journal, offer it as a resource. Something told me that wouldn't be the case, that she'd continue her private investigation while the rest of us ran around playing pretend.

Monica, however, ate it up, jumping onto the stone bench by the window and crouching to our eye level. Her loafers crinkled under her weight like smiling eyes. "Revolutionary," she said.

"Okay, no," Josie said, standing up. "Have you guys lost it? Why would we dig further into something that involves a female student being found *dead*?"

"Huh," Monica replied, scratching her chin. "I thought you didn't believe in any of this."

"I don't."

"Great! It's purely for research purposes." Our ringleader smiled at her logic.

"It's all academic, Josie," Alice said, winking at her. The sight made my stomach drop.

"And don't worry," Monica said. "I think we all know what's really down there."

The rest of us were silent, watching as she climbed down and approached us slowly.

"You've heard the rumors," she continued. "They say that, beneath the school, you'll find…a…cask…"

Josie rolled her eyes, but Meg gasped, standing to join in the parody. "You don't mean to say...of Amontillado?"

"That's exactly what I mean to say!" Monica pointed at her

SHOT: Monica lunges at Meg, tackling her onto the couch.

"For the love of God, Montresor!" Meg yelled dramatically on the way down, giggling when they hit the green cushion.

Alice smiled at the Poe reference as well, no doubt content with the direction we were heading in. I knew better, though. And the more I thought about it, the more wary of her I grew.

Just what were the odds, that the year a new student transfers to a school, cryptic messages begin to appear regarding an incident of which she had prior knowledge? For twenty years, the myth had remained nothing more than a whisper. For twenty years, it hid in the shadows. Then Alice showed up, looking for it, maybe even hoping to bring it out into the spotlight. The painted door, the poem sent to Monica, it occurred to me that the author of those "messages," could very well have been in our midst, all along.

CUT TO:

We submitted the project topic to Professor Shaw, Monica running in mere seconds before class started. She'd stayed up all night perfecting the proposal, and even if Meg hadn't told me, her smudged mascara, parted bangs, and half-tucked undershirt were all dead giveaways. But, as I had said, don't be fooled. She was, in fact, beaming.

After glancing over the page-long outline, Professor Shaw looked around at each of us. For once, her expression was clear. She looked surprised.

"This project requires research. It requires evidence," she said. "The topic only works if the application is real."

Alice spoke up for the rest of us. "Who says it isn't?"

And that, folks, is what we call *dramatic irony*.

The other girls were blissfully unaware of the sincerity behind Alice's statement. And I, despite the perspective I'd gained, could not have predicted the way things would play out from that moment on. I do, however, distinctly remember thinking, *You know it's real, Alice.*

And, now, so do I.

SCENE 22

It was incredible how much work you could get done in a real library.

(As opposed to one that had zero writing surfaces and furniture that functioned best for a cozy read or a quick or long nap.)

With my World Cinema midterm coming up, I had decided to join a study group that planned to meet back in civilization, where students crowded around long, mahogany tables and stayed put for hours, especially at that point in the semester.

We'd managed to cover both the postwar Japanese and Italian units before my mind began to drift elsewhere, such as to the fact that the others were coming to meet me at some point so we could establish our plan of attack for the mythology project. I hadn't even figured out my *own* plan of attack, yet, and I needed to soon. Because I hated lying to them. (At the time, I preferred to think of it as *omitting key details*, but I try to no longer delude myself.)

My internal debate was interrupted when Study Group Steve tapped me with his pen, redirecting me toward the conversation about the Andreotti Law of 1949.

"Because it was counterproductive to their postwar agenda," said a junior boy named Collin.

"Right," said Molly, another sophomore. "That guy called it, 'Washing Italy's dirty linen in public.' What was his name?"

Collin cringed. "That was...who was that?"

SHOT: Clay and Jamie walk in through the door nearest to our table.

I smiled and quietly called over to him, "Clay."

A mistake, clearly, as everyone at the table turned to look at me, their confusion evident.

"It definitely wasn't Clay..." said Molly. "Clay who?"

A senior began flipping pages. "I don't remember learning about a Clay."

"No, no," I said, trying to diffuse the light panic. "Sorry, that's someone else. Completely irrelevant."

I could see the tension leaving their bodies, an invisible puppeteer releasing the control bar and allowing them to sink down into their seats.

When the study group parted ways for the afternoon, I grabbed my belongings and walked over to Clay's table. He waved when he saw me, pulling out the chair next to him and motioning toward it.

"From what I could tell, you seem like the worst study group member," he joked in reference to my earlier distraction.

"I have been told I hold everyone back," I said.

"I believe it."

He pulled out a copy of *Great Expectations*, along with a notebook and pen. "How's Monica doing?" he asked.

Ah yes, Monica. Who did end up publishing that poem in the paper, and did, as Josie had predicted, face repercussions. Nothing too drastic in the grand scheme of things, but the administration seemed to know how to hit her where it hurt. She faced trial by her peers on Judiciary, and ended up being suspended from the council for two weeks. Not that bad, right? *Wrong*, according to Monica.

FLASHBACK:

"I didn't get to take down Ben Fritz. Sent in on plagiarism charges, gets off with a warning. They just don't have an edge without me," she had said, sulking in her room.

FLASHFORWARD:

"She's managing," I told Clay.

"And you?" he asked.

"What about me?"

"How are you? Everyone's been kind of on edge now that there was a second mention of it."

I nodded, looking around and trying to distract myself with something other than lying to Clay. There was a couple that sat a few tables down, holding hands while reading, which didn't seem very practical. I preferred not to focus on that. There was also a group of boys having an animated debate over the upcoming election. I happened to notice that three of them wore the same navy sweater, and five of the six of them wore similar glasses. (They say our school has a "type.") Watching them go back and forth, one pacing with his arms crossed, another sitting on the table, it was all entertaining enough until Clay quite literally snapped me out of it, the image of his hand pulling away from my face coming into focus.

"Well?" he asked.

"I'm okay," I said. Part of me wanted to tell him everything I'd learned since we had last seen each other. About the journal, about Alice. But as much as I trusted him, I didn't yet know what I was getting myself into, and the last thing I wanted to do was drag him down along with me. That being said, having all those thoughts constantly rattling around in my head had grown overwhelming, and I needed to hear anyone else's thoughts except my own.

I think that's why I asked, "Do you think there's a chance that any of it could be real?"

He looked up from his notebook. "Could what be real? The whole 'Girl in the Tunnels' thing?"

I shrugged. "That, or the tunnels in general. Could there really be something down there?"

CUTAWAY TO: Alice wanders into the room, her dark hair producing a subtle, red glow where the sunlight coming in through the window meets it.

She glanced around for a familiar face, her lips molding into a smile when her eyes caught mine.

"In all honesty," Clay said. "I think somebody's just trying to mess with all of us."

"Huh. That's exactly what Josie said."

"Well, Josie and I are, as you know, perfectly in sync."

Alice suddenly appeared at my side, offering a quick greeting to Clay. "Should we grab a table?" she asked.

Relocating once more, we managed to find a smaller table in one of the back corners, setting our stuff down and waiting in silence. I realized I didn't know what to say to her. Anything I could think of tied right back to those tunnels. I didn't even want to start working on the project with her, because one misstep and she would figure out that I knew at least part of the truth.

"So, how have your midterms been so far?" she asked, her face indicating that she was aware of the awkward tension between us.

"Fine," I said, trying to keep anything I offered brief. "You?"

"*Fine,*" she mocked. "I still haven't quite figured out my design for my term project, though."

The *term project*. I don't know why it had only occurred to me then, what role Alice's architecture assignment played in all of it. But I remembered her asking Professor Aldridge if she could have access to the older building plans, "for inspiration," as she called it. As the lightbulb went off, I thought of another explanation.

She wanted to see if they could show her something the campus had been hiding.

Something like, I don't know, any ways to get underground?

Why else would she have asked for the ones to the oldest buildings? Stylistic motivations aside, anything resembling an underground network of tunnels would have been around from the start, so she likely thought those blueprints could tell her how to find them.

"Did you end up getting access to those plans?" I asked her.

"Plans?"

"To the older buildings. To help you with your design."

Realization washed over her face, as though she had forgotten that I was a part of that conversation at the football game.

"No, I didn't." She shrugged. "Professor Aldridge said the higher-ups wouldn't budge. Which is fine. I'd made sure not to get my hopes up."

I decided to test the waters, see what she might give away. "That's a shame. I was going to say, I thought they might have helped with our project."

Her eyes narrowed momentarily. "How so?"

"Well, you know, if we're supposed to prove that these tunnels exist, wouldn't you think that having what are essentially original maps of the campus would be helpful?"

She took her time, studying my face before responding. "I hadn't thought of that."

"Really? I would've thought that you had." I shook my head and leaned down to take out some paper. "Oh, well. We can definitely figure something else out."

She nodded, reaching down for her bag as well.

I used the rest of the time before the others got there to start outlining a Critical Film Theory essay, keeping my head down and aiming to appear busy, thus warding off any further conversation. My strategy faltered only once, when I let my guard down and looked up at the girl sitting across from me.

I couldn't be certain, but it seemed like she had been watching me the entire time.

SCENE 23

—

What is it that your mother warns you when you prepare for a night out? "Nothing good happens after two a.m.," I think it was?

Well, it was only twelve-thirty that night, but I think the idiom can make an exception.

With the rest of our midterms behind us, the plans for our Tuesday evening were taken to a vote, the result of which was almost unanimous: we would drink. (Any guesses as to who the lone supporter of a cozy night in was?)

My former drinking habits had gone down the toilet along with my career as the "life of the party." (Hence my despicably low tolerance.)

And, such sweet sorrow, parting was not.

I realized that I preferred to remain lucid, in control. I preferred to be able to keep an eye on things. To keep an eye on them.

To keep an eye on her.

Besides, someone had to do it. Otherwise I, too, would have been sprinting around the quad that night, traveling in circles and reciting Keats at an above-average volume.

So, while Monica spun in circles to the first stanza of "Ode on a Grecian Urn," and Josie tried to initiate a duel with a less than enthusiastic Meg, and Alice was busy taking a photograph of another bird that had landed on a nearby bench, I stood on the sidewalk, looking out for other observers while my dark overcoat did little to warm me in my sober state.

Their performances came to a halt when a bright white fissure formed along the sky, the ground beneath our feet vibrating with the thunder that accompanied it. Poetry was replaced by screams as the four of them raced down the quad to take cover. We would have made it back to the dorm, I think, had the rain not started falling as we passed the steps that led to the Dining Hall. Monica veered to the right and lunged under the arches, the others following her like ducklings.

I looked up at that third-floor window as I headed for the front doors, quickly skipping up the few steps on the way.

"Well," Meg said with a giggle. "Did anyone know it was going to rain?"

"Zeus is far too *fickle* to listen to the weather report," Monica said. She grabbed hold of the brick wall and leaned out from under the cover, letting her face become drenched until there was another flash and thunder rang out. "He's angry," she said, wiping her bangs away from her eyes.

Josie leaned against one of the doors, shivering. "I say we make a run for it."

"Or," Alice said, "we could just go upstairs."

"Oh, Alice." Monica came over and put her head on Alice's shoulder. She sighed dramatically. "A lovely thought, but tell me, how would we get in?"

Alice lifted Monica's head up gently and walked to the right, counting the doors as she passed them. When she reached the fourth one, she wrapped both her hands around the door handle and faced it head on. "Like this." Bracing herself, she quickly pulled backward and a loud click was heard. The heavy oak door swung open, and Alice held it with her right hand while executing a dramatic, *after you,* motion with her left.

"How the hell did you know you could do that?" asked Josie as she passed through the doorway.

"Just another one of my secrets I picked up," she replied, shooting a quick wink my way as I went inside.

CUT TO:

The room looked different when lit by the glow of the moon, even the dull one that evening, dimmed by the storm outside. Shadows cast themselves over the walls, telling stories of the past. I shuddered at the thought.

SHOT: our faces as we pass through the silver rays of light, growing illuminated before disappearing once again into darkness.

What followed began as arbitrary conversation, nothing out of the ordinary for us. Nothing I remember in too great of detail.

I do remember hearing a faint clicking noise followed by the appearance of a tiny orange flame that reflected in Josie's eyes.

"Not in here, please," Monica said, her head resting back against the stone windowsill.

"I'll open a window," Josie said.

"These windows don't open."

"Fine."

The flame disappeared.

I also remember the moments that passed in silence, each of us observing different areas of the room. My head heavy,

I summoned whatever strength my neck could muster to turn toward Meg, who sat to my right, her back propped up against the green couch like mine was. Her corduroy-clad legs stretched out in front of her. Her lashes hung low.

"You've been quiet tonight, Megara," I said, lazily reaching toward her and poking her arm.

She looked over and simply nodded.

"Meg is always quiet," Josie corrected from across the room.

To this, Meg gave no response. She sat still as though she hadn't even heard the remark. But I knew she had. I could tell by how she appeared to be holding her breath, her chest still and her face straining subtly.

"Well, that's simply not true," I said, looking at her.

Josie smirked. "I'm just saying that's what I've experienced."

"That's because you don't know how to listen."

My words surprised everyone, including myself. I'd never been one to initiate confrontation, or humor confrontation, or diffuse confrontation. I suppose I'd just grown tired of the condescending remarks and the interruptions every time I had something to say. I'd forgotten to remove the lid on the instant noodles already in the microwave, the container expanding until it was ready to explode.

The room was uncomfortably quiet for a beat or two, until Monica let out a delayed laugh.

"Yes, that's really funny, Monica," Josie said, her words still slurring a little. "But Stella, if you need to take your issues out on me, then please, continue."

"I'm sorry, I didn't mean—"

"You absolutely meant it," Josie interrupted. "But like I said, I can play therapist. Purge all your dark and brooding feelings, if that's what you need. I think we'd all appreciate it."

"What is that supposed to mean?"

"Oh come on, Stella," she looked around the room, as if the answer were obvious. "Don't pretend you haven't changed. What happened to the girl who was up for anything? Who actually wanted to spend time with me? If you even agree to go anywhere with us these days you just stand there, sulking, wishing you could leave."

"And?"

"What's *wrong* with you, Stella?"

"Josie..." Monica warned, her face matching the sobering exchange.

"There's nothing *wrong* with me," I said.

My face had grown hot with the increasing interrogation. Who was she, of all people, to comment on my feelings? To belittle my behavior? She was the one who couldn't read a room to save her life. Who truly believed that people worshipped the ground she walked on, and who discarded those she suspected might not.

"You need to get off your high horse, Stella," she said. "It's more obvious than you think, the way you look down on me for the choices I make."

If we were really going to do this, I decided to make my point.

SHOT-REVERSE-SHOT: Josie and I, our voices rising.

"The only thing I look down on you for is the way you treat us. Like we're dolls who are only there so you can complain about how unhappy you are. And then you leave us the second some boy gives you an ounce of attention."

"I'm perfectly happy."

"Is that what you tell yourself? I can't count the number of times you *keep* bringing up Scottie—"

"Don't talk about Scottie," she snapped. "You know what? You're right, I'm not happy. But I'm not unhappy, either, Stella.

I don't *care*. About any of it. In fact, you should try it. Maybe then you'll be able to dislodge that stick up your—"

"I think," Monica said, her tone uncharacteristically serious. "That we're all really tired, and have had too much to drink, *certainly* for a Tuesday night—"

"You have to stop caring, Stella," Josie said. "God, it's exhausting. The second you let it all go, you'll see. Looking at the world and feeling nothing..." Her voice went quiet. "That's the best feeling in the world."

There was nothing to be heard, save for the sound of our breathing. A full minute passed in silence, the hypnotic and slow movements of our shadows lulling me back into a state of calm.

"Bullshit."

Her voice sliced through the air, jolting it awake.

"Excuse me?" Josie asked.

Alice looked at her. "That's bullshit."

The shocked expression on Josie's face rendered her incapable of responding. Alice capitalized on it.

"That whole being numb, feeling nothing, spiel? It's entirely transparent," she said. It was Josie's turn to suffer an interrogation. "Why would you ever want that? How could you possibly expect us to believe that you do?"

"Well, of course you wouldn't, Alice," she said. "No, *you* have it all together. You're more emotionally evolved than the rest of us."

Alice shook her head and stood, pushing her bag to the side and walking over to the window. I looked at Monica who shook her head. Her eyes were tired.

"What?" Josie asked, noticing our reactions. "It's true. Alice is good at everything. Alice is always three steps ahead, and she takes these cute little pictures," she picked up Alice's bag and rummaged through it. "Like this one right here. Let's see, aah, look at that, a campus squirrel." She turned the photo for the rest of us to see.

"Maybe we should just head back," Meg said, staring at her hands.

Josie ignored her, continuing, "Then you have this one, ooh, I look good in this one. And the lovely window right there, would you look at that? And now we have…what is this?" she asked, looking up at Alice. She turned back to the photo, moving it closer to and farther from her face.

Alice turned away from the window to look, but when she saw the picture, she froze. I'd never seen Alice at a loss for words before. It was unsettling.

I stood and grabbed the picture from Josie's hand. It was of Alice when she was young and a girl who looked like a slightly older version of her. The resemblance was truly remarkable. I glanced down to see what she had labeled it.

Demeter + Demetria

I froze. It was a photo of Alice and her Aunt Daphne.

Demeter.

D.

"Demeter," Josie said, echoing my own thoughts. "So that's where you got the name from." She sat down with the photo, and I watched as pieces of the puzzle slowly rearranged in her head. "It's almost like"—she lifted the rug with her foot—"*this* Demeter carved into the floor."

Had Alice's poker face been better, had she not been caught so off guard, she might have managed to convince Josie that her observation was baseless. But she was unable to hide the fact that Josie was onto something.

Josie's buzz had at that point become a dull hum, if even that, allowing her to dig deeper. "You knew," she said smugly. "You were the one who found this room. Never told us how you did that, by the way. But it was because of her." She looked down at the picture again. "Your…sister? Mom? She looks too young to be your mom. She's Demeter, isn't she?"

Alice said nothing.

"Isn't she?"

"Yes."

"Who is she?"

"My aunt."

Josie laughed proudly. "I knew it. Don't underestimate me, I can piece these things together. So, your aunt was in the first class of women, she and her friends met here, what else?" Her eyes lit up. "That was her journal, wasn't it?"

"No," Alice said quickly. "It wasn't."

Josie was practically beaming. "I don't believe you." She ran to the bookshelf and dug around for the journal, Alice behind her, unable to get to it first. Josie lifted the book in the air, out of her reach, and tried to look inside without losing it.

In all honesty, I was as uneasy as Alice about all of it. I knew what Josie would find in those pages. Even though Alice's aunt hadn't been the one to write those entries, the implications were larger than Josie was prepared for.

D was very clear. We can't trust any of them.

They exist, hidden underground. I've seen them.

I'm terrified of doing this. But I don't think I have a choice. I have to go back down there. Tonight.

I watched, nauseous, as Josie flipped through the book, much to Alice's discomfort. Alice wasn't one to take anything by force, I knew that, so all she could do was stand by helplessly and prepare for what was about to come to light.

I knew the exact moment Josie read what Alice and I were both dreading.

SHOT: Josie's smug smile drops. Her brow furrows.

"Josie? Everything okay?" I asked, despite the fact that I was already aware of the answer.

My voice seemed to wake her up from her trance, and she looked over at Alice angrily, suddenly lucid.

"What the hell is this?" she asked, holding open that last page.

"Josie," Alice said, guilt written across her face.

She dropped the journal on the floor, Monica picking it up when she turned to walk toward the window. She looked outside, the pattern of her breathing visible from the rise and fall of her shoulders.

"That's not all you knew," Josie finally said. She turned back to Alice. "Your obsession with the tunnels, your theories. You already knew it was all real—"

"I didn't—"

"Oh, you didn't know? You didn't know that the people in this room had been in the tunnels? You happened to skip over the part where this girl talks about going back down there, about how she's terrified, and she needs to tell the truth. It's the last thing written in here, Alice. What exactly did you take away from all of that?"

"I didn't know for certain until I found that journal," Alice said.

"And then you *agreed* that we should pick the Labyrinth for our term project," Josie said.

Monica looked up from the entry warily, glancing over at me. Her head tilted, and I wondered if she could tell that none of this was new information to me.

When Alice still hadn't responded, Josie shook her head. "Well, forgive me for leaving before you realize you're in over your head." She started toward the door, stopping momentarily before opening it. "Was it you?" she asked. "Were you the one behind those messages?"

I held my breath, scared to hear Alice's answer. But when she looked at Josie, and calmly said, "No," I believed her.

Without another word, Josie left, the thumping of her footsteps gradually disappearing.

It felt like minutes before Alice finally turned to me and said, "You figured it out, didn't you?"

I ignored the stares Monica and Meg gave me when I nodded. "Yes, I did."

Alice exhaled and slumped onto the couch, her face masked in a look of exhaustion, and defeat.

"You do still need to explain, though," I added.

And so she did.

She explained how her aunt had gone to our school in 1972, and how she and six of her friends found the hidden room and started to meet there. Their own secret society of women who would read and eat and talk about mythology and hide from the world.

"When I was younger," she said, "she would tell me these bedtime stories. Tales of the Seven Goddesses and their adventures. Their time spent in a secret room. She would tell me ghost stories, in the context of myths. Like the girl who went into the Labyrinth and never came out. I loved listening to her talk about it, but as I got older, I noticed that she'd get more distressed. She'd recount things that felt very personal. About that one semester, and how she had been convinced that something terrible had happened. That something happened to one of her friends. Something about tunnels. And I would think back and wonder if those had been more than just bedtime stories. With time, the narrative would get darker, more detailed. She'd insert herself into it, saying it was all her fault, that she couldn't find the girl in the Labyrinth. I tried to ask my mom about it a few times, but she'd never want to talk about it."

Alice reached up and played with the "D" pendant that fell against her chest. "My aunt would see my necklace, and she'd get upset. She'd say it wasn't mine, that it didn't belong to me. I'd tell her that she had given it to me, and she'd insist that wasn't true. When she heard the name Demetria, or Demeter, it was like someone had flipped a switch, and she'd return to the stories all over again. It devastated me to see her like that, and to hear her say those things. I remember this one time, she started crying, talking about how no one had believed her. 'I tried to explain,' she'd said, but no one had cared. She would just repeat, over and over again, 'I have to go back. I have to find her.'"

She told Monica and Meg what she had already told me, under the moon, but with the missing context. That when her aunt passed the previous year, she knew she had to transfer, to find out just what had happened. She was desperate to prove that Demeter had been right. That semester, in 1972, had presented one of the people she loved most with a heavy snowfall that eventually became an avalanche.

"I have to know the truth," she said, after all that.

I waited for the other girls to speak first. I already knew how I felt about the situation, but it wasn't my place to persuade them. Not after I had kept so much from them.

Eventually, Monica took a deep breath and said, "Well, we have already committed to the project, so I'm not sure we really have a choice."

And with that, it was settled. For Alice, and for the sake of our GPAs, we would find out what really happened in the tunnels in 1972.

Minotaur be damned, we said. The only thing we had to fear was a hit to our transcripts.

SCENE 24

———

I believe the biggest oversight I made in my fight with Josie was the fact that I still had to live with her.

And the days that followed played out in montage, only not one that told the story of physical or emotional growth. *This* montage detailed the series of uncomfortable encounters that came with having a roommate who was no longer speaking to you.

The night of the fallout, I went home to find that Josie wasn't there. I tried to chase down the hours of wasted sleep, but around four in the morning, I was awakened by the sound of her stumbling in no more delicately than she usually did in her belligerent states, knocking over our trash can as well as the glass bottle of perfume on her desk as she maneuvered through her nightly routine. A good twenty minutes later, she finally found her way into her bed, only to jump up after about thirty seconds to bolt back to the trash and puke. Leaving the contents of her stomach to sit there, she climbed back into her bed without so much as brushing her teeth and fell swiftly into a deep, snore-infested sleep. Meanwhile, I was left to stew freshly in my thoughts until tired enough to drift off once more, doing everything in my power to ignore the stench of vomit emanating from the corner.

The next night, I didn't have that problem, because I was already dreaming before Josie came home. The rather unfortunate part of that day, however, was waking up in the morning to find an unidentifiable boy sleeping naked on our floor. I wasn't sure where she'd found him on a Wednesday night, but I *was* sure that I didn't want to know.

Now, don't get me wrong—Josephine was free to do whatever she wanted, and it wasn't my place to judge. But that didn't mean I had to enjoy the eight a.m. small talk said mystery boy tried to maintain as I packed my bag for my morning lecture.

"Film?" he asked. "That's cool. Did you see *Back to the Future Part Three*?"

I got ready quicker than usual.

At the end of the week, I walked in to see a semipacked bag sitting on top of Josie's bed. She was at the sink packing up her makeup, and when she saw me in the mirror she offered a simple, "Hi."

"Hey," I said. "Going somewhere?"

She threw more stuff in the bag. "I'm going to be staying at Katie's for a little bit. Not sure how long, it's more of a play-it-by-ear situation."

Katie was one of Josie's friends from her old dorm, whom she once called "too happy" when I said I thought she was nice. "It's kind of annoying, you know?" she'd said. "She laughs a lot, and like, *really* loud."

"Have fun," I told her as I walked in to put my stuff down.

When she'd gotten everything together and was heading out the door, I realized that in all the ends we'd left undone, there was one I needed to tie up. No matter how angry we were at each other, or how blindsided she felt by Alice's secret, she needed to understand how serious the situation truly was. I had to make sure she did, for my own peace of mind.

"Josie," I said, before she could leave.

"Yes?" she asked.

"You can't say anything. About any of it. Not yet."

She turned and closed the door behind her.

SCENE 25

———

As much as I would like to think that I had been Sherlock in this story, there is no doubt in my mind that I was often Watson. Alice, on the other hand, *she* always knew the right place to look. The right questions to ask. Normally, the realization would be a slightly disappointing one, but in the years since then I slowly confirmed what I knew, deep down, all along.

None of it would have happened if not for her.

With Josie living across campus, taking her space, and even going so far as to sit in a new seat in class, it was up to the four of us to figure out what our first step would be. I watched as Alice paced around the attic, thinking through different scenarios of how to attack the problem. Possible avenues we could take.

"What if we tried to get the blueprints again?" Monica asked from the couch. "Maybe you could go straight to the department head and express how passionate you are about recreating that older style. Maybe he'll be impressed by your enthusiasm."

Alice shook her head. "I don't think enthusiasm alone will sway him."

"You're probably right," she said, frowning. "Can you flirt a little?"

"*Monica.*" I glared at her, suppressing a smile.

"Okay, I'm sorry. We'll think of something else."

Meg had been chewing on her pen, occasionally stopping to blow her caramel-blond hair away from her eyes.

"What if we just looked for them?" she asked. "Actually went around snooping, searching. It could take a little longer, but it might be the most discreet option."

"It's harder than it looks," Alice said. "I never found anything, and I looked around everywhere for almost two months."

So I noticed.

"Well, obviously not everywhere," Monica said. She was bent over, holding her head in her hands.

I went over the different possibilities in my mind. The plans to the grounds were likely the best option, but almost certainly impossible to get our hands on. No one would entrust such important archived materials to one sophomore architecture student.

Especially if they had a secret hidden within them.

As for simply looking for the way to get down there, if Alice hadn't found it by then, I was sure none of us would have any better luck. But, unfortunately, it seemed like we were running out of options, and would one way or the other have to figure it out ourselves. Despite the possibility that it could all have been some big misunderstanding, and there may have been nothing sinister lurking beneath our campus, no one could know what we were up to.

"I need to read," Alice said. She once said that reading helped her think.

She examined the books at her disposal, pausing on the left end of the shelf.

SHOT: Alice slowly reaches for that small, black hardcover.
The Shadow in the Veil *by George Everett.*

I'd seen Alice browse through almost every one of those books throughout our time there, but I knew she'd never picked that one up. I remembered the way she looked at it on that first day she brought us there. With recognition. With longing.

Alice looked at that book the same way she had looked at the journal when she first found it. Like there was something about it that called out to her, and begged her to look inside. Yet, up until that moment, she had refused to touch it.

When she sat down across from me, I asked, "What made you pick that one?"

It was then that I realized her eyes were misty, on the verge of welling up. But she didn't look sad. She looked nostalgic, if anything.

"This was my aunt's favorite," she said. "I've seen it up here, before, I just couldn't bring myself to read it. But I figured, now is as good a time as any." She smiled softly.

I motioned toward the book, indicating that she should go ahead, and then I left her to it.

It was strange, thinking about where we were at that moment as opposed to days, weeks, months earlier. Alice had gone from someone who fascinated me, to someone who stumped me, who concerned me and who surprised me. She'd already undergone significant character development within one semester. I wondered what could possibly be left in store for her. For us.

Several minutes had gone by when the sound of flipping pages started to grow louder, and more frequent. I looked over and saw Alice frantically turning through the book, counting.

"Alice?" I asked. "Everything good?"

She didn't answer. She just kept sectioning off multiple pages at a time.

"I need a blank sheet of paper and a pen," she said.

I dug through my backpack and produced both, handing them to her quickly. When Meg shot a questioning look in my direction, I shrugged. At that point, I was willing to follow Alice's lead.

She moved through the pages again, writing down a single letter for each page she stopped on.

"Care to explain what you're doing?" Monica asked.

"Aunt Daphne," Alice started, remaining entranced in her work. "She always used to say that you should remember to mark the pages that matter."

She scribbled down some more letters.

"This book, her *favorite* book, has very specific pages folded in. Not only that, but each page that's folded has one letter circled. At first, I didn't know what to make of it, but then, I saw the pattern."

She showed us, holding the book up and flipping through the marked pages.

"And by writing down all the circled letters, I'm willing to bet that we're going to have—"

"A bunch of gibberish," Monica deduced, peering at the sheet of paper.

"An *anagram*."

She proceeded to shift the letters around, writing out different combinations and phrases. It took her a while, working with so many letters, but, finally, she stopped and sat back on her heels. A smile spread across her face.

She picked up the paper and turned it around for us to see. At the top, there were sixteen letters:

LUIMTNESENDAURNN

Below all the scribbles and tested combinations were three words:

TUNNELS

UNDER

MAIN

I felt my stomach drop, staring at the phrase.

The answer was entirely logical. The assumption was that these tunnels were as old as the school itself, and so why wouldn't the entrance be somewhere in the oldest building? In the Main Hall?

But, at the same time, knowing the answer meant that we were one step closer to actually going there, and the idea of that was mildly nauseating.

"Don't get me wrong, Alice, this is all impressive work," Monica said, surveying her craftsmanship. "But to be the voice of reason, this all seems a little too good to be true, doesn't it? Why would the location be sitting here, all these years? It's not like she could have left the clue for you."

Alice chewed her lip, thinking it over. "It could be possible that she left it for someone else to find. I don't know who that could be, but right now, this is the best thing we have to go on."

"Tunnels under main," I reread, nodding at her. "But, assuming that this is correct, we still don't know *where* the entrance is."

Alice sighed, looking it all over again. "That's the problem, I've checked the Main Hall, I couldn't find anything. Not even when I managed to get down to the basement."

"Okay, but it's not like they're going to put a flashing sign above the entrance saying, 'Tunnels this way! All are welcome!'" Monica looked over the piece of paper again.

There was something about the way Monica had said it that sent alarm bells going off in my head. In a building full of rooms and hallways and offices, how could you expect to find the one, right doorway out of so many? At the same time, there was no way of monitoring who did what in that building. Students and visitors went in there every day, so how could they possibly ensure that no one would find the one thing they'd managed to keep hidden since the school's founding?

The answer was so obvious that it would go undetected.

That's why I said, "What if I told you that, in a way, I think that's exactly what they did."

SCENE 26

———

Halloween. Known to most of the general population as the day you can become anything. Live out your wildest dreams of becoming a rock star, or terrify others by becoming a monster. In college, October 31 becomes a roughly four-night-long excuse to throw themed parties. Campus would be crawling with unrecognizable peers, and professors would be hurrying home to avoid becoming collateral damage.

Halloween fell on a Saturday that year, so while almost everyone was distracted and partying, we were provided the optimal conditions to go snooping. The four of us met in Monica and Meg's room, and while no, we weren't planning on attending any social events, we did still plan on dressing up. (To blend in.)

We'd made Alice go as Veronica from *Heathers*, because, as we'd told her many times, she did bear resemblance to Winona Ryder. Meg really wanted to go as a witch, and I ended up purchasing a black wig to go as Wednesday Addams. Monica had insisted on dressing "to theme," as she'd called it, although she hadn't told me ahead of time what that meant. But when I walked into her room that evening, I caught on pretty quickly.

She wore a white, floor-length gown with a slit up the right leg and golden rope tied around her waist. Her chocolate brown hair was adorned by a gold headband. She told me it was labeled at the store as "Grecian Princess," and when she saw it, she instantly knew it was the closest thing to perfect for our *main* activity of the evening.

"An Athenian maiden sent off to Crete," she said with flair. "Preparing to enter the Labyrinth and face the Minotaur."

"I'd prefer we not make jokes right before we go down there," Meg said while adjusting her pointy hat.

I had shared my theory with the three of them right after I'd solved the riddle myself. If the entrance to the tunnels was somewhere as crowded as the Main Hall, I explained, then it would have to be hidden someplace they knew no one would dare go.

Like the back entrance to the building, perhaps?

When Alice came over, I saw that she had with her the— what had I called it? Ah yes, the Ultra-Mega-Super 500-Watt PowerLight 3000. The moment I saw it, I realized that what we were about to do was likely the reason she'd bought it that day in the bookstore, when we first met. Before I bumped into her, she'd already been planning on doing a lot of investigating in the dark. I also made the resolution to stay out of its way for the evening, lest we forget what happened the last time we went up against one another.

Minutes later, we walked across campus quickly, trying not to look suspicious in front of partygoers and other students out and about that night. We were banking on the fact that, ideally, anyone we passed would be moderately to severely inebriated.

When we got to the Main Hall and ran around to the back, I realized that I had never actually seen it before. (The superstition, to their credit, was quite effective.) The stairs led down, instead of up, to a set of double doors, with windows peering into the building. More interesting, however, was the fact that, hidden off to the side, expertly masked by a row of bushes, there was another set of stairs that would take one down to a small wooden door. Anyone else would think it entirely irrelevant, but we'd had luck with small wooden doors in the past.

"Well, here's to risking not graduating on the off chance that *this* is the entrance to the tunnels," Meg said with above-average attitude.

"Please," Monica said. "If the tunnels are behind that door and we can get down there, we likely won't make it out to graduate regardless." Her comment was, again, not appreciated by Meg.

LOW ANGLE SHOT: the four of us look at the door ahead, preparing to go inside.

The door opened slowly to reveal a long flight of stairs leading down into the darkness. We each looked at one another (Alice clicked on her flashlight) and we went on our way.

Even just stepping through the threshold, the change in temperature was noticeable. My skin was met with a burst of air that made me shiver, the hair on the back of my neck rising. For a little while, it felt like the stairs would never end, and walking into nothingness was unsettling.

Eventually, however, we'd made it to the bottom, and the first corner we turned revealed a long pathway. Alice's flashlight, shockingly, could only reach so far. We continued on tentatively, stepping slowly and occasionally jumping at an echo induced by our own movement.

"I really, *really* do not like this," Meg said.

"I'm with you there," I said, rubbing my arms. "It's freezing down here."

"Well, so far, a twenty-year-old myth is becoming more and more real by the second, as is our A on the project, so I say we suck it up and keep looking." Monica sped up, taking the lead.

It surprised me how each of us seemed to be forgetting what we'd read in that journal. A girl had been frightened, *terrified*, actually, of what was down there. Of the fact that she had to go back down. That was the final entry, and it made us realize that what we'd read was not just any primary source. We'd read the journal that belonged to *The Girl in the Tunnels*. So, tell me. Why were we there in that moment, following in her footsteps, so willing to walk into circumstances we still didn't understand? I'd told myself that I was doing it for Alice, that after all we'd been through, and all she'd set out to do, I wanted her to have closure. Monica, as you know, claimed she was in it purely for the academic research element. But I think each one of us, deep down, was desperately curious to know the truth, as well.

We came to a dead end, but it wasn't clear how exactly we'd gotten there. All we'd seen were walls, but there had to have been a turn we missed, so we backtracked. And sure enough, it was there, about twenty feet back.

Starting off in a new direction, I felt the four of us gravitate toward each other, craving the security of our collective presence. Alice asked me to hold her flashlight and I complied, taken aback by the sheer weight of it. Granted, I'd been neglecting many forms of physical activity for around twenty years or so, but I hadn't expected a flashlight to put up such a fight.

I watched as she pulled out her Polaroid and snapped a photo of this turn, one of another.

"We aren't sightseeing, Alice," Monica joked.

"It's for research purposes," she replied, taking another picture.

For a moment I thought I heard the sound of running water, and I looked upward, wondering what was directly above us.

POV SHOT: I watch the stone ceiling above me.

I wondered who it was who had no idea that we were there, below them. I ignored the sound as we pushed on, only stopping when we reached two diverging paths.

"Well, what do we do now?" I asked.

Monica grinned. "How about we—"

"If you make a Robert Frost joke right now I swear, Monica, I will leave you here." Meg could be feisty when provoked.

"Geez, all right." She looked down to the right. "This way."

"Why?" Meg asked.

"Because if you'll notice, there's a faint light at the end of this tunnel."

"Isn't that typically a bad sign?"

We followed Monica ten, twenty, thirty feet down, and she was right. There was a light coming from a turn down at the end. At first it was reassuring, knowing we would soon be out of the dark. But that feeling was quickly replaced with dread, and apprehension. Because if there was a light, someone had to have put it there. And if someone put it there, then the tunnels weren't just empty pathways.

Approaching the turn, I could practically hear the sound of my heartbeat. We carefully peered around the corner.

And I can honestly say I did not expect to find what we did.

We had, believe it or not, come face to face with a *formal seating area.*

Couches lined the walls. A table sat off to the side. There were books, lots of books. On shelves, on the table, on the couches.

It looked like someone had taken our hidden library and recreated it right there, underneath the school.

We broke off in various directions, inspecting our discovery further. I moved toward a glass case, filled with china teacups. They wore complex, blue designs, converging to form some sort of crest, it seemed. There was an intricately woven wreath, and perched in the center, there was a crow, its beak open and ready to attack. I stared at it closer, and I remember feeling like there was something about it I recognized. Something I couldn't put my finger on. Before I could try to place it, I was startled by the sound of Alice's camera shutter.

I turned to see her bent down by one of the couches, inspecting something on the ground.

"Is it just me, or does this look very much...lived in?" Monica asked, looking around.

I nodded. "This stuff doesn't look old. It looks like someone was just here"—I ran my hand over the beige couch in front of me, noticing the dips in the cushion—"today, even."

FADE IN: footsteps echo from a distance.

We shot up, looking at each other, our panic palpable. I looked at each of the paths that diverged from the area. The footsteps sounded like they were coming from every one of them.

Meg mouthed, *No, no, no, no...*

"What do we do?" I whispered.

Alice spun around, facing the same dilemma I had. Unlike me, she made a choice, pointing toward the path on the left, in the opposite direction from which we'd come. We followed her, speeding up to a silent jog, operating purely on instinct and choosing turns solely to make sure that whoever was out there couldn't find us. The pit in my stomach told me we were beginning to get lost, with the passages all looking the exact same and our sense of direction practically nonexistent. Thankfully, Alice noticed something the rest of us hadn't.

"You guys," she whispered. "The stairs."

I looked and sure enough, there was another set of stairs. We raced up, climbing as fast as we could until we reached a door and pushed, not thinking about what might be waiting for us on the other side.

It was more darkness.

But as our eyes adjusted and we stopped to breathe, we realized exactly where we were.

We were in the basement of the Dining Hall.

SCENE 27

The next day, the four of us didn't leave each other's sides.

Easy enough to do on a Sunday, but the sense of unease that we felt made the decision all the more necessary. After returning to the dorms the night before, I hadn't been alone in my room for more than two minutes before the sound of echoing footsteps filled my mind, the damp chill caressing my skin. I ran over to Meg and Monica's, and, when I knocked, Alice had been the one to open the door. Apparently, she'd arrived only a minute or so before I did.

Our voyage through the tunnels, like many of the abnormal things I'd experienced that fall, would play over and over like a film. I saw myself looking up at the ceiling as we walked. I saw myself studying the design that ran along the china teacup. I saw darkness as we sprinted through it, with no idea what we were heading toward.

Or who we were running from.

I even saw the most plausible scene heading: INT. TUNNELS; NIGHT; VERY MUCH REAL.

That last part was perhaps the most interesting of them all. I knew that the tunnels existed before we went down there, and yet, there was something inside me that wouldn't let me fully believe it until I was walking along the concrete floors, grateful that Meg felt the need to squeeze my hand so hard. Once we had been there, and seen what we had seen, and heard what we had heard, there was simply no turning back.

But as I said, there would be no turning back, *together*. We snuggled into the two twin beds, and awoke to agree that we wouldn't let any of us out of our sight for the fore-seeable future. As such, we had initially planned to stay in their room the whole day, but found it impossible to prepare for more approaching assessments. There was also the question of eating *meals*, so the verdict was: to the attic once more.

But for just one day, we didn't want to talk about the project. We didn't want to talk about the girls, or the "T" word, or mythology at all, for that matter. (Which was rare.)

It would appear, however, that we couldn't always get what we wanted.

Rather than venture for small talk during study breaks, Monica had brought her Sony Walkman with her so that she could listen to the student radio station that evening. (There was supposed to be an announcement made on behalf of the Judiciary Council, from which she was suspended for only a few more days.) We listened to the various segments to drown out all thoughts that had been banned, and things actually started to feel a little more normal again.

But our moment of bliss was short-lived.

It came on a commercial break, when we were planning on leaving, the sky falling asleep around us. The student host of the hour had said, "And now, a word from our sponsor."

But what came next made me think there had been a slight misunderstanding.

What came onto the air was *not* a message from Ed's Tires, but rather a mildly darker one, played on a loop, the speaker's voice tainted by the effects of a voice modulator.

The message managed to play two times before it was abruptly silenced and the voice of the flustered (and soon-to-be fired) radio host could be heard, apologizing profusely.

The haunting words that rang out through the room were these:

Watch your step. You are not as safe here as you think.

After the commotion on the other end of the transmission subsided, Monica clicked the off button, and everything stilled.

Each of us waited to see who would be the first one to speak. The first to say what each of us already knew.

"We have to talk about it."

It was Monica, her knees pulled up to her chest, and her hair obscuring her eyes. She sighed when none of us accepted the invitation to begin. "Well, given what we know, I think it's safe to confirm that these messages are not simply pranks. Which means, there is someone else here who knows what happened in 1972. Now, I will admit, Alice, when you told us about your aunt, I did think you were the responsible party. No offense."

Alice shrugged. "None taken."

"But," Monica continued, "we, of course, know that's not the case. So, the question is, who is it...?" She trailed off, losing steam at the realization that there was so much we still didn't know.

I stood up, determined to lift our spirits and get us brainstorming. "We should consider what the messages tell us about perspective," I said, encouraged by the sight of Monica nodding. "The first read as an accusation. The second, a story. And the third..." I took a deep breath.

"The third was a warning?" Meg asked.

It would be reasonable for anyone to assume that the voice behind that message meant to warn us. To convey that there was something dangerous in our midst. But we were in the position to know better. Each of these messages had a target in mind.

"The third was a threat."

But what type of threat? Of exposure? Of something worse?

"It's a recipe for revenge, folks," Monica said, her spark reemerging. "Like I said, someone else knows what happened. They know how The Girl in the Tunnels died, and they're looking for justice."

"Do *we* know anything about how she died?" Meg asked.

"Nothing concrete," I said. "There was almost a month missing from her journal entries, so there's a lot we don't know. But she did mention Demeter, "D," and how she'd said that they couldn't trust them."

"Them?" Meg asked.

"The other girls. There was a bit in there about how she couldn't recognize them anymore, she said they'd changed. There was tension. In her last entry, when she talked about going back down to the tunnels, she said they would be there, that there was something happening there that she knew of. They had a secret, and she needed to tell someone, but it scared her."

Alice had been sitting on the floor, her eyes closed. I could tell she was working through it all in her mind, searching for something that we'd missed, anything that could fill in the gaps that the girl left us.

Monica picked up where I left off, muttering what she could remember from her own read-through. "Right, she felt like she was in over her head with whatever was going on here. She wanted to come clean." She nodded to herself as the picture began to form more clearly. "She wanted to come clean, but as we all know, you don't leak the secret of a secret society, so one of the other girls stopped her before she had the chance, does that sound right? Good. Yes. But, of course, the question still stands, who?" She fell back onto the couch, sighing in frustration. "There has to be something we missed."

It felt impossible that we could have missed something when there had been so little there in the first place. But still, we didn't have all the pieces. So, either other action was needed, or we did, in fact, miss something.

"Let's check the journal again," I said, heading for the bookshelf. "We can go over it all one more time."

I slid the books we kept in front of it to the side, stretching as far as I could to reach the back of the top shelf.

But my hand was met with wood.

I slid more books and kept feeling for it along the back wall. Nothing.

I took off all the books that were on the top shelf, dropping them onto the floor, frantically grasping for anything else up there.

"It's not there," I said.

Alice opened her eyes and looked up at me. "What do you mean it's not there?"

"It's not there," I repeated. "Did anyone move it?"

Monica shook her head, her eyes wide with alarm. Meg started chewing her nails. A nervous habit.

I turned back to the shelves and removed books from each of them. Fourth, third, second, first. Alice helped. The blue journal with the missing initial was nowhere to be found. And none of us had moved it. None of us *had* it, at all. So that meant someone else had taken it.

That meant someone else had been in this room.

"Josie?" Alice asked.

I considered it. It wouldn't have been entirely out of the question, but I still doubted that she'd been the culprit. It would've been below even her to mess with us after her big exit, storming off the set.

"She's stubborn," I said. "She wants us to believe she doesn't care. Stealing the journal would betray her front."

But if Josie hadn't taken it, then who did? Who else knew it was there?

As the thought crossed my mind, the sound of creaking wood pierced the air. We looked at each other, no one moving. Seconds passed, the silence heavy, pressing down on me, suffocating me. Holding my breath, however, didn't prevent the feeling of ants crawling up my arms, up my spine. An awareness that we may not have been alone.

The second creak came, magnified by our intent to listen for it. It was nearly ear-splitting, sending another wave of ants up out of the floors and in through the soles of my feet, traveling all the way to my neck. I saw Meg's breathing pick up, panic in her eyes. I looked to Alice, who motioned forward, and I silently agreed. The sound had come from outside the door.

Monica had been standing the closest to it, so I mouthed to her, *The door.*

She looked over at it and nodded, taking a few deep breaths as she counted down. *Three, two, one.* But when she stepped forward, the wooden floor whined beneath her own foot. She cringed.

We then heard footsteps, the sound of someone running. Leaving.

"Go," I said.

On that cue, Monica darted over to the door, lunging for the handle. And we were close behind. But when she swung it open, the stairwell was empty, quiet.

But there had been someone there, listening to us.

Someone knew about us.

SCENE 28

———

Meg wouldn't stand up.

She had rolled herself into an upright ball, rocking back and forth gently in the middle of the room.

"We need to go home, Meg," Monica coaxed. "Don't you want to go home?"

"Yes," she said, but she didn't move.

Realizing we would be stuck there for a little longer, we took action. Someone had been listening to us outside the door. Probably the same someone who took the journal. Someone who knew about all of it. The only way we were going to figure out who that someone was, was to work with what we had, and find more clues.

We followed Alice's lead and looked everywhere. Under the couch, under the rug (again), in the books we'd just thrown off the shelves, behind the shelves, on the ceiling. We tried to cover every inch of the room, putting on our detective hats and looking for the smallest traces of the women who had stood there twenty years ago.

After repeatedly coming up with nothing, Monica ripped the seat cushion from the red chair out of frustration. She threw it across the room (almost hit Meg, actually), and followed it to pick it up and throw it down again. She was about to pick it up a third time when she stopped, tilting her ear to the ground.

"Did anyone else hear that?" she asked.

She bent down, examining the cushion first with her eyes, then with her hand. When she turned it over and did the same, she looked up at me with a half smile, her hand still moving over the fabric.

"What?" I asked.

"Hand me a pen," she said.

I reached into my bag and gave her the ballpoint pen I'd had in there. "Why—"

She raised the pen above her head and swung downward, stabbing the cushion.

"Monica!" She had snapped Meg out of her haze.

Monica grabbed hold of the cushion and tore, gutting it like a fish.

"Monica, there's a zipper *right there*," Alice said, horrified.

Ignoring our protests, she stuck her hand into the recently dissected specimen, and pulled something out of the stuffing. A small wooden box.

Eagerly, she maneuvered around the clasp and looked inside, her smile growing wider.

She let out a sigh of relief. "Jackpot."

"What is it?" Alice asked, hurrying over from the far window.

Monica took out the discovery and held it up for us to see. It was Polaroid. Not one of Alice's, obviously. This one was dated 1972, and it was a picture of seven women.

The Seven Goddesses.

They had their arms around each other, and they were smiling.

Alice took the photograph, quickly locating Daphne and tracing her finger over her face. It really was remarkable how similar the two of them looked when they were about the same age.

Monica pointed out the same thing. "You look just like her."

"That's what we were always told," she replied.

"So, one of these girls is *the* girl, then," I said, glancing at each of them.

"Yes," Monica said. "And another could be the one who killed her."

Alice frowned. "I wish she could tell us which one," she said, referring to her aunt.

I skimmed over each of their faces. Their smiles looked so genuine, so hopeful. They'd created something for themselves there.

But somewhere along the way, something went wrong. Horribly, *terribly* wrong.

"There has to be some way to figure it out," Meg said.

I sighed and moved toward my bag. I left the pen, since it had been part of a crime scene. It seemed like we were all ready to go, until Monica gasped.

"You guys," she said. "I think there is a way to figure it out."

I walked over to her. "What do you mean?"

"I *mean* that there is someone in this picture who can tell us." For someone who had discovered an important lead, she looked rather sad. Frightened, almost.

I took the photo from her, looking over it once again. I had been sure I hadn't recognized anyone the first time, but perhaps I'd missed it.

It wasn't until the third scan that I noticed her.

The back-left corner, five girls away from Alice's aunt. She had dark brown hair, and a slightly chubbier face. Her youthful glow and lively eyes made her practically unrecognizable. And, that smile. It was a smile I'd never seen her wear before.

The realization was a punch to the gut. The realization that we did know another woman in the picture.

A woman who knew The Girl in the Tunnels.

A woman who, as it had occurred to us earlier, may have killed her.

The woman was Professor Madeleine Shaw.

THE CLOSE-UP

SCENE 29

———

All right. This is as close as you're going to get.

Everyone had received letters in their mailboxes again the next morning. This time, however, they didn't simply offer apologies or reassuring remarks from the administration. This time, they called for an assembly. There would be a quasi-mandatory meeting in the Basilica that evening, and all those who could make it were strongly encouraged to attend.

And somewhere among the students who were either genuinely concerned about it all or simply had nothing better to do on a Monday evening, you would find us, arriving thirty minutes ahead of time, as per usual.

You could tell President Gallagher was displeased from both the slight tinge of red and the thin film of sweat that coated his face. (The innumerable creases that formed above his brows and the bulging veins that branched outward from his eyes were indicators, as well, but I'll spare you a tight shot.) It was a relatively drastic departure from his tranquil and even sanguine disposition, especially given the way his voice faltered when attempting certain words and quivered upon ending certain sentences. The message was clear. Someone had managed to spook him.

Someone had managed to spook us, as well.

"I want to assure you that this attempt to shake our community has not gone unnoticed, and will not go unresolved," he'd said. "We will extinguish this flame that attempts to burn us, as well as whoever dares to fan it." (He was big on metaphors, which played a large role in the aforementioned predictability of his speeches. There are only so many ways one can describe the "blooming" of a new class of students, all of which, as you might assume, involve a flower or some other plant derivative.)

In retrospect, I can't help but feel that it was all very *jamais vu*. We had been there before, merely a few months earlier, and yet, everything had become almost unfamiliar, if but for a moment. I looked around, at the lifeless stained-glass windows, seeing nothing but darkness beyond them. We sat there, in the fifth row, with Alice instead of Josie.

And *she* sat there, in the second row, with her Hitchcock Blonde hair soaking in the candlelight and the warmth, leaving the rest of us in the cold.

I watched her as I had that first time, the image of her altered since we'd seen her in that photograph the night before. It suddenly made sense. The way she had frozen the first time she saw Alice. The way she had continued to look at her since. When she saw Alice, she saw Daphne, and perhaps she'd felt haunted by her the same way I'd felt haunted by the ghost of the girl whose journal I'd read. The Girl in the Tunnels.

I also understood why she'd taken such an interest in Alice's middle name. It was more than a simple link to the goddess at the heart of the Eleusinian Mysteries. It was a link to the girl she once knew.

I saw her within the context of something larger. A secret society in which something appeared to have gone wrong.

Something involving a girl, the tunnels, and a monster. And I was worried, in that moment, that the monster in question could have been sitting just three rows ahead of me.

No matter what role she played, however, there was no denying the fact that Professor Shaw had been a cast member in the story we were trying so hard to understand. Which in and of itself had meant three things:

1. She, we assumed, had taken the journal from the attic library (of which its existence, she would have been aware).
2. She, we assumed, had been the one listening to us outside the attic door the previous night.
3. As deduced from numbers one and two, she knew that we knew.

Whether it had been a cue from off-screen or the hole my eyes were burning into the back of her head that had prompted her to turn around, she, nonetheless, did.

SHOT: Professor Shaw peers over her left shoulder and stares back at me.

No matter how badly I wanted to, I couldn't look away. All I could do was remain trapped in her gaze, my breathing stilted and my thoughts spiraling. I felt relieved when her eyes flicked to my left, but the weight on my chest only pressed down harder when I remembered who was sitting there.

It was the least composed I'd seen Alice in the time that I'd known her.

In addition to her usual knee-bouncing, she was wringing her hands and pulling her fingers individually as though she were trying to free them from their joints. A hue matching the one on President Gallagher's face had begun to creep up her neck, a myriad of emotions flooding beneath her skin.

Anger. Confusion. Resentment.

I looked down at her hands once more before reaching out and grabbing one of them, holding it for her. (Although I did almost instantly regret it as I realized that I'd vastly underestimated her strength.) Any semblance of calm that had settled in was short-lived, as President Gallagher's speech took a rather ill-timed turn with our professor's eyes still set on us.

"This rumor has gone on long enough," he said. "The absurdities surrounding it not only carry dangerous implications, but furrow deeper with each passing generation, bringing us further away from the truth—that this 'story' is simply nothing but a lie."

With my fingers still interlaced with hers, I felt Alice's breath catch. I felt the dagger slice through her heart as we were all told that the events her aunt had lived through had never taken place. That the reality she had sworn by was merely fiction.

I still remember the way my stomach somersaulted for the duration of what took place next. My hand was suddenly empty, the girl next to me standing up before an entire room of students and faculty. But she didn't object or fight back. She simply stepped out from the pew and turned in the direction of the door. I had been too stunned to move, but the second I felt Monica put her hand on my shoulder, my feet took over. I stood next, followed by Monica and Meg. President Gallagher only briefly stumbled over his speech before continuing, more forcefully than before.

TRACK backward as the four of us walk down the aisle toward the door.

CUT TO:

TRACK forward. The camera follows closely behind us.

I tried to ignore the weak feeling in my legs brought on by the rows and rows of eyes watching us, the minds in which our faces were becoming seared. That feeling followed me long after we'd let the doors close behind us.

Alice didn't say anything for the rest of the night. She simply parted ways with us when we came to the path that would take her back to her own dorm, and despite everything that had happened, I wasn't worried about her.

She seemed different, yes, but this shift had in no way appeared to be one that would hinder her in any capacity. What had begun as heartbreak had become fury. What had begun as a desire to know the truth had become a refusal to remain in the dark.

If anything, that night made Alice even more determined to finish what we had started.

What had happened in those tunnels was not absurd, or a lie. Alice was going to prove it.

No matter the consequences.

SCENE 30

—

"If I were our next clue about what happened in the scary tunnels under the school, where would I be?" Monica asked.

She was lying on her bed with her legs stretched upward against the wall, settling alongside her *MacGyver* poster. She held her fingers to her forehead as though she could telepathically will the answer into existence.

After a minute or so, she squeezed her eyes shut even tighter, the grimace on her face growing until she finally relaxed with a sigh. "Nothing."

"Don't get me wrong, I'm enjoying this project as much as the next person, but I can't help but feel it would have been easier to research something that gave us actual tangible *material*," Meg said.

The three of us were lounging around their room, having unanimously agreed to no longer meet in the hidden attic library after what had happened. Meg continued to jump every time she heard footsteps approaching (a frequent and unavoidable occurrence), and I myself had no issue staying away until further notice. Crowding into Meg and Monica's dorm room was different, with other students constantly milling around outside and occupying the space on the other side the walls.

Knowing our surroundings, that was what made us feel safe.

"Easier, sure," Monica said. "But 'easier' isn't as fun, is it?"

Meg sighed. "I suppose not."

"Where's Alice?" I asked. "I don't think we'll make much headway without her." Noticing the look of utter betrayal on Monica's face, I continued. "She brings a key perspective to this. Considering her aunt and all."

"Alice is in her drawing class," Meg said. She squinted up at the clock. "But she did tell me she'd come here afterward, so I don't think she'll be long."

Monica rolled over onto her stomach. "Speaking of Alice, how do we think she's doing?"

"Like Stella said, she has more stake in this than any of us. She seemed fine when I saw her, but we all know how good she is at hiding things."

I thought back to the other evening in the Basilica. The way her hand had practically crushed my own. The way we followed her as she walked out, earning the unwanted attention of everyone seated around us.

"Did you guys see Gallagher's face?" Monica had asked, later that night. "I was tempted to stop at a payphone and call a doctor."

We had, I'd realized after she brought it up, caused a scene during that assembly. Nothing had been said, and all had continued on without us, but there was still an unspoken statement we made. One that everyone there heard. There was always the chance that I'd been imagining the intent behind the way people looked at me in class the next day, but I couldn't help but feel I'd lost a bit of that coveted anonymity I'd mentioned at the start of our story.

And if I hadn't, I would soon enough.

We hadn't seen Alice for almost forty-eight hours following the assembly, and while her radio silence didn't concern me, as I'd previously said, not having her around to help brainstorm was presenting a serious roadblock to our productivity.

Because Meg was right. This project didn't give us any real, tangible material to work with. All we had were rumors, and dead ends, and a Polaroid of seven women who met in an attic twenty years before we did.

That was when it hit me.

Polaroids.

"Are you sure Alice didn't say exactly when she'd be here?"

"What is it with you and—"

There was a knock at the door.

ENTER ALICE.

She walked in, with impeccable timing, it appeared, and dropped her bags to the ground. She sat down slowly, eyeing the three of us as though she could tell she'd just been the subject of discussion.

"What did I miss?" she asked.

To spare her the knowledge that we had, in fact, been talking about her, and to relieve Monica of her apparent wrestling match with her own tongue, I offered the thought that had occurred to me mere moments earlier.

"Have you looked through your photographs recently?" I asked.

Alice's surprise was evident, her eyebrows arched and her next words probing. "Not for a few days. Did you think of something?"

I shrugged, remembering that I was operating solely on speculation. "I just thought, since you record so much, that we might be able to see something we hadn't noticed before. We don't exactly have a ton of sources at our fingertips, here."

Alice nodded. "We can try. It would be nice to have someone other than me look at them. Eventually they all just start to blend together, and nothing seems to stand out."

She grabbed her camera bag and, after removing the device itself, dumped her photos onto the floor.

AERIAL SHOT: the camera moves upward as the four of us sort through the Polaroids, rearranging them on the floor so that each one can be seen clearly.

At first, everything looked familiar. Insignificant. I'd seen the photo of the third-story window, and the bookshelf, and the bird on that bench from the beginning of the year. I started to notice some others, like a shot of the tunnels stretching out in front of us, the only thing illuminated by the camera's flash being more darkness. I saw the carvings etched into the floor beneath the rug, and the first message painted across the doors to the Main Hall. I saw the anagram Alice had solved in her aunt's favorite book, and I saw the poem Monica had published in the paper.

And despite never having laid eyes on some of these photos before, I already knew all the information they could possibly provide. These clues, however integral they had been in our progress, had already been uncovered, and led us nowhere other than where we were sitting in that moment.

But then I saw the one that had found its way over to Meg, on the other side of the grid we'd constructed. I reached over and grabbed it.

The subject of the picture was upside down, a series of numbers followed by a letter. I rotated it and recognized it as what I'd seen quickly scribbled into the very last page of the journal in the attic.

3401029B

"You noticed this too?" I asked Alice.

She peered over and nodded. "Yeah, I couldn't really make sense of it at the time, but it looked like it might be something."

"What do you think now?"

"I still don't really know. The only thing I took from it is that she was in a hurry when she wrote it. My guess is that she thought of it, or saw it, but didn't have much time to get it down on paper, so she grabbed the journal and flipped it open, not minding that it was upside down and she had opened it to the last page. The only thing that mattered was making sure she would remember it."

I studied the numbers again. I hadn't thought much of the scribblings the first time I'd seen them, likely assuming something similar to Alice's hypothesis. The girl simply needed a place to write the numbers down in a hurry, and she grabbed the thing closest to her. The journal.

But looking it over again, it seemed to be the only discovery we hadn't really questioned. The only avenue we hadn't explored.

It could've been that those numbers did mean something. Something she had been looking for. Or…something she had found.

"It's the only thing here that we haven't looked into," I said, handing the picture to Monica. "Right now, we have nothing to go off of. Nowhere else to begin. So maybe we start by figuring out what those numbers mean."

Monica squinted at the photo, rotating it a few times. She opened her mouth to say something, but stopped, shaking her head.

"Don't hold back on us now, Monica."

She grinned. "I was just thinking, what if she may have forgotten something?"

"I don't follow," Alice said.

"What I mean is, in line with Alice's theory, what if, in her *moment of haste*, she had been writing carelessly and forgot to include a key detail?"

"What do you think this key detail is?" Meg asked.

"I think she forgot a decimal point."

Monica looked around at each of us, checking to see if we had caught on.

"I think it's a call number."

SCENE 31

We practically sprinted to the library, the frigid air stinging our faces.

"I have class in thirty minutes, so let's make this quick," Monica said.

But it wasn't just our busy schedules that had us in such a rush. At least, it wasn't why I found myself traveling at a pace faster than a light jog, for once. Time was of the essence for a number of reasons. We had to verify that the lead was not another dead end. If Monica's assessment had been correct, then we had to make it to the book before anyone else could check it out. And if it wasn't there, we might've lost a critical piece of evidence. One with the power to make or break our final conclusion.

There was also the chilling possibility that we wouldn't find the book because someone else knew that we were looking for it. Whether it had been Professor Shaw or someone else who'd taken the journal from us, whoever it was could've assumed that we'd read everything inside and been well aware of our next move.

One step ahead of us.

The warm air that greeted my skin as we went inside only magnified the icy pain imprinted upon my hands and face, before gradually melting into a dull, numbing burn. Monica led the way since she'd checked out more books than any of us, what with all of her different research papers and idle curiosities.

She took us to the second floor law section, right by the rows of tables we'd studied at for our midterms. The area was still busy, with students passing left and right to search through this shelf or that one. There didn't appear to be a single table open in the entire stretch of the room.

It made me nervous.

We were trying to find a potential new clue amidst what appeared to be half of an entire class of students. (A mild exaggeration.) Either this call number was leading us to a book our mystery girl had simply hoped to check out, or a monumental discovery for our "research project" had been hidden in plain sight.

As it would turn out, however, it was neither.

We had been skimming the wine and navy spines, tracking the numbers on the white labels that decorated them, when Monica said, "That can't be right."

I looked to find her hunched over a lower shelf, her pointer finger grazing over a book still lodged between two others.

"I'm assuming you didn't find it," I said.

"This is the call number," she said, her mouth fixed in a frown. "But this doesn't make any sense."

Alice stood from her crouched position on the ground. "What is it?"

Monica shimmied a thin book out from the row and inspected the cover. From what I could see of the back of it, it wore a white book jacket (a stark contrast with the others around it) and appeared to have illustrations on it. She turned it so that the cover faced us.

"*The Lost Culinary Art of the Fire Roast*," she said, suppressing a laugh. "I mean, unless she was trying to make waves at her next barbeque, I don't think—"

"That's not it," Alice said.

I walked over and grabbed the book. Sure enough, there were illustrations on the cover. Drawings of different foods that could be prepared with a traditional fire roast, some of which you wouldn't expect. (Blueberry muffins, for example.) What managed to catch my attention was that, when I turned it over to inspect the label, the call number was there.

340.1029B

But why would we find a culinary book in a section filled with law dictionaries?

I stared harder at the letter that followed the call number. "B." It didn't match the initial of the name of the author whose book I held in my hands.

My eyes followed the label as it traveled onto the back cover. Part of the plastic was peeling away. I used my finger to lift it further, feeling it pull upward with little resistance.

"Someone switched the books," I said.

SHOT: they look at me, eyes wide. Alice appears hopeful for the first time that afternoon.

"What makes you think that?" she asked.

I held the spine out in their direction. "The initial of this author's last name, 'F,' see? It doesn't match the letter that follows this code." I then showed them how I was able to lift the label off the book jacket. "This peels off too easily, so the seal had to have been broken before."

Monica's face conveyed pride. Or amusement. Regardless, I had their attention, so I used the momentum.

"It might be nothing," I continued. "But finding this book here with its correct call number would have been less surprising than finding it with the number we were looking for. So, I'm willing to bet that our book is in the same spot where this one is supposed to be."

It was our next best option, trying to figure out where this book on fire roasted delicacies belonged. And, thinking about it more clearly as we went to do just that, it made more sense by the minute.

I wondered if the girl who had looked for the book had found the same one we did, but she hadn't looked any closer. I wondered if she just assumed what any other reasonable person might have. That it wasn't there. I also wondered if she'd figured out the switch like we had.

Or if she had known about it the entire time.

We eventually found the section that housed food and culinary-related materials only a hop, skip, and a *catapult* away from any and all people. It was in the basement, a sad, ill-lit area with brown carpeting and plenty of workspaces that no one ever used. The shelves that lined the room were made of a lighter wood that looked sticky as opposed to glossy, likely because of the harsh fluorescent lighting. It was worlds away from the lively elegance found just upstairs.

As we passed through the rows of books, I felt the hair rise on the back of my neck and shot a look to the right, through an empty space on the shelf next to me.

"Stella?" Monica asked.

I squinted in that direction for a few more seconds before shaking my head. "Does anyone else feel like—"

"Like we're being watched twenty-four-seven?" Monica passed me on the left and patted me on the shoulder. "Just you, I think."

We found the book in the back-right corner of the room after searching for roughly ten minutes. Meg had been the one to spot it, and though you would have thought it should have stuck out like a sore thumb amidst the books along the lines of *The Lost Culinary Art of the Fire Roast*, it had been tucked safely away on the top shelf, away from the average set of wandering eyes.

Black's Law Dictionary. First Edition. That was the book The Girl in the Tunnels had made note of in her journal.

TIGHT SHOT: Alice runs her hand over the rough wine-colored exterior and the gold lettering on the front.

"Open it," Monica urged impatiently.

So, she did, and the worn pages we found inside signaled just how old the book truly was.

The edges had been stained brown, some torn in certain areas. Others hung onto the binding by threads, threatening to give at any moment. I watched the way they shifted flimsily, even in reaction to Alice's delicate touch. It was clear that it had been subject to years of use.

And something told me that not just anybody had been making trips down there to pay it a visit.

I leaned in closer to get a better look at the pages Alice had been flipping through, noticing the annotations that had been made in some of the margins. She passed by them quickly, but I caught glimpses of numbers, and occasionally letters. Initials, maybe.

"What do you think those mean?" I asked her.

She grabbed a couple hundred pages and moved past them. The annotations continued.

"They look like dates," she said.

I looked closer and saw she had been right. The page she was skimming had dates lining the margins: 2.21, 2.28, 3.05.

And below each date there was a set of initials. MC, MH, NS—

Zoom in. Right there.

DH.

"Dining Hall," I said, waking the others out of their collective trance.

"What?" Meg asked.

I pointed to the letters. "Dining Hall. They're dates and buildings."

"Meeting places," Alice said, a look of realization dawning on her face. "Dining Hall, for the hidden library?"

"Maybe," I said.

But something was off.

We knew the girls had been meeting each other in the attic consistently. It was their spot. But if the initials did represent places on campus, what did the society have to do with all the other ones? Should we have assumed they'd found hidden meeting places all over campus? Or did each of those buildings have something in common?

I scanned over the letters once more, trying to decipher a pattern, and finally succeeding when I noticed the initials MH reappear.

Main Hall.

There was a pattern. Something that connected the Main Hall to the Dining Hall. (Literally and figuratively.)

"They're not just meeting places," I said. "They're entrances to the tunnels." I took a step back to deliver my hypothesis. "We went into the tunnels through the Main Hall, but when we found that second set of stairs, it took us out through the Dining Hall. After all, why would there be only one entrance? What purpose would that serve? The tunnels don't simply exist down there, they connect various parts of the campus. And these building names," I pointed to the annotations, "must be where the other entrances are. So, these are meeting times and places, yes, but I think they were meant to indicate which entrances the girls were supposed to use and when."

I paused to catch my breath, waiting for their reactions. It was the only explanation I could think of as to the role that book had played. It was a ledger of sorts. An account of the times they were to meet in those tunnels. An account of the ways they would get down there.

It had been hidden thoroughly enough, though I wondered why exactly that was. If these girls were as close as they seemed to have been and spent time with each other every day, why would they have needed to communicate in such a clandestine manner?

"Stella's on her game today," Monica said. "Though I worry having too many Sherlocks in the group might disrupt our dynamic."

"I feel like I'm definitely not in the running for that title," Meg said.

"But you are valued, nonetheless, Megara," Monica assured her with a pat on the head. Meg batted her hand away, and she continued, "I'm positive I'm already late for class so I have to run, but let me know what else you find?"

"I have class, too," Meg said.

I did as well, and it seemed Alice could tell from the apologetic smile I flashed in her direction.

"You guys go ahead," she said. "I'll just check this out and take it to Studio. I can definitely find some time there to look more closely at everything. We'll reconvene tomorrow night?"

As she started to close the book, she lingered on the very first page that had flipped back into view. Below the printed title there were three handwritten words:

Imperium in Imperio

Empire within an Empire.

We parted ways for the day, each of us off to the more mundane parts of our lives. Those that didn't involve investigative work masquerading as academic exploration or reading secret society ledgers instead of textbooks. Those where we could forget the mess we'd gotten ourselves into, despite the fact that each of us had managed to convince ourselves that it wasn't a mess at all. We'd told ourselves that the battle was being fought elsewhere. A clash between a murderer and someone who wanted revenge.

But how could we have expected to be the leading ladies of this film if we didn't take part in the action?

Whatever our fantasies may have been at the time, reality was about to set in. Any good storyteller knows the line between good and evil is never quite as solid as one may think. It's blurry, and easy to cross, often without any conscious agency of one's own. And sooner or later, we would realize that we were no longer navigating the Labyrinth by choice.

We just couldn't find our way out.

SCENE 32

There's nothing like a good old-fashioned threat to make you realize you're onto someone.

Finding the head of a horse in my bed would have been fairly effective. The same goes for Inigo Montoya knocking on my door and yelling, "Prepare to die!" But these cinematic warnings paled in comparison to what someone at school had in store for us.

They delivered lovely typewritten notes directly to our mailboxes.

In all honesty, I would rarely check my mail at school. I never received any letters or packages (apart from the occasional "we're sorry someone is threatening our community" notice, but that had only happened during that one year), so I wouldn't even bother getting my hopes up.

The day after we found the dictionary in the library, it seemed my postal drought had been granted a lucky forecast.

I had been just about ready to go meet the others for dinner when there came an incessant knocking at my door. I opened it to find Monica, breathless.

"Check your mailbox," she said.

I didn't know what for, as she seemed intent to withhold that information from me until I completed the task, so I started down the steps, both she and Meg hot on my trail.

When I reached the mailroom, I saw that I did, in fact, have a lone slip of paper waiting for me. I pulled it out, silently reading the message I found with it. It said:

Stop looking.

And there was also something on the back.

Actually, it turned out that what I'd *read* had been typed along the back of a photograph. A black and white print of a library card.

Alice's library card.

I turned around to find Monica holding her own slip of paper up to my face, the same words typed across it. And the same print on the other side.

"Do you think—" she began, interrupted by the sound of someone running down the hall.

We turned to see Alice jogging toward the steps, stopping only once she saw us standing there, looking at her. She held what looked like a crumpled-up piece of paper in her hand.

Back in Meg and Monica's room, we sat and talked through our options.

"We can't stop now," Monica said.

Meg frowned. "Are you sure? Cause it sounds like someone wants us to."

"That's because we *found* something, Meg. Something that matters."

"Do we know that for certain, though? What can we gather from that book, other than the fact that the society met in the tunnels, which, by the way, I thought we already knew."

"Alice." Monica held her hand out. "Would you care to present your findings to the group?"

Alice hesitated, her eyes glued to the floor. Maybe she hadn't found anything else and didn't want to admit we were in for another let down. Maybe she felt defeated, like we'd been running in circles all this time with no real payoff.

Or, maybe she had found something. Something she was afraid of sharing with us. Something that scared her.

"Well?" I asked, shooting for encouraging, but admittedly coming off as impatient.

She pulled the book from her backpack and stared at it. "From what I could tell, Stella was right. All the initials listed by the dates in the margins seem to correspond to campus buildings, particularly the old ones. The Dining Hall, the Main Hall, the theater, even. So, we can assume that each building mentioned holds a tunnel entrance, and that on the days, or nights, listed, the society had planned to use the assigned entrance to meet. Or, do whatever it is that they did."

She stopped and waited for someone else to speak. All she had contributed, however, was a confirmation of what we'd known the day before. She had more to say, I could tell, but I didn't understand what was keeping her from sharing it with us.

Monica, too, looked unconvinced. "Is there anything else you came across?"

CLOSE-UP: Alice's fingers play with the pages in front of her.

I swore I saw them shaking.

I moved from Monica's bed to the floor, lowering myself slowly so that I could draw her attention. I looked at her reassuringly, hoping to convince her that she could tell us whatever it was that she'd found. She looked back, and her nod was almost imperceptible.

"I did, actually," she said. "But it's big."

"How big?" Monica asked.

Alice sighed and flipped toward the second half of the book. "You saw the dates listed in these margins. They're everywhere. A month and a day, and an entrance. Correct?"

We nodded.

"But when I took the time to go through it all more thoroughly, I noticed something else, as well. There's another temporal marker. A year." She found the page she'd been looking for. "For example, 1972, of course."

I already saw where she was headed.

I wasn't sure I liked it.

"But every however many pages, new years are marked: 1977, 1982, 1988." She listed years as she passed them in the book.

Eventually, she stopped turning pages, and looked up at us. "It goes all the way up to 1992."

The air had grown thin since she'd begun talking. Each of us, I assumed, had to be aware of what this meant. It had been quite literally spelled out for us, in that book.

The society hadn't just existed among that first class of women. It had persisted.

It wasn't simply an issue of the past. It was our present.

And to come to the realization that those women were still out there, living among us, hidden behind the faces we passed every single day, was to watch the world dim, to feel the ground begin to crack beneath our feet. It was to look around and find that you no longer recognize what you see.

Meg was the first of us to speak.

"So," she said. "Should we stop?"

At first, none of us objected. None of us said anything. It had all become more complicated, knowing that we weren't just dealing with a mysterious mythology professor and journals from the past. Someone noticed that we took that book. A book that was still in use. Someone wanted it back.

"We don't stop."

Her declaration was short and to the point. But the speech that followed was, in Monica's typical fashion, anything but.

"It appears, ladies, that we've struck a nerve. Someone doesn't like that we're digging. Or, multiple someones in this case."

I saw Meg's face fall.

"But now, our job is to figure out what we're up against." She paused like a teacher hoping to be prompted for further explanation.

I indulged her. "How do we do that?"

"Thank you for asking, Stella. It's simple, really. It's the manipulation of risk."

When none of us responded, she looked around, realizing we were lost.

"The manipulation of risk? Thomas Schelling? No?"

We shook our heads.

"Okay, quick lecture. He was a theorist, dealing primarily with strategies concerning the Nuclear Revolution, and essentially, there was this theory called MAD. Well, MAD was something else, but it's relevant, you see. MAD, or Mutually Assured Destruction," she said, emphasizing each word with her hand. "It was basically a theory that argued that the widespread distribution of nuclear warfare would actually promote more peace than war, which is what *made* it so revolutionary actually—"

Alice cleared her throat. "The condensed version, perhaps?"

"Right, so the idea was that no nuclear power would want to launch a nuclear attack on another, because that would essentially ensure a retaliation, and they would both burn. However, this presents a sort of conundrum, because you want the enemy to fear you, but you don't want to have to employ the big guns. *So,* the manipulation of risk was essentially a way to overcome this issue of credibility. You test the limits of your opponent. It's like a game of Chicken. Ooh, or Stella, Ms. Film Major, it's like that movie, the James Dean one. He wears the red jacket."

"Rebel Without a Cause?"

"Yes, exactly. The scene where they drive toward the cliff, and the one who jumps out of the car first loses. That's the whole idea."

I almost laughed. *Almost.* "You seem to be forgetting that, while Buzz technically won the game of Chicken, he still ended up driving off the cliff to his death."

Monica sighed, her voice lowering. "Well, that's the thing. It only works if you're willing to lose everything."

"Oh. Great."

It was valiant, in theory, and part of me felt we had come too far to turn back at the first sign of trouble.

CUT. Take Two:

The first (painted door), second (suspicious journal entry), third (ominous poem), fourth (discovery of tunnels), fifth (radio threat), sixth (missing journal), seventh (creaky floors), *eighth* sign of trouble.

But those are the things we do in the pursuit of knowledge. Ah yes, and for Alice.

She didn't look sold on Monica's "drive off the side of a cliff" plan. In fact, that same hesitant, almost fearful, look was still plastered on her face. She didn't like where any of this was going, and that worried me, considering how she had been the most invested of all of us. She wouldn't have been planning on stopping, either, but that didn't mean she felt confident about what we were up against. When her eyes met mine, I saw what she had been wrestling with in that moment.

There was still something she wasn't telling us.

I tried to ask her, *This again, Alice?*

I believed she answered, *Trust me.*

Monica was sitting on her desk by that point, swinging her legs back and forth as she attempted to rally us together. "Think about how close we might be. We could actually figure this all out." She hopped down and crouched to my level, her face inching toward mine. "So, the only question is, how much are you willing to lose?"

SCENE 33

It appeared we were actually willing to lose quite a bit.

Sitting in class, waiting for Professor Shaw to arrive, we couldn't ignore the way some of our classmates would glance in our direction. The boy three rows ahead had turned around casually, but the moment his eyes crossed our path, he quickly leaned over to his friend and whispered something in his ear.

Something, I assumed, along the lines of, "It's them."

And it hadn't been the first time.

At that point in the narrative, we'd had no way of knowing just who was responsible for what came after the notes. Throughout the course of the semester, there were a few different persons of interest we'd stumbled upon with regard to this *investigation,* if you will. Alice, Professor Shaw, and the latest, the not-so-dead society. We had ruled out Alice, of course, so unless Professor Shaw felt inclined to target our deepest fears and insecurities on a school-wide level, our bets were placed on someone we, unfortunately, could not name. Someone we could not see.

But let's circle back to our deepest fears and insecurities.

Remember when I told you how I thought sophomore year would have been different? How our status as freshmen would no longer paint targets on our backs? How our class rank would no longer be the source of any ridicule or gossip that came our way?

Well, it turned out that we were about to be the subjects of a lot of attention. But the "freshmen" element obviously had nothing to do with it.

Now, had I considered the possibility that a sudden increase in notoriety could have been brought about by something entirely unrelated? We did, after all, make ourselves known to a decent portion of the student body by ever so boldly walking out on a speech meant to denounce anonymous threats. ("The Coward's Playthings," as President Gallagher had so affectionately called them.) So, to answer my own question, of course I considered it. And truthfully, I wish it had been unrelated.

But when you and your four closest friends all fall victim to baseless claims perfectly tailored to the darkest innermost workings of your minds and egos, all within the span of a weekend?

That, I decided, simply could not have been a coincidence.

It started with Monica.

Thankfully, Monica had always had incredibly thick skin. While there were certain things that managed to breach her defenses every once in a while (the God complex was, after all, only a figure of speech) she rarely let anything truly get to her. It was a good thing, then, that she had been the first to gain her fifteen minutes (give or take a few weeks) of fame.

CUT TO:

She had arrived to her shift at the paper like on any other day, with an appetite for authority.

She could tell almost instantly, however, that something was amiss. Whether it was that many staff writers failed to meet her eyes, or that her senior editor seemed a tad snippier than usual, Monica's unfailing intuition hinted that the tides had changed, and she was determined to find out why.

Now, the university newspaper, unsurprisingly, acted as a sort of hub to the intricate web that ran along the campus grounds, the staff members some of the most connected individuals within the community. Any conjecture, therefore, would never fail to make its way back to headquarters. And, conjecture regarding their editor in chief? Well, that was a whole other story.

Whispers had grown louder, suddenly, about Monica's position of leadership. Everywhere she looked, someone had been talking about the same thing. The thing they'd heard from so and so who'd heard it from this acquaintance who'd heard it from the talking childhood stuffed animal that had appeared to them in a dream. It was decided, very suddenly, that Monica had obtained her role as editor in chief by sleeping with her predecessor, Danny Nelson.

"The insinuation is entirely unfounded," she had said at dinner when we caught people staring. "If I'd slept with Danny Nelson, I sure as hell wouldn't want to spend all my time in the one place that would remind me of it."

For the most part, as you can tell, Monica managed to brush the rumor off pretty easily.

But poor, sweet Meg wasn't so lucky.

CUT TO:

Arriving at orchestra practice had always been the highlight of Meg's day, where she could lose herself in the chorus of strings for two or three hours and remember how much easier it was to speak with Vivaldi than with words.

When she sat down in her (well-deserved) second chair that one afternoon, her loyal neighboring musicians broke the news to her, gently. And whoever it was that had decided to speak on her behalf chose a narrative that succeeded at hitting her where it hurt.

It was said that Meg, as brilliant as we all knew her to be, had only been admitted to the school because her father had donated a large sum of money to make it happen. Meg, whose one significant insecurity was rooted in whether or not people believed she belonged at our school, had become subject to the overwhelming opinion that she did not. Seeing her crack under the weight of this particular accusation had been painful, and despite how hard she tried to hold her head high, we each knew how truly broken she was over it all.

CUT TO:

A myth about yours truly came next, although it wasn't as much of a cohesive story as the others. It was more that my character had come into question, the intimacies of my personal life up for debate. But, as you know, my life wasn't all that interesting during my sophomore year (from a social perspective, that is), and Josie certainly hadn't let me hear the end of it. Therefore, the reassurance that my calendar was all but uneventful only allowed me to ignore the fact that I could have miraculously been deemed a prude, a slut, a tease, easy, and frigid all at once. It was nothing more than a failed attempt to resurrect my past. It wasn't me anymore.

Yet, despite my indifference, I couldn't help but feel like the camera had been on me at all times. Watching me. Stalking me. The POV shot was someone else's, rather than mine, but any time I'd look over my shoulder, there would be no one there.

CUT TO:

A painted door. A published poem. A radio threat.

As far as actual damage to be done, Alice's rumor took the cake.

The opinion had somehow spread that Alice was the party behind the three messages that had revolved around the generation-old ghost story. And when you stopped to think about it, she hadn't done much that would convince someone otherwise. There was the fact that she'd earned the reputation of the "mysterious new girl" among peers in our class. But that, in conjunction with her decision to leave, visibly upset, during the assembly held to condemn such messages, simply didn't cast her in the best of lights.

How much people really believed the gossip, we weren't sure, but we did know that, if word traveled back to the administration, or if anyone with enough influence actually gave credence to it, Alice would find herself back under the microscope. Only I wouldn't be the one inspecting her.

Now, you'll recall that I did say that my *four* closest friends fell victim to these claims.

Which means it's time for Josie's return to the big screen. *CUT TO:*

We had been sitting in my room, huddled around a tearful Meg as she remembered what had been said about her over the previous few days. We did our best to comfort her, but our attempts to offer kind and reassuring words were interrupted by a loud voice approaching from the hall.

"Charlie Morgan!" it yelled, right before the door burst open.

Josie marched inside, her face as red as the hair that framed it. She faltered for a moment when she saw the four of us sitting there, but rest assured, her rant was quickly resumed.

We'd heard the opinions circling around her that week as well, that the reason Scottie had broken up with her was that she tried to make a pass at his older brother, Charlie.

She paced angrily. "Charlie isn't even my *type*. I mean, sure, he's cute and all, but I was dating Scottie for a reason. To say that I would do something like that is, frankly, insulting."

As abrupt as the intrusion had been, it seemed to be distracting Meg from her own feelings of self-pity. Taking note of the drying tears on her face, Josie slowed to a standstill. She exhaled as if it were the first time she'd done it all day. Then she sat down, tears welling in her own eyes.

She looked at us with remorse. "I'm so sorry about what I said, Meg. You too, Stella. And Alice. I just—"

"And me?" Monica interrupted, batting her eyelashes.

"It's okay, Josie," Alice said with a comforting smile. (She was quicker to forgive than I was.)

"It's not okay." She shook her head, the tears spilling over. "I was horrible to you, Alice, and what you were trying to do was way more important than me trying to get over my breakup. I was taking it out on you."

It suddenly hit me that it was the first time I'd seen Josie cry. I think it was the first time any of us had, like her declarations about wanting to feel numb, however genuine they had been, were beginning to thaw and melt away.

"You never did tell us how that happened," Monica said.

Josie threw her head back and laughed, as though it were the funniest thing in the world.

"I'm glad you asked," she said, wiping a tear from her cheek. "As it so happens, Charlie made a pass at *me*."

"No," Monica said, her mouth agape.

Josie nodded. "On their family vacation, no less. He kept making all these comments, under his breath, or whenever we had a moment alone. The day before we were set to leave and go home, he cornered me in the pool house, saying all these disgusting things about the 'messages' I was sending him. As though me smiling at him across the dinner table meant I wanted him." I saw a shiver race up her spine. "I bolted out of there just fine, thankfully, but...it didn't matter that he never physically touched me. There was something about the way it made me feel. Gross isn't the right word. I felt humiliated, for some reason. Like I'd done something wrong."

"I'm so sorry, Josie," Meg said.

"That wasn't even the worst part," she said, her voice sinking as her anger dissipated, turning into something else. Hurt. "The worst part was, when I told Scottie, he didn't believe me."

I'd figured Josie wasn't being honest when she'd said her breakup hadn't bothered her. It didn't seem possible to me that she could be so in love one moment, and so completely fine the next. And to know that, all that time, she'd been dealing with something much bigger than vapid insecurity made me feel like I didn't deserve to be the one holding the camera. It made me feel like, for the first time, I'd truly missed something.

I couldn't blame her for not telling me the truth. Because we all put up fronts to feel safe, don't we? If other people believe you're okay, it's easier for you to pretend that you really are.

In that moment, all I wanted was for Josie to believe it herself.

CUT TO:

We were back in class, the clock still ticking, the students still settling in.

Some of them still staring.

And I know what you're thinking. This is *college* we're talking about. People don't care. It's too big a pond for word to spread so easily.

But you'd be surprised. Films will often tell you that, by the time you're off to college, you've grown up. That you're ready to strike out on your own because you've finally found yourself. Truth is, most of the people you meet in college are still stuck in high school, convincing themselves that the decisions they make are justified because they're "adults." And they don't have any real adults around to tell them otherwise.

So, yes, people do care. And, yes, word does spread.

And, truthfully, it only takes one stranger thinking they know you to make you feel alarmingly on display.

"So, what now? Do we think we have anything *left* to lose?" I asked, trying to distract myself from the fact that Professor Shaw would be there any minute.

Josie, who was sitting with us again, sighed. "I personally feel like withdrawing from society entirely. Does that answer your question?"

Monica leaned over from the other side of Meg, propped up on the table by her elbows. "What is this, *Nineteenth Century England*? Our reputations have not been irreparably tarnished."

"Speak for yourself," Meg said. "Though I'd describe it as being run through a woodchipper, perhaps."

"When did you get to be so dramatic, Meg?" Monica asked. "But if you all want to behave like we have, in fact, transported back to The Regency, then I'm sorry to inform you, Miss Josephine, you have one more societal obligation to attend."

She groaned. "And what would that be?"

"Why, the Presidential Gala, of course."

SCENE 34

The Presidential Gala was held annually at our university on the Saturday before Thanksgiving Break. Students donned ball gowns and tuxedos, faculty became virtually unrecognizable in their evening wear, the orchestra, the band, and the choir all replaced Sir Mix-a-Lot, and the Main Hall's palatial gallery transformed into a ballroom worthy of any Hitchcock political thriller.

Naturally, there was a lot to do before then, and students were already running around buying clothes, securing dates, "somehow" obtaining copious amounts of alcohol, and doing anything they could to ensure that what was considered the grandest night of the year was one to be remembered. (Or, in many cases, forgotten.)

So, you might ask why, with only four days remaining until the infamous event, we were instead on our way to the campus broadcast studio, our ears subject to the numbing pain brought on by the harsh November winds.

Valid question.

FLASHBACK:

"Please tell me you checked that book back into the library."

Monica had all but cornered Alice the moment she walked through the door on that Tuesday afternoon, her appearance signaling that she was more frazzled than usual. (A dangerous state.) She'd missed not one, not two, but *three* buttons on her blouse, and a dark blue stain ran down her chin from when she'd been chewing her fountain pen minutes earlier. She had been startled to feel her teeth rupture the barrel and reservoir, the ink proceeding to bleed out onto her lips and drip downward toward her clavicle. She'd spent the time leading up to Alice's arrival scrubbing, and scrubbing again, to no avail. She'd have to try again later.

Alice's eyes swept over the streaky remnants before making the wise decision to refrain from commenting, instead saying, "Yesterday. Right after class."

Monica exhaled, her trademark self-assurance reappearing with each passing second. "Smart," she said. "But just so we're all on the same page, this does not mean we're giving in. Or giving up, for that matter."

I held my hands up in surrender, well aware that she would be unwavering in the matter, and not daring to even suggest I thought otherwise.

"So, walk me through it again," said Josie, who was still trying to catch up from her mid-production hiatus. "Shaw was also in the society?"

I nodded. "She was. And we think she was the one listening to us outside the room that night."

"You mean, the night after you all went down into the tunnels," she clarified.

"Correct."

"Because the tunnels are real." She had to force the words to leave her mouth.

"The tunnels are, in fact, real," Monica said as she hopped onto her bed, reclining on her side. "We know that, Shaw knows that, and the entire society knows it."

"Right. The society that apparently still exists after all these years." Josie frowned. "Are you sure about that one? How could we possibly not know about it?"

Alice shrugged. "It's called a secret society for a reason. Clearly they weren't happy with our efforts to figure out more."

The rumors were still circulating. I wasn't sure when they'd die down, only that none of us really had the time to concern ourselves with them. The fact that they'd felt the need for retaliation meant that we were a little too close for comfort. Perhaps closer than any of us realized.

That was why Alice returned the book.

"Make them think that we've stopped looking," Alice said. "We'll wave the white flag, all the while searching for another way in. One they won't see coming."

"A new angle." Monica nodded, lightly chewing on her nails.

I examined the tops of my shoes, and my face as it was reflected in the patent-leather surface. I looked to the mirror, noticing the dark circles under my eyes, the same shade as all of theirs. That was what we got for trying to be full-time students with penchants for embarking on the occasional wild goose chase. The only thing that had been keeping us going at that point was the fact that it wasn't so "wild" anymore. There was an element of truth to it all, and all that was left to do was to separate fiction from reality.

A trivial task, I was sure.

"Have you considered the messages?" Josie asked, surprising all of us. When we didn't answer, she elaborated. "From what I understand, my opinion that this was all a prank was entirely off base. If Shaw really is a killer, and not just The Professor from Hell, then clearly someone wants us all to know that. I think we'd have better luck figuring out who that person is and piecing it together from there."

"Work from the outside in," Alice said. "I like that. Any objections?"

I didn't have any of my own. Only questions. I agreed that we wouldn't get anywhere near the society itself since it was likely on high alert, but there was an element to Alice's proposal that didn't seem genuine. There was something about that dictionary that she left out, I was sure of it. And suddenly, she was steering us in the opposite direction. I wanted to know just what storm she was trying to navigate away from, and what would happen if we found ourselves lost at sea, either way.

But I wouldn't ask her, yet.

"Good," she said. "Besides, we'll have to clear my name somehow, won't we?"

FLASHFORWARD:

That's how we ended up on our way to the east end of campus. Meg pointed out that the radio mishap was the most recent of the three messages and would therefore leave behind the most fingerprints. We didn't know what we'd find there, if anything at all, but the odds seemed better than trying to break into an armed fortress on our own.

And if it did turn out that someone else was trying to do the same (only, far more successfully, at that point), Monica pointed out, "Anyone opposed to a little Trojan Horse scenario?"

We reached the Student Center as Meg was telling us all about her friend who DJ'd a show on music in film called

Rated R for Sax and Violins and ended each session by putting on an Austrian accent to deliver a convincing, "I'll be Bach."

"You should really listen to it, Stella," she said. "He's a *genius*."

We passed the first-floor study spaces and the groups meeting there, the readers and the chess players and the kids debating the pros and cons of coeducation. We made a beeline for the stairs. The broadcast studio was in the basement, the student booth at the very end of the hall.

The bare, white walls and the dim fluorescent lighting made for a less than picturesque journey as the destination approached on our right. The red "On Air" sign was off, but I'd always been one to proceed with caution.

"You should knock," I said to Monica, who was up ahead, leading the expedition.

"No one's going to be in there," she said.

She turned the handle and leaned into the door, using her weight to push it open. The lights were on, and sure enough, there was someone there.

Someone, I was certain, none of us were expecting to find, huddled over a box of vinyl records. The sound of the door opening jarred him, prompting him to turn around and identify us. The intruders. But we recognized him immediately.

It was Professor Aldridge.

SCENE 35

He looked surprised to see us.

"Alice. Ladies," he said, still trying to piece together exactly what we were doing there.

I was wondering the same thing about him.

Even Alice was caught off guard.

"Prof—Max, I mean," Alice said with a smile. "Are you… what are you doing here?

He gave a lopsided grin, as though he should've been the one asking that question.

"I'm the faculty supervisor. For the student station," he said.

"Really?" she asked. "I had no idea."

He frowned and pointed toward Monica's chin. "Did something happen?"

Monica's eyes widened as she felt the area with her hand. I'd forgotten what happened as well, the sight of the left-over blue ink stain something my mind had simply begun to pass over.

"No big deal," she said, forcing a laugh. "A little brawl with my pen. The pen lost."

"Right. Is there something I can help you all with?" he asked.

"We were just..." Monica trailed off, looking to us for assistance. We hadn't planned for a scenario such as that one. We figured we would've been able to dance around any other students using the booth. How could they have known better? But the faculty supervisor? He was aware that we didn't belong there.

I looked around the room, taking in the shelves of CDs and the record sleeves pasted onto the walls, the soundboard lit up with oranges and greens and the microphones that hung over the edge of the counter. The dark carpet that ran beneath our feet was monochromatic to the extent that it was dizzying, like you could fall into it, and keep falling.

When none of us came to her rescue, Monica improvised. "We were hoping to inquire about any available showtimes," she said cheerily.

"No, we weren't," Alice said.

CUTAWAY TO: Monica shoots a pointed glare at Alice.

But Professor Aldridge looked amused, if anything.

"What Monica meant to say was that we're doing a group project for one of our classes," said Josie, who'd been surprisingly quiet up until that point. "A project on...radio broadcasts."

The seconds ticked away in silence. We waited for him to take the bait. To accept the narrative we were feeding him as truth and run with it.

The silence had just begun to feel uncomfortable when he said, "So, you wanted to interview someone, I assume. Someone in the field."

"Exactly," she said. "Would you be able to answer some of our questions?"

He shrugged. "Of course. I can try."

This all would have been lovely had we actually prepared any questions to ask him. Like I said, we weren't expecting to have to talk to anyone. We just figured we would do what we did best. Snoop and theorize. But we'd found ourselves in a situation that seemed inescapable, so the only thing left to do was work with what we had. Namely, average to above average skill in the fields of distraction, observation, and deduction.

Josie kept the conversation rolling.

"Could you tell us a bit about the types of people who work here? How you select student hosts, for example. What criteria do you use?"

He thought about it for a moment. "Well, we try to, for the most part, allow those who are passionate about radio to get their chance to explore it. That being said, there are a limited number of slots in the schedule, so we look for students who will take a unique angle with their show, do something we haven't seen before."

"Like my friend, Michael," Meg said.

Professor Aldridge smiled at the connection. "*Rated R.* Absolutely. That creative twist plays a huge role in earning some airtime."

CUTAWAY TO: Josie looks at me, nodding her head in the direction of the rest of the room.

A signal.

"Can I have a look around?" I asked.

He glanced toward the rest of the room. "Go ahead."

"I'd love to know more about the scheduling process. How you manage to coordinate all the different shows," Josie continued as I stepped away from the group.

SOUND CUE: the conversation fades into the background.

I made my way over to the back wall, looking more closely at the album covers that decorated it. I settled in on The Police's *Synchronicity,* taking my time to get lost in the layered images, the blue, red, and yellow streaks, the textured look of it all. I had my back to the rest of the group, unsure of whether or not I was being watched. I needed to look convincing.

I moved to the bookcase that housed the CDs, quickly glancing over my shoulder to confirm that the others still had Aldridge's attention occupied. He seemed fully immersed in explaining the ins and outs of scheduling, particularly when it came to assigning the night shifts. I turned back to the alphabetized rows of cases but angled my gaze toward the soundboard and the box of records we'd found him going through. The top of a Van Halen album was peeking out, *1984*, I gathered, from the child-sized forehead sprouting blond hair I could make out as well.

I inched closer to the recording area, noticing the stacks of tapes on the counter. I didn't know what it was that drew me to them. It could have been the five that sat apart from the rest of them, spread out like they had been examined. Juxtaposed. On the other hand, it could have been the labels that started to come into view the closer I got.

Zoom in.

ED'S TIRES

I passed behind the five of them, their exchange coming into earshot briefly once again.

"Did you want to write any of this down?"

"I have a really good memory."

The tapes that had been pulled away from the others all wore the same label, that of the advertiser whose recording was meant to play the night the third message was broadcast to anyone on campus who found themselves listening. They looked almost identical.

I say almost because one of them was tagged with a Post-it note that had a simple question mark written on it.

I picked it up, turning it over in my hands. Other than the attached note, I had trouble distinguishing it from the others. They all just looked like black cassettes labeled and ready to be aired.

"Ah, I see you've found our mystery tape."

I jumped, nearly dropping what had apparently already been deemed evidence. I placed it down quickly.

"Sorry, I was just looking."

Professor Aldridge gestured to the tape and walked over. "No apologies necessary. I've been trying to figure out how this one got in the mix since the," he paused, searching for the right word, "the incident."

The panicked look on Josie's face melted away as an opportunity seemed to naturally present itself. Maybe we were able to speak more directly than we'd thought. Given that I was the one who prompted the discussion, I was the one who had to lead it.

"Any luck?" I asked. "I don't know much about this stuff, but it seems odd that something like that could slip in undetected."

He shook his head. "To be honest, I'm still just guessing. Obviously something like this doesn't reflect well on us as a department, or on me, as supervisor. But there really isn't a whole lot to go on. The tape was labeled correctly, so how could the host have known any better?"

"The tapes are prerecorded?" I asked.

"Yes, they're 'production spots.' Essentially, the company records the ads and sends them over, then we add them into the lineup." He picked the tape up. "Someone switched the tapes, I believe, but that would mean that they figured out the ad lineup, labeled it properly, and did it all without being seen."

The others had slowly made their way over, joining the conversation. Monica peered over at the tapes. "Without being seen?" she asked. "Surely someone would have had to notice a person who wasn't meant to be here."

Unless, of course, they were meant to be there.

He shrugged. "It's very possible to get in here undetected. As you girls proved earlier, the doors aren't locked. Not during the day, at least. So, whoever switched out the original tape for their own would've needed to have done their research."

They'd have needed to be familiar with the lineup. They'd have needed to be familiar with the labels. They'd have needed to be familiar with the schedule.

I couldn't be certain, but at the time, it sounded like they already knew what they were doing.

It sounded like an inside job.

SCENE 36

——

I don't want to tell you about what happened in class over the next few days.

I don't want to tell you about how Shaw ignored us, and we her. I don't want to tell you about the homework I did, or the debates we had over what to do with what we learned at the broadcast studio.

I'd rather tell you about the morning of November 13. The morning after the first snow of the school year.

The five of us had decided to walk to our classes together. Amidst a span of dreary days and dark clouds that had made the campus appear sad and damp, the sun had decided to come out, its bright rays reflecting off the icy layers on the quads that had been decorated the previous night.

It was beautiful, even though I had to squint nearly the entire duration of the walk.

We clambered together down a pathway that cut straight through the snowbanks, walking shakily with our hands in our pockets. The paths had not yet been plowed, so we had to follow along the areas of snow and ice that had been flattened by previous students on their walks earlier that day.

I didn't hear what Meg said to Josie when we reached the middle of the quad (I was too busy concentrating on where I placed my foot with each step) but the next thing I knew, Josie had playfully bumped her to the side. Meg had no choice but to step directly into the tall bank of powder (her other option was falling in entirely), and she gasped, a shiver running visibly through her body. I cringed at the sight. Her stocking-clad leg knee-deep in the frigid substance, her patent-leather loafer submerged. A chill ran up my own leg just at the thought. Josie bit her lip, a laugh attempting to bubble to the surface.

What happened next was one of those real moments in life that you look back on as beautifully cinematic:

Meg grabs a handful of snow with her mitten and chucks it at Josie.

Josie attempts to evade the attack but gets nicked in the ear, anyway.

I had been caught up in watching the spectacle when I felt a sharp stinging at the back of my head, a few droplets of water sliding down my neck and into the back of my shirt. My shoulders pulled toward one another, and I slowly turned to find Alice with her hand over her mouth, delight in her eyes. It was, however, quickly replaced with fear as she watched me lunge toward her, shoving her backward and sending her toppling into the snow. She lay there for a second, eyes wide, limbs frozen, until she started making snow angels, laughing away the shock.

At some point, clouds had reappeared and snowflakes came down from the sky, with rays of sun still peeking through and illuminating them. Illuminating us. We chased each other down the path, grabbing whatever fistfuls of snow we could on the way, narrowly dodging some other students.

Monica abandoned the fight and started running with her tongue out, attempting to catch whatever she could.

We'd come to a natural stop near the architecture building, the white marble blending harmoniously with its surroundings. I bent over to catch my breath, a warm burn radiating from my chest, a cold one prickling the bottoms of my feet due to the melting ice that had found its way into my shoes.

Alice turned to face the four of us, breathing heavily. "Well," she said, a wide smile on her face. "I'll see you."

I saw her in a close-up, the camera roaming over her features, revealing what might not be noticed by the human eye alone. Her cheeks were tinged red, the rest of her face pale as ever and lightly covered with a few strands of her dark hair. Her brown eyes were layered in a light, shiny film. Reflective. You could almost see yourself in them. Tiny snowflakes decorated her dark eyelashes. To this day, the image is seared in my brain.

I remember feeling like I was floating that morning. Like someone had shaken me awake, the air inside my body expanding. I felt like I'd never feel tired again.

And I wondered if that was what Alice had meant when she told me what she did under the moon that one night.

What she'd meant when she told me I'd fall in love again.

Because, for the first time, I started to believe her.

SCENE 37

———

It was around noon that same day when Alice knocked on my door.

I'd just finished a mind-numbing reading on the semiotics of cinema and was hoping to sneak in an afternoon nap, but as luck would have it, answering the door was on the agenda instead.

She was standing there, bundled up in a long, navy overcoat with the collar of her cream blouse tightly hugging her neck. Her hair was tucked behind both of her ears to reveal small pearls. I realized I'd never seen her wear earrings before.

She wore heels. Not high enough to look entirely out of character but enough for me to have to look up to meet her eyes.

"Where are you headed?" I asked.

She didn't answer the question. She only asked in return, "Do you want to go for a drive?"

By "a drive," I pictured a quick, serene journey around the outskirts of campus. By "a drive," I pictured traveling mere miles off the grounds, perhaps to a local coffee shop or bookstore to simply browse. By "a drive," I pictured staring peacefully out the window as the rows of snow-covered corn passed.

I didn't picture merging onto the expressway with no destination in sight.

But when I asked Alice where we were going (for the third time, actually), the only information she offered was a playful grin, and it occurred to me that the answer might be something I could very well do without.

Thirty minutes into our impromptu adventure, I looked down at the hunter green velvet trousers that flared loosely around my legs. After I had agreed to the drive, Alice glanced up and down, surveying my turtleneck and jeans, and asked, "Is that what you're going to wear?" Given that I had absolutely no idea what occasion I would be dressing for, I took the hint and tried to match her level of flair without sacrificing my partiality for pants. Apart from the knots in my hair that I didn't have time to tackle or the aforementioned bags under my eyes, I believed my efforts paid off nicely.

But I wanted to know where she was taking me, and why she felt she couldn't have told me before we were well on our way. I wanted to know what was so important that she decided to ask a boy from Studio if she could borrow his car for the day. I wanted to know why she took me with her, and not the others.

We were hitting the forty-five-minute mark when she looked at me out of the corner of her eye and said, "Ask me again."

I knew what she meant, but I played the fool anyway.

"What?"

"Ask me again, about where we're going. I'll answer this time."

"Where are we going, Alice?"

She nodded her head in the direction of the glove compartment. I took that as my invitation to open it. Inside, I found the car's registration, the owner's manual, and a lint roller.

I also found the Polaroid. The one of the seven women. The secret society.

I held it up in front of my face, looking at each of them once more. Aunt Daphne, whose raven hair, even though longer than Alice's, enhanced the canvas of her skin the same exact way. She smiled the same closed smile, too. My eyes drifted across the frame to Professor Shaw. Madeleine. It was a wonder how much of a difference her hair could make. How her brunette waves radiated warmth, a youthful joy only reinforced by her smile. It was one that seemed to take up her whole face. I thought of the Madeleine I knew, the woman she'd become. The icy blonde radiated a fitting chill, her smile frozen in the past. Despite the fact that she seemed to be the only piece of the puzzle in our midst, she was also the one we couldn't seem to place. She just didn't seem to fit.

I looked to Alice, unsure of what exactly I was meant to take away from the picture in the glove compartment. She kept her eyes on the road.

"I found one of them," she said.

For a moment, we froze, time standing still as the cars, trees, and the rest of the world continued to move past us. Alice was taking me to one of the women from the photograph. One of the women from the society.

I couldn't even begin to formulate a response.

"Well, I found many of them," she corrected herself.

Apart from the obvious reasons, such as gaining a much clearer picture of what we were dealing with, the decision to show up on the doorstep of one of these women without so much as a phone call (I assumed, at least) seemed unpredictable. I liked knowing what we were walking into.

"You found many of them," I repeated, looking out the window and focusing on one tree at a time. A grounding technique of mine.

She nodded, waiting for more of a reaction than the one I'd given her.

"How?" I asked.

"It was the day I returned the dictionary to the library," she said. "I was curious, so I found the archived yearbooks, and looked through the one for the class of seventy-six. I tried matching faces, and once I got names, I got addresses, current information. Anything that would help."

I'd thought Alice wanted to steer us away from the society, but there she was, driving us right to its door. If this didn't worry her the way reading that dictionary did, I needed to know why.

"I thought you wanted to take a different angle."

"I did. This is another one."

"Did you consider what we read in that journal? It wasn't exactly an episode of *Full House*."

She smiled sadly. "We need more information, Stella. We're in the dark about too much to move forward with this. This project, this, whatever you want to call it."

CLOSE-UP: Alice's hands grip the steering wheel tighter.

She needed more information. She needed to meet the woman. After everything she'd gone through to get that far, she needed answers.

And I realized I wanted to get them for her.

I sighed. The moving landscape was easier to watch than her.

"Which one?"

"Bottom left," she said. "Jeanne McLeod. The only one who settled within driving distance."

She had short, chestnut hair and pale green eyes that pierced through the hazy quality of the long-expired film. She had been mid-laugh when the picture was taken, with her head tilted back ever so slightly.

"And you found the others, too, you said?"

"Almost all," she said. "There were three girls in that photo who weren't, from what I could tell, in the yearbook."

Three girls didn't graduate with the rest of them.

"Aunt Daphne, as you know, dropped out at the end of the semester." She paused before continuing, "Professor Shaw wasn't in there either."

Madeleine Shaw hadn't graduated? The information came as a surprise, naturally, as it seemed out of character. It made me wonder what had happened between freshman and senior year that made her leave.

Before I could ruminate too heavily, I realized the magnitude of what came next. The third girl—the one Alice couldn't find in the yearbook. The third girl who didn't make it to graduation.

The only girl whose whereabouts were unknown.

"Which one is she?" I asked.

Alice glanced over at the photo before returning her eyes to the road.

"Next to Daphne."

There she was, with pale blond hair, wearing a plaid skirt that stopped just above her ankles. Daphne had her arm around her, cradling her head close to her own. It was a peculiar feeling, looking at her. Knowing that it was her ghost that had haunted me.

Around ninety minutes into the trip we exited into the suburbs, and continued on back roads, Alice entrusting me with the map. Eventually we came to a stop in front of a blue house with a stone walkway that led to the front door.

When Jeanne made her first on-screen appearance, the only attribute consistent with her headshot was that of her eyes. They glowed like sea glass, shifting through a pattern of emotion when she saw Alice and me standing before her.

From surprise, to confusion, to disbelief.

I remembered who she had actually been looking at when she uttered merely two words.

"My *God*."

SCENE 38

———

I'd begun to sink into the yellow couch cushion when Jeanne brought us each a cup of tea.

The scent that reached my nose before the liquid could reach my lips made it difficult to suppress a wince, tea never having been my refreshment of choice. But I wouldn't tell her this. Instead I smiled and glanced around the room to look otherwise occupied.

The tall, arched windows provided a view into the backyard. There was a swing set placed near the back fence, and a slide fit for a small child, though, from what I could tell, she was the only one at home.

I studied our reflections in the gold, ornate mirror that hung above the fireplace, making note of the way my cheeks had hollowed further over the recent weeks and the way Alice stared into her teacup rather than making eye contact with our host.

Jeanne sat down in the olive-green armchair to our right, smoothing down the fabric of her dress before crossing one leg over the other. She smiled.

"I apologize for my, frankly, inappropriate reaction earlier. It's just, my goodness, you look so much like her."

Alice smiled politely, although I was sure she'd grown tired of hearing that. She took a sip of her tea.

"Please, don't apologize," she said. "I'm just happy to be able to talk to someone about her. Someone who knew her, back then."

Jeanne nodded. "Yes, of course, well, tell me. What is it that you'd like to know?"

We'd entered her home under the guise that we were there to learn more about Daphne. That Alice was hoping to understand what she was like when she was younger. We'd planned to only talk about the society if it came up naturally. And no matter where the conversation took us, there was one subject we would not broach.

We would not mention Madeleine Shaw.

"I think I'd just like a clearer picture of her back then." Alice stared wistfully at the floor. "I remember bits and pieces from when I was young, but unfortunately, it wasn't until I'd grown up that I felt I could really start to understand her."

"I see," she said. "I can tell you that Daphne was always the most sparkling person in the room." She leaned forward and placed her cup on a saucer set on the table between us. "She had this zest for life. She was always trying to get us to do this or try that, and, to be perfectly honest, I was always envious of how adventurous she was."

I watched Jeanne's expression as she spoke, soft and gentle, the complete opposite of Professor Shaw.

She leaned back in her chair and continued, "I'll never forget, this one time, we were walking back to the dorm late at night. And, you know the fountain on the west end? Well, it was hot out, and she dropped her things, ran over, and jumped right in."

She laughed at the memory and studied the ceiling. Looking down at Alice next, her smile fell.

"I'm so sorry to hear she passed," she said. "I always wished we did a better job of keeping in touch, but after she left, it was difficult. What with still being in school, and she didn't really say goodbye. We didn't have a chance to get her information, or anything."

"From what my mother told me, she came back a different person," Alice said. "She hinted that something happened that semester."

Alice waited for Jeanne to take the bait, but when all she did was sigh and nod, Alice pressed further.

"What was it, do you know? Was there some turning point?"

"Well, I would have to agree with your mother. Toward the end of the semester, she certainly didn't seem like herself." She paused, hesitating. "I'm not sure how much you know about that year, but if I had to pinpoint a moment when things started to change, I'd say it was after our friend Becca left."

Alice perked up. "Becca?"

I thought back to the third girl who hadn't graduated. The blonde that Daphne had her arm around. I thought of the journal entries, the nameless author. It was her.

I then considered her wording. She said she *left*.

"Yes, she was another one of the girls in our little group. She and Daphne were actually the closest of friends at the time, and Daphne took it pretty hard when she left school. Wasn't quite the same after that, and then she herself decided to leave." She picked up her tea and took another sip. "As you can see, our group took quite a hit."

She laughed lightly, but there was something in her eyes that conveyed discomfort. Alice seemed to notice it as well. I saw her look down, trying to understand what we'd heard.

As the silence dragged on, our host grew increasingly perplexed. I decided to step in and cover for Alice while she worked through the information.

"Why did your friend Becca leave?" I asked.

"She actually never told us," Jeanne said. "One day, out of the blue, she was just gone."

Her answer only added to my confusion. Not only did our mystery girl leave the school of her own volition, according to Jeanne, but the reason for her departure had been undetermined. How had there been so much she didn't know?

"Surely you had some theories," I said, gulping my tea. (Anything to mask my uneasiness.)

"Oh, of course we did."

She moved to the edge of her chair, as if she were about to let us in on a secret.

"It actually wasn't uncommon for girls to drop out that year. I knew one or two from different groups who left as well. I think a lot of the new female students didn't really know what they were getting themselves into. It's hard work, after all, thriving at such a prestigious school. And there was a lot of pressure on us as the first class, so it was no surprise that some couldn't handle it."

"So, what," Alice said. "You thought she dropped out because she couldn't keep up?"

"Something like that, yes. She had started acting strange around the end of our second month there. She stopped going to Mass, she stopped hanging out with us, even. We couldn't really keep track of her. Then, one day, she was gone. We figured she didn't tell us because she was embarrassed. Which is understandable, but I would've hoped she'd known that we wouldn't have judged her for something like that."

I thought of the gap in time I'd found in the journal. The days that were missing.

A lot has happened since my last entry. Things I couldn't have predicted.

Could it have been the truth? That she'd left the school for some perfectly logical reason?

But in reality, they're more than that. They exist, hidden underground.

No. She had been down there. She had been scared.

When I looked at Alice, I desperately hoped that she could read my mind. That she could tell where I thought she should steer us next.

When she looked back at me, she seemed to understand.

"You said my aunt didn't take that well, correct?" she asked.

Jeanne sat back once more. "She didn't. From the moment we realized Becca was gone, she started to panic. She swore something had been terribly wrong. Of course, none of us knew where this was coming from. We all thought she'd seen as little of her as we did over the course of that, what was it, a month? But apparently they'd still been in regular contact, and Daphne felt she had reason to believe that she didn't just up and leave. She even…"

I felt myself lean forward involuntarily, as if I could will the words to leave her mouth.

"She even started saying all these things about tunnels. That they existed, and they had something to do with her 'disappearing.' It actually got to the point where rumors had spread around campus, these mutated versions of Daphne's fears. Suddenly everyone was saying they found a body down there."

The teacup I held began to shake. I put it down on the table, balling my hands into fists.

Assuming what she had told us was correct, Daphne had been the one who started the rumors about The Girl in the Tunnels. She'd been responsible for the inception of the myth, the one that had woven itself into the fabric of the school.

But there was something else about the way Jeanne spoke of the tunnels that didn't add up.

She spoke as though she didn't believe they existed. As though she'd never been there.

"So, you didn't think the tunnels could have had anything to do with it?" I asked.

She looked at me like I'd just insulted her choice of lampshades.

"Of course not," she said. "Everyone knew, deep down, that they didn't exist. But the drama of it all, well, college students eat that up, as I'm sure you know. So, the rumor gained traction anyway."

"But...my understanding was..." Alice searched for the right words. She didn't want to give away our sources, after all. "From what I'd heard from my aunt, it sounded like you had all been down there."

Jeanne appeared to be stifling a laugh.

"My goodness, no," she said. "They were always just rumors. I always did find it odd that Daphne turned to them as an explanation for Becca's leaving. I suppose it was her way of coping. Finding someone to blame."

"But your society?"

I shot Alice a look, worried that she'd ventured too far. Her face told me she hadn't meant to say that out loud.

But Jeanne nodded.

"Oh, yes, there was that. We'd always met in this little hidden room. I trust you'll understand when I say I won't tell you where. Because of the *secret*, of course."

Too late, unfortunately.

"We ate, we talked, we studied," she said. "We were all very studious, hence why we were selected in that first year. Let's see, what else. We listened to music. I gained a new appreciation for the classical stuff. Vivaldi was Becca's favorite. I can't count the number of times we listened to "Summer," terribly bleak but it really does grow on you, doesn't it? It did become our song, in a way. But I'm getting off track."

She paused, looking between the two of us.

"But I don't see what that has to do with the tunnels."

"It doesn't," I said quickly. "I think we were both just curious."

Alice tugged on the hem of her skirt. I could tell she was uncomfortable with the conclusion being drawn. A conclusion that strayed away from any of the routes we'd imagined prior to arriving. Our understanding of the situation had been so different from the account we were hearing, so either Jeanne was telling the truth, and they really had no idea that the tunnels existed, or she was lying to us.

"It's unfortunate," I said, improvising. "The way it all went down, I mean. That she left without saying goodbye, and that she stopped spending time with you all. Probably trying to keep up with all that work."

I watched for any sign of a falter, anything that might suggest she wasn't faithful to her story.

Her face showed nothing of the sort. She seemed to only want to elaborate further.

"Although, of course, that may not have been the only reason she'd been distracted. At one point we did actually think she had started seeing somebody, but she was always so secretive about it. Would never admit to anything, would never give us a name." Her eyes lit up suddenly, like she'd remembered something. "Actually, *one* time I remember that she did slip up, not enough for us to learn anything valuable, granted, but I just remember that she had called him D."

I could feel the color draining from my face. I could see it in the mirror, too.

I watched Alice put her teacup down out of the corner of my eye. Her leg had started bouncing.

I reread the journal in my mind.

But D was very clear. We can't trust any of them. And I trust D.

I silently repeated the words over and over again. It had never occurred to me that D would have been anyone other than Demeter.

But what if I'd made a mistake?

What if there had been another player involved all along?

Jeanne studied the two of us from across the table, and I didn't want to know how we looked to her in that moment. The two of us were silent, neither knowing what we could possibly say next.

When Jeanne's eyes moved from me to Alice, I saw them widen with recognition. She reached out and pointed at her.

At her neck.

"That's so funny," she said. "Becca used to wear a necklace just like that."

SCENE 39

———

"She was lying."

Alice walked back and forth across my room with her hands clasped behind her back. Monica sat at my desk, playing with an old Super 8 camera I'd gotten at a garage sale, and Meg stood at the mirror with Josie, helping her hold her forest green gown for the Presidential Gala up to her shoulders.

The minute we'd walked through the door after returning from our afternoon excursion, the three of them had been there, waiting for us like parents staying up to make sure we got home before curfew.

"And just where have you two been?" Josie had asked, peering over the top of her book.

Once they overcame the shock of hearing who we had been visiting (and once Monica overcame the offense of not having been invited), they wanted to hear every detail. So, we told them what Jeanne told us.

And they were just as confused as we were.

"What does she mean they never went into the tunnels?" Meg asked. "It was all right there in the journal."

"Technically, it wasn't," Monica said. "I'll admit, we did a little bit of inferring, as all historians must, but I still don't buy it."

"She was lying," Alice repeated. "She had to have been. It just doesn't add up otherwise."

"Not to be the one who doesn't believe, again," Josie said. "But what if she was telling the truth? What if this girl just couldn't handle the work and left without telling them?"

Except we knew she didn't just leave. We knew for a fact that she'd been in those tunnels. We knew that it was the last thing she wrote in that journal.

It was the rest that didn't seem to fit together.

I closed my eyes, reclining on my comforter as I listened to all of them theorize back and forth. I'd been pretty quiet throughout the whole discussion, going over everything in my head as it was offered up for debate.

"My aunt had to have known something the others didn't. That's why she started the rumors."

But how could she have known something the rest of the society hadn't?

"Well, we know that this Becca character went down there. So, what if she was the only one?"

"The society still exists, though. And they meet there, we know that."

So, Jeanne had to have been lying, right?

"How the hell did you get that necklace, Alice?"

And who did the initial belong to in the first place?

That final detail had certainly thrown me for a loop earlier that afternoon. I had been so sure that the D in the journal had stood for Demeter, and that it was simply another tactic to remain anonymous. Then again, I knew that still could have been the case. But learning that there had been another

D in Becca's life made the chances slim, and I couldn't seem to figure out just what role he might have played.

I remembered what Alice had told us the night she revealed the truth about her aunt.

FLASHBACK:

"She'd see my necklace, and she'd get upset. She'd say it wasn't mine, that it didn't belong to me. I'd tell her that she had given it to me, and she'd insist that wasn't true."

FLASHFORWARD:

"Stella."

I opened my eyes, pulling back into focus. The scene in front of me consisted of the four of them, staring wide-eyed in my direction.

"Yes?"

Monica walked over and jumped onto my bed.

"It seems we're in a bit of a standoff. Two against two regarding whether or not Jeanne was lying," she said.

"Wait, Monica," Josie said. "I thought you agreed with me and Meg. Which side are you on?"

"Murder. Always."

She turned to me and leaned forward onto her elbows.

"So, what's it going to be, Stella? You're the deciding vote. We can either pursue Shaw and the society or do something else that we haven't thought of yet."

Slim pickings.

But aside from the conjecture and the "he said she said" of it all, there were a few things that had remained constant throughout our investigation.

1. Becca had found the tunnels.
2. She disappeared right around the same time.

3. There was someone on campus who knew what happened. Someone who wanted to expose it.

There was only one course of action that would allow us to find out what it was that needed exposing.

"I say we go after the society."

Monica smiled, pleased with the verdict, and Josie conceded more willingly than usual.

Alice somehow looked both relieved and anxious, and I realized I still hadn't tried to find out what she was so on edge about.

"That's what I like to hear," Monica said. "Speaking in academic terms, if I may, we have researched, gathered evidence, and have now come to the part of our project where we need to form a conclusion. The maiden's identity has been uncovered, we've navigated the Labyrinth, so all that's left is to unmask the Minotaur."

She'd moved off my bed to go and stand on my desk chair.

"To catch a monster," she said. "We need to set a trap."

CLOSE-UP: Alice's face as bits and pieces of a plan visibly form in her mind.

"Meg," Alice said. "How likely is it that you can add a song to your set for tomorrow night?"

"Depends on the song, but it shouldn't be a problem."

"Good."

There was a desperation in her voice that I couldn't ignore. She almost appeared nauseous.

In all honesty, I wasn't feeling much better. I had agreed to moving forward with whatever plan they put together, but I couldn't shake the feeling that we were still missing something.

I knew, deep down, that there was something I had been forgetting.

"Using the Gala?" Monica asked. "Doesn't that seem risky? There will be a lot of people there."

"Exactly," Alice said. "Everyone will be there."

She grabbed a piece of paper and a pen off of Josie's desk and started scribbling.

"I think that our best move is to send the fourth message. A message that everyone will hear, but only one person will understand."

OVER THE SHOULDER SHOT: Alice holds the paper toward Monica, who smiles.

"Well, it's a good thing I do my best work last minute," she said. "It looks like we have just about twenty-four hours to prepare our final presentation."

SCENE 40

——

If we're being honest, there were far less glamorous ways to catch a monster.

Though you can't reasonably hold a premiere prior to the film's release, we certainly felt like we were on the Red Carpet, striding toward the newly refurbished doors of the Main Hall. I looked down as we reached the top of the steps, curious as to whether or not I'd find any remains from that first message. In the wake of all that had happened since then, that day had begun to blur in my memory, a flashback getting harder to locate.

Meg had arrived an hour or so before us to warm up with the rest of the orchestra. I watched as she traveled down the staircase to meet us, her slate-blue gown falling so that she looked like she'd been floating. With her blond hair knotted up onto the top of her head and her sheer, puffy sleeves, she looked, simply put, ethereal.

Monica whistled as she approached, but Meg was more focused on easing Alice's questioning stare.

"All set," she said as she looped her arm with mine.

Other students had already started to fill the ballroom, the larger-than-life chandelier lit to fill the space with a gentle, warm glow while a string quartet played opening melodies in the corner.

CUT TO: our slow-motion entrance.

Unfortunately, I felt those who watched the five of us walk in did so not simply because we'd caught their attention, but because we remained shrouded in myth. At least, that's what it tends to feel like, doesn't it? When you walk into a room, and no one can take their eyes off you, you assume the worst.

Our reunion with Meg was short-lived as she left to rejoin her musically inclined companions and make final preparations for their set. I scanned the room, going through the plan again in my head. It was risky, what we had in store. There was no guarantee it would work, or at least, that it would work in the way we had intended. What if the message was too obvious? We couldn't cause chaos. It would get in the way. But what if it wasn't obvious enough, and not even the person we were targeting took notice? A missed opportunity. I didn't know when we'd get another chance with everyone together like we were that evening. I was afraid that we'd have to withstand more time wondering, plotting, filming. I was afraid of it all crashing down around us.

But I was also afraid that it would work perfectly, and we'd find ourselves in over our heads.

We stood by the refreshment table, each of us noticeably on edge. Even Monica couldn't stop running her hands up and down the velvet fabric of her mulberry dress. Alice looked like she might hurl, and Josie busied herself with drinking innumerable glasses of the apple cider they'd put out for students in champagne flutes.

It occurred to me then that we were some of the only students with a rigid lucidity about them. Those around us were already laughing and moving without care, unaware of those outside their immediate interest. It made me think everything might go according to the script.

The camera pans around the outskirts of the room, inspecting each of the faculty members in its path.

Stop.

There she was.

She wore a black silk gown that fanned toward the floor and an emerald-green shawl that hung loosely around her shoulders. Her hair was pulled up and around to the back of her head, providing a clear view of her face. I didn't know what it was about the way she looked in that moment that sent sirens shrieking in my head. There was something about her I couldn't place. That same nagging feeling had returned, the one that told me there was something I still couldn't see.

I turned away quickly when her eyes searched the crowd. I could feel them land on me. On us. But I refused to look back, to even hint that her presence was something we took note of. Especially that night.

Somewhere in the time since we'd arrived, the quartet had ceased its operation and joined the larger body of instruments, the music having grown only to be trapped by the ceilings that told stories of angels and the heavens. Two songs in, our countdown began, and I touched my hand to my neck as I felt the shallow burning that made a home there, my skin clammy with anticipation. Josie clutched her stomach, having just tossed away another flute of cider. She fanned her face.

I was about to try and offer words of encouragement when the three of them flashed award-winning smiles in the direction of something, or someone, over my shoulder. I spun around.

Clay was making his way through the crowd to us, and I felt bad for not wanting to see him in that moment. It wasn't the best timing, after all.

"You all look beautiful," he said as he approached.

"Clay," Monica said. "Looking dapper, as always."

He grinned and pushed his glasses back up his nose, then straightened his bowtie for effect. Placing a hand on my shoulder, he guided me a few steps away from the group.

"How are you?" he asked.

I looked back, not wanting to be separated from them for long.

"I'm good," I said, distracted.

He tilted his head.

"Are you sure?"

"Why wouldn't I be?"

"Well, with everything going on, with what people are saying, I just wanted to check in on you."

I remembered the past week of chatter and stares, but the bead of sweat traveling in my hairline took the front seat. I shrugged.

"It's just talk, Clay. Nothing I haven't heard about every other girl at this school."

His face dropped. His eyes filled with worry.

"Stella," he said. "I know that's not how you feel."

SOUND CUE: Clay's voice fades into the background.

My breathing quickened as I checked to make sure the girls were still behind me, by the drinks. The beat of my heart attempted to catch up to the swift pacing of the music. I could hear it. It was almost time.

SOUND CUE: Clay's voice fades back in.

"Stella, you can talk to me about this."

"Can I?" I snapped, regret instantly washing over me.

He looked like a hurt puppy, standing there, unable to meet my eyes. It wasn't fair of me to lash out at him, I just couldn't shake the feeling of the walls closing in around me, with no way to stop them. The music slowed as the final notes were played.

"I'm sorry," I said. "I need to find—"

The sound of a microphone being tapped rang throughout the room. Everyone's attention was drawn to the main stage, where our student body president, Sam Hebert, stood awkwardly.

Zoom in. Meg, who sits behind him, looks for us from the stage.

"Excuse me, folks," he said, nervously glancing around the room. "I hope we're all having a wonderful evening so far. Let's have a quick round of applause for our dazzling orchestra."

He held his arm toward them. Claps filled the air.

"I just wanted to fulfill a quick request. It seems we have a dedication for this next song."

He reached into his jacket to pull out a piece of paper, unfolding it with shaking hands.

"Huh," Clay whispered. "I didn't know you could do dedications."

FLASHBACK:

"I caught him cheating on our History of Medical Sciences midterm last spring while he was in the running," Monica said. "I knew it would come in handy."

"Ladies and gentlemen," Josie mocked. "I present, our Judiciary."

FLASHFORWARD:

Sam cleared his throat before continuing. "Let's see here, yes. This next song goes out to someone, 'You know who you are,' with a special message," he squinted at the paper, "11.14, MH, for one last dance. See you there."

From a brief sweep of the room, it didn't seem like anyone found the message to be anything other than a love-induced shout-out.

Sam glanced up with a confused smile. "Romantic. Anyway." He motioned toward the orchestra again.

The conductor raised his baton and they proceeded to play "Summer" by Vivaldi.

I ran my hands down the sides of my dress, ridding them of sweat. When I looked back to the refreshment table, Alice, Monica, and Josie were gone. I started to walk in that direction, but Clay grabbed my hand, stopping me.

"Let's dance," he said.

"This isn't really a dancing song."

"Yet, people are dancing. Come on."

He pulled me out into the center of the floor, twirling me around like he did on the night of my birthday. Only with less exhilaration and more paranoia. My mind was all over the place as I tried to catch a glimpse of the others. They had disappeared. The only faces I saw were those of strangers, crowding around us. I struggled to get air to my lungs.

"Clay," I said. "I need to find them."

He ignored me, pulling me in for a quick dip. We were halfway into the song. The clock was ticking. The room looked fuzzy.

When he went to spin me again, I felt a hand on my arm. Alice.

"Stella," she said. She looked at Clay. "I'm so sorry, I need to borrow her real quick."

And with that, she pulled me away, dragging me to the periphery. My heart rate slowed, my vision clearing and my legs regaining their strength. I followed her toward the door, toward our destination.

"Where are the others?" I asked.

"Waiting for us," she said.

I looked back toward the stage. Meg was set to join us as the band replaced the orchestra for the evening. Our song was winding down, coming to a close.

When we exited the ballroom and made a path for the stairs, Alice stopped abruptly, forcing me to almost stumble into her. When she faced me, I saw that she no longer looked nauseous or nervous. Instead, the color that had drained from her face and the way her hand shook holding mine told me a completely different story.

She was scared.

"Alice," I said. "What haven't you been telling us?"

She exhaled, her breathing shallow, her eyes looking anywhere but my face.

"You can't keep things from us anymore. We're all in this with you now."

If our message had worked, we were going to be walking into something serious. Something real. She couldn't continue to leave us in the dark.

"I know," she said.

I heard clapping coming from the ballroom. Meg, I assumed, was on her way.

When Alice still hadn't spoken, I added, "I've had this feeling, for the past week, really. Like we're missing something. Like there's something we skipped over somewhere."

"I think we have," she said, finally looking at me.

I urged her to continue.

"Stella," she said. "I can't help but feel like this is all a lot bigger than we realize. That we're walking into something much more serious."

My stomach turned. "What makes you say that?"

"The book. The dictionary, I mean. Remember how I showed you that the years continue all the way up to this fall?"

I nodded. How could I have forgotten? It was like the rug had been pulled from beneath us.

She breathed deeply. "Well, they don't just go forward."

I searched her face, trying to understand. Although, I thought I was beginning to.

"They go backward, too," she said. "They go way back, before 1972."

The sound of someone running toward us interrupted my ability to process what Alice had just told me. Meg arrived, breathless, some of her hair falling into her face.

"You guys," she said. "Are we going?"

CUT TO:

We traveled down into the darkness once more, Alice's flashlight (which she'd hidden in a bush near the back of the building earlier that morning) guiding us. We didn't know how long we had to get down there, only that, if all went according to plan, she would be following us. She would find us down there, waiting for her.

"Monica," Josie whispered. "Do you think Sam knows you potentially screwed him?"

"There's always plausible deniability," she said. "But if that doesn't work, don't worry, he deserves it."

We reached the bottom of the stairs, the concrete cool against my bare feet. (You didn't expect us to trek down there in heels, did you?)

SHOT: our gowns drag along the ground, our feet peek out from beneath the hems.

We traveled the rest of the way in silence, should anyone have been listening, as I tried not to look behind me into the nothingness. There was a chalk drawing we passed, on the wall to my right. A crow perched within a wreath. It was the same crest I'd seen on the teacup. The same one I swore I knew from somewhere. Seeing it a second time, I still couldn't place it.

Coming to a clearing, we stopped and looked at the differing pathways that branched from it. There were six of them, all leading to destinations unknown. We hadn't been there before. I was sure of it.

"Alice," Meg said. "Are you sure we're going the right way?"

Alice turned in a circle. "I swore I made the exact same turns we did last time."

Monica sighed. "I suppose we never discovered an 'Ariadne's String' type of parallel in our research. A map, or something."

We stayed huddled together, following Alice as she shined her flashlight down each of the seemingly identical paths. We were lost.

"Maybe we retrace our steps," Alice said.

But after turning in circles and trying to tell the difference between the routes, there were two that could have been the one we had taken to get there. Alice's flashlight shifted back and forth between them.

"Oh no," Meg said, lowering herself to the ground like she had that night in the attic.

"It's okay," Monica said. "We'll just pick one, right? They all lead somewhere."

Alice shook her head. "But that ruins the plan. We were supposed to make it back to that same spot."

Just as the damage began to feel irreversible, Monica held her hand up and shushed us.

I listened. At first I couldn't hear anything. Nothing but the cold breeze that flowed past us. But, suddenly, it came into earshot. A sound, getting closer.

Footsteps.

Heels.

SCENE 41

I would've recognized the sound of those heels anywhere.

They seemed to be coming from the left of the two routes we'd been torn between, the noise bouncing off the walls that funneled it straight to us.

We couldn't see her. Not yet.

SHOT: *Meg, hunched over on the ground, looks up, slowly.*

As she got closer, I could hear the swishing of her dress, the fabric scraping against the concrete. Alice kept her flashlight trained on the darkness. But that was all there was.

Seconds, almost a minute later, she appeared, shading her eyes with her hand. We didn't say anything. We just looked in shock as she sped up, striding all the way to us until she put her hand on the flashlight and pushed it, directing it toward the floor. She stared down at us.

"Are you insane?"

It wasn't the reaction we were expecting, I'll say that much.

But she was there. In front of us. It had worked.

And yet, seeing her, I didn't feel that sense of accomplishment I'd thought I might. I didn't feel proud, or pleased, or relieved in the slightest. Perhaps, it was because she'd asked us if we were insane. Perhaps, it made me stop and think that maybe we *were*. That maybe we'd gotten it all wrong.

That we'd made a serious, potentially fatal, error in judgment.

"It was you," Monica said, her mouth slightly agape. "We were right."

Were we? She looked angry, but not like someone who'd just gotten caught. She looked angry like someone who was concerned. Someone who was worried. For *us*.

But she'd understood the message. She had met us down there, which meant she had to have thought it was real. That whoever had sent the other three messages decided to send one more. A request, for one last dance.

So, I asked myself, yet again, what was I forgetting?

"You have no idea what you've done," she said.

"What *we've* done?" Alice asked. "We know everything, Professor."

What was it?

"You know nothing," she said.

"We know about the journal. We know you took it."

The journal. There was the journal.

"I was trying to keep you away from all of this."

SHOT: the camera inches toward my face.

Their voices echoed, bombarding one another. I tried to block them out.

"Keep us away from what, exactly? From your society? From the truth?"

Think, Stella. Think.

"What secret was so dark that you had to kill her?"

I couldn't remember. It didn't make sense.

"Why did you kill Becca?"

Becca.

The name hit me like a ton of bricks, pummeling me, scraping away at my skin. The temperature dropped further. I thought I saw my breath materialize before me, a cloud of ice soon whisked away so that the fog could clear. I saw her there, through a new lens. A clean one.

Becca.

Rebecca.

"It's you," I said.

The voices stopped. They disappeared, right into thin air. I ignored the way my friends were looking at me. I spoke only to her.

"Isn't it?" I asked. "You're her."

I was met with silence, and a wary look she couldn't shake. I'd reached into the back of my memory to produce that theory, but her hesitation only confirmed its validity. She was the missing piece. She had to be.

"I'm who," she challenged.

"You're Becca. You're Rebecca," I said.

FLASHBACK: Sister Catherine approaches her after the Opening Mass, extending her hand.

"Rebecca?"

"No, I'm sorry. I'm Madeleine Shaw. The new classics professor."

FLASHFORWARD:

"She recognized you," I said. "Sister Catherine. Despite how different you look, there was a part of you she remembered. She was your teacher."

Her name was, oh gosh, not again…Sister Kate, I think?

Despite her unwavering expression, I saw her facade crumbling before my very eyes. The anonymous author, The Girl in the Tunnels. She was alive.

How was she alive?

What did that mean?

The disoriented look on Alice's face stung me, the way I could see her putting together pieces we didn't even know were in play. She had expected this the least of all of us. That the answers she had been searching for were under our noses the entire time.

"Is that true?" Alice asked, looking at our professor.

"Are you *her*," she stressed, when she received no response.

She, Rebecca, deflated. "I am."

A stunned quiet. A theater after the last person leaves, the lights shutting off, the reel of film slowing to a stop.

Only this movie wasn't over yet.

"You've been alive this entire time?" Monica asked. Though, it wasn't as much a question as it was a statement of disbelief. A realization that a key ingredient had slipped right through our fingers.

For the first time, Alice looked truly, undeniably lost. She stared at the floor with her shoulders slouched. I wanted to help her, but I didn't know how.

Her voice was weak when she said, "You couldn't have let her know that you were okay?"

She didn't say who, but she didn't have to. We all knew, even Rebecca.

"I didn't have a choice."

"She thought you died."

"I *did* die."

There was a sharp edge to her voice. It made me flinch, cowering away from the invisible blade she'd swung. I waited for her to speak. We all did. It was her turn to talk.

"The girl who went into these tunnels twenty years ago was not the same girl who came out. I knew I could never be her again, and not just because of what happened. I couldn't look in the mirror and see her. I couldn't let anything remind me of that night. It ate away at me, it..."

She trailed off, clutching her chest.

"It *hurt* me. I had to become someone else, so I changed my hair, my name, practically everything about me. And, all of a sudden, I didn't see her anymore. I could breathe, I could live."

I let the information I'd just heard sink in. She had lived through whatever happened down there, but in another sense, she hadn't. What had happened to her? What did it have to do with the secret society?

The more I thought about it, the more the answer seemed to be...nothing.

They exist, hidden underground. I've seen them.

She said, "*I've* seen them." She never said, "we've." And Jeanne had insisted they'd never been down there.

But if she went down alone, as she seemed to be implying, what did she find? I needed to know the big secret.

I tried to remember what Jeanne had told us.

She had started acting strange around the end of our second month here.

At one point we did actually think she had started seeing somebody, but she was always so secretive about it...I just remember that she had called him D.

But D was very clear, she'd written in the journal. *We can't trust any of them. And I trust D.*

"The boy you were seeing," I said. "Did he have something to do with this? With the tunnels?"

She looked at me, and despite how much we were coming to understand about her, her face continued to reveal nothing.

"I'd met him in one of my classes," she said. "We had so much in common, we both loved mythology, it just seemed to work. I guess we thought we were in love, and one day, he said he wanted to show me something. I never could have imagined that this was what he meant." She motioned to our surroundings. "He was very clear, though. He told me because he loved me, but I couldn't tell anyone. No one else could know, not even my friends. I agreed to keep their secret."

Their secret. I looked at Alice, who returned the gaze. The dictionary, the dates that went further back than 1972. There was a society down there, but it didn't involve the Seven Goddesses.

Alice had been right about one thing. The entire time, we had been so focused on figuring out what those seven women had to do with the tunnels, that we never once stopped to think that the reality may have been much larger. We never considered the possibility that they had been just as in the dark as we were.

"But what made you change your mind?" I asked. "What was going on down here that you needed to expose?"

A look of confusion spread across her face. She tilted her head.

"I didn't come down here that night to expose their secret," she said. "I needed to tell him my own."

A lot has happened since my last entry. Things I couldn't have predicted...I have to tell someone. But I don't know if D will understand.

It wasn't supposed to happen like this...I'm terrified of doing this, but I don't think I have a choice.

She had to tell him something that she didn't think he'd understand. She'd been acting strange, and she had been avoiding her friends. She clearly felt a sense of urgency.

Could that mean—

"You were pregnant," I said, looking up at her to gauge her reaction.

For the first time since I'd met her, I saw her expression soften. Behind the hard exterior she always wore I saw a young girl. A girl who had been scared. A girl who had a secret, and who needed to tell the boy she loved.

But something had gone wrong.

"What happened?" I asked.

It was the tipping point. She could turn back and leave the way she'd come, her new reality remaining almost entirely intact, or she could offer us the final key, and risk everything by revisiting that night.

Her movements were slow and careful as she tugged her shawl closer around her shoulders.

Her voice was faint as she abandoned her shield of armor.

Timid, as she said, "I was eighteen, at a Catholic school during the first year they even let women into this place, and I'd gotten pregnant. I wasn't ready for any of it. I didn't expect him to react well. I was terrified. But I thought that, if I explained it correctly, we'd be able to figure it out. I'd put it off for too long already, it was becoming obvious. So I made the decision to come down here, where I knew they'd be gathering. Was that stupid of me? In hindsight, perhaps, but I tried to time it so that they'd be done with their meeting. I wasn't thinking, I was scared. When I got down here, there was all this commotion. The boys were freaking out because I'd seen them, because I knew. I remember the way they looked at me, and the way they surrounded him, threatening him. 'You better take care of this,' one of them said. He assured them he would, so they cleared out, and when I tried to talk to him, he was so angry. He had this crazed expression on his face. I've never been able to forget it."

She stopped to catch her breath. I noticed her hands trembling.

"I told him what had happened. I begged him to help me, to stay with me, but he just kept yelling. He didn't care that my reputation would be destroyed, he didn't care that I'd have to do it alone. All he cared about was what would happen to him, now that they knew he'd revealed their existence. It wasn't something they took lightly. He kept repeating that it was my fault. That I ruined him. And, of course, that made me angry, so I yelled back. That's when I made my biggest mistake. I *did* threaten to expose them. All of them. I said that if I was going to go down, then I was going to drag him down along with me."

Her voice sputtered out, an engine that no longer had the strength to run. I had a feeling I knew where she was headed, I think we all did, but it still came as a shock, to hear her finally muster the will to say it.

"The last thing I could remember was lying on the ground and him kicking me," she said.

I looked at the woman who stood in front of us as she desperately clung to the identity she'd cultivated over the twenty years that led to that moment. But with each new piece of information she shared, Madeleine Shaw seemed further and further out of reach. I worried that, by the time we were done listening, she'd find herself unable to look in the mirror yet again.

Josie spoke up. "But you made it out. Couldn't you have told someone? The administration?"

"Who do you think it was that cleaned up his mess?" she replied. "I woke up the next day in the hospital with a stranger telling me the baby didn't make it. And the next thing I knew, they were paying me to leave quietly, to never breathe a word of it to anyone. I shouldn't have been surprised. His family practically owned the place. Christ, all those boys were Legacy. They were untouchable, no matter what rules they broke, no matter who they hurt. And they wanted me to disappear, so, I did."

"But you came back," I said. "You came back to expose the truth. You were the one behind all the messages."

She nodded, and the events of the previous few months reworked themselves in my mind. An accusation, a story, and a threat. Not for her, but by her.

Because there had been a life taken in those tunnels, it just wasn't hers.

It frustrated me, how wrong we'd been. Although, I supposed I had answered correctly in class that one day. A lack of consequences could prove quite dangerous. It could prove dangerous to the people who walked above ground without any idea of what was taking place below, and who were made vulnerable to ensure someone else's safety. Like Rebecca.

"I didn't just want to expose him, I wanted to expose all of them. They're the monster, the entire society. They believe they're invincible."

Immortal souls, I remember thinking, they do not fear death.

But then I froze, the realization dawning on me. "Wait. That means he's still here, right? D?"

"Yes, and that's why we have to leave. He heard your message, too. I'd assume he thinks I was the one who sent it."

Alice had been quiet for some time, the blank look on her face telling me she had been absorbed in her own thoughts.

"She fought for you," she said. "And no one believed her."

"I never told her about any of this," Rebecca said, her voice laced with a sense of urgency. "Never concretely, at least. I'd hinted at it a few times, more after I realized what I'd gotten myself into, but I was serious about keeping my promise to him. The furthest I went was leaving those clues for her, before I went down here. I left the location of the entrance in her favorite book. I left the necklace, which she clearly found." She motioned to Alice's neck.

Alice yanked off the piece of jewelry, the clasp bursting. She held it in the air.

"This was his, then. He gave this to you, with his initial."

Rebecca's head shot toward the direction she'd come in. "Did you hear that?"

"What was his name?" Alice asked, tears threatening to spill over. "What does D stand for?"

I suddenly heard what Rebecca had. I listened closer. More footsteps.

Someone else was coming.

"Alice." I put my hand on her shoulder. "Alice, she's right. We need to leave."

Meg looked queasy again. Monica shifted back and forth.

"What does D stand for?" Alice repeated, insistent.

"It's not *his* initial," Rebecca said, her voice rising. "It was for his code name. It's a D because I called him Daedalus."

Alice's face fell as she lowered her hand to her side. The footsteps had grown much louder. It sounded like they were right there, just beyond us.

"Why did you call him that?" I asked quickly, looking over my shoulder.

But Alice answered on her behalf, her voice gentle, all of a sudden.

"Daedalus," she said. "He's the architect."

SCENE 42

———

CLOSE-UP: Josie's devastated face as Max Aldridge emerges from the darkness.

I, like the others, was surprised to see Alice's charismatic architecture professor striding toward us.

Actually, I can't use the word, "surprised," like it was some trivial coincidence. Like we'd turn and say, *Oh, hello, Professor! Fancy seeing you down here!*

Take Two:

It was bone-chilling, seeing him step out from the same tunnel we'd taken. The fact that our eyes had somewhat adjusted to darkness only made him look more menacing. A shadow of a person. A shadow of a monster.

And when Alice directed her flashlight toward him, real shadows were cast all along the walls, a mammoth, mirror image of him.

I took a step backward, startled by the feeling of an elbow grazing my back. I looked behind me. It was Monica's, and there was nothing between me and him but what little distance I could create.

When he saw the six of us there, he sighed. "I guess we both failed at keeping the kids out of this, didn't we, Rebecca?"

He paused, tilting his head back. "Or is it Madeleine, now? It is, isn't it?"

He smiled, like it was all an amusing game to him.

"Although, I will admit I wasn't expecting to find all of you down here. I guess you five are more resourceful than I thought." He looked around at each of us, before settling again on Rebecca. "I take it you weren't the one who wanted that last dance, then. It's a shame, I was really looking forward to it. But, I have to hand it to you, you did have me spooked with that first message. I had no idea who it could be. It was like a ghost, haunting me."

He waved his hands through the air with mock drama.

"And then there was that football game. The funniest thing, I saw you, and I knew there was something about you that struck me. Something I couldn't quite put my finger on."

FLASHBACK: Her stare is cold, and pointed, and personal. But it's not directed at us, or Alice. It's directed at him.

"Then, finally, when I read that poem in the paper, it hit me. It woke me up." He placed his thumb and middle finger together and snapped. "It was *you* that I saw. You'd come back."

He stepped forward again, and it felt like I had nowhere else to go. I prayed he couldn't hear my heart beating the way I could.

"And then you actually used *my* station," he said. "That stung a little. I suppose that's what I get for taking you there all those years ago, showing you the ropes. It made me look bad. But I think, deep down, we both know that it doesn't matter how I look." He smiled and spoke like he was pushing a dagger further into her heart. "I will always be safer here than you are."

I didn't know if she couldn't think of a response or simply had nothing left to say to him. Perhaps she didn't want to give him the satisfaction. But I did notice her grip on her shawl tighten. I noticed her eyes glance around to a few of the paths open to us.

"You should've stayed away, Rebecca."

She winced when he said her real name again.

"We could've avoided all of this." He paused and turned to Alice. "But you. You still would've looked."

I didn't turn around to see Alice's reaction. I kept my gaze trained on him. On the direction of his feet, on the subtle movements that might have told me his next move.

"I was curious when you first asked me for those plans. You weren't as sly as you thought you were, I'm sorry to say. But it was seeing you reading *Black's Law Dictionary* in Studio that really did the trick, and confirming it with the library records was easy enough." He looked at the ground. "I did try, you know. To keep you all out of it. I mean, the boys even volunteered. They said they could handle it. They insisted they knew what would make you break."

My stomach twisted.

He shook his head. "Pity it didn't work."

I felt my throat threatening to close. The rumors, the lies, it was them.

"I assume you've already heard, but I found myself in quite the predicament that night. My very first semester. I wasn't left much of a choice in the matter. I had to clean up my mess, and even then, they never let me hear the end of it. We had to be careful, from there on out. Move even further underground. Any hint of our existence had to be snuffed out entirely, and it was all because of you, Rebecca."

"Any repercussions from that night were of your own doing," she said, finding her voice.

"If you hadn't come down here in the first place, none of it would have happened."

"None of it *had* to happen. No one forced you to do what you did."

He ran his hands down his face. "What don't you understand? We have a *code*. It was bad enough that I told you about us at all, and then you said you were going to tell everyone. I mean, what did you expect, really? The society takes precautions, they have insurance, they know what to hold over your head."

He took a step back and leaned against the wall, crossing his arms. Calm. Collected.

His voice was light as he added, "But I say we leave the past in the past. You already know what happens next. You leave, we compensate you for your trouble. Only this time, I'd really prefer it if you didn't come back."

"You can't just make me disappear again," she said. "I'm going to tell them. Everyone. It's all going to come out."

He stifled a laugh. "Rebecca, darling, I appreciate the challenge, but let's be realistic. You do know they won't believe you, right? I'll make sure of it. We all will. I can't tell you how many allegations we've had to squash over the years. It always ends the same way."

"You certainly weren't this confident twenty years ago. If you had been, I doubt you would've reacted the way you did."

"I was a kid, then. I thought my life would be over. I thought they'd get me expelled, and I'd lose everything. I couldn't let that happen. And then you kept pushing me, and I'll admit, I lost it. But in the end, I'd taken care of it. And when you left, without a word, that was when I realized how all of this works. You honor the code, and you're protected. And it only gets better as you get older." He shrugged. "Better for me, that is. But that's why I know how this ends. We'll always find a way to get rid of you."

Rebecca stepped forward. "You can't possibly do anything worse to me than what you did that night."

"Maybe not," he said, turning to address the five of us. "But I can do far worse to all of you. Those rumors were nothing more than whispers, in the grand scheme of things. If anything, though, they laid a foundation. I could have you all out of here in a heartbeat, on any charges. What do you think would happen if they believed you were the one behind those messages, Alice?"

Max moved toward her, only stopped by Rebecca's hand on his chest. I glanced to the passage on my right, wishing I knew where it led. Wishing I knew it could get us out of there.

"Let's not make this any harder than it needs to be," he said.

I took the brief intervention to look back at Alice, who shook her head. We didn't know what to expect next. Was that it? After everything we did, was *that* how the story would end?

But Rebecca wasn't ready to give up.

"You know people aren't just ignoring the messages I sent," she said frantically. "They're nervous. The press is already showing interest. What do *you* think would happen if I talked to them?"

"Come on," he said. "We've dealt with the press. It isn't hard to get ahead of stuff like that—you'd be wasting your time. Especially since we'd get to them first."

"And what if I already talked to them?"

A pause.

He studied her face, looking for hints of a lie beneath the stone mask she managed to reconstruct. His eyes narrowed as he tested the waters.

"You're bluffing."

There was a tremor in his voice. She noticed it, too.

Capitalizing, she asked, "You really never considered that? You didn't think they might already have all the answers they need?"

I could see his nostrils beginning to flare, his jaw tightening. For the first time that night, she smiled. "I told you it was all going to come out, Max. You didn't believe me."

His movement was swift. I almost missed it, him grabbing her arms, his grip so tight that he had to have been crushing them.

"What did you do."

When she didn't answer, he let go, running his hands through his hair.

She took a step toward him, rubbing her arm. "Those messages weren't for show. I meant what I said; you're not as safe here as you think. I don't care about some code. I don't care about insurance. I don't care that you think you know how this ends, Max. Because you don't."

As cornered as I felt, he was the one who looked it. He paced back and forth like a caged animal, and she took full advantage of his captivity.

"And how do you think the society will feel about *finally* having to go down for your mistake?"

What happened next made me wish that I had done more in those twenty years of my exercise-free life.

Because I certainly wasn't strong enough to try and defend her when he lunged.

Yet, I did it anyway

I saw the move coming, stepping out in front of her to bear the burden when he crashed into me. Down we went, the back of my head colliding with the cool ground. Needles poked and prodded at my skull. Tiny bugs crawled from the center of my brain outward, the surrounding environment worlds away.

I barely saw the two arms wrap around his neck and pull backward.

I barely heard the commotion going on around me.

I barely felt the hands that grabbed me, lifting me into a seated position.

The camera was out of focus, the audio on the fritz. I could provide you a blurry picture only.

SHOT: *a face, Alice's, I think. She looks at me, holding my head up.*

She says, "Stella, go."

So, I did.

I rolled over onto my stomach and crawled. The concrete scraped against my palms. My dress began to catch beneath my knees, pulling me back down to the ground. I managed to lift myself onto my feet, only to fall against the closest wall. I followed it, traveling deeper into one of the tunnels.

The ground shook beneath me, though for a moment I thought I'd imagined it. I felt more hands grab me, steadying me, and I looked to my left and saw that it was Alice.

"Are you okay?" she asked.

I didn't get to answer before she turned in the direction we'd come from, her eyes widening.

"Keep going," she said as she left me, and ran back there.

My vision was clearing, the ringing in my ears growing duller by the second. I heard voices from the clearing. I heard Josie say, "Meg, this way." There was arguing I couldn't make out.

I told myself to keep going. Just a few more steps, Stella.

I stumbled into the wall once more, leaning on it for support as pain morphed into dizziness.

I'd just made it to another turn when I heard it.

The scream.

THE DELETED SCENES

THE DELETED SCENES

—

Alfred Hitchcock once famously said, "The trouble today, is that we don't torture women enough."

Eloquently put, Hitch. But I'm afraid I'm going to have to play devil's advocate on this one.

Hitchcock believed that there was a great deal of the psychological within the visual, as well. His belief that to torture the woman was to torture the audience, his admittance that his male leads shared his fears, those that prompted them to watch, stalk, and punish the female characters, it's all very telling, don't you think?

But, more than anything, it goes to show just how seriously each cinematic experience both influences and is influenced by the director's psyche.

Your experience was, after all, certainly influenced by mine.

I'll admit, every film, every story, really, has something that's missing.

It could be entirely accidental. A simple, coincidental omission. It could be the shortcoming of the storyteller's perspective, POV, limited scope. But it could also be intentional, a manipulation of the facts. A carefully curated set of scenes designed to send a message of one's choosing.

It can be an effective strategy, rewriting a story. It can, as Alice so astutely mentioned, give you control over a situation in which you had none. A situation in which you couldn't have known any better. An answer that you wanted to ignore.

But that's not facing your fears, is it?

And, unfortunately, I think the only way that all of this is going to work is if I tell the complete and unedited truth.

Because I'm afraid I haven't been perfectly honest with you.

It's nothing too major, don't worry, just the stubborn, inner workings of my mind facilitating the withholding of certain vulnerable, yet critical, pieces of information. Typical, really.

You see, I've told you a story. A classic mystery with bold heroines and despicable villains. A tale in which our leading ladies battle adversity and may even emerge victorious. They solve the case, try and take down the bad guy, and the world, you assume, will be a better place.

But while there are certain, important clues I may have purposefully, accidentally omitted, you'll notice that I haven't yet told you how it ends.

Figuring out where to begin the end. That's tricky, isn't it?

I suppose I'll tell you that another thing I learned from my studies is that sometimes the best villains aren't always the most obviously despicable. No, the most *common* villains are complex. Their wrongdoings are not the only defining elements of who they are.

And these common villains are often those you allow into your life.

They're pesky things, rumors. They eat you from the inside out, taunting you because they know that anything you try to say or do to squash them only feeds them. But isn't it easy, you might wonder, to ignore a rumor that isn't true? If it's simply a myth, does it matter? And I might say, perhaps you're right. Perhaps remembering that the baseless opinions of others don't define you is all there is to it. It's certainly a level of security to strive for.

But I told you that my own rumor, the one started by the secret society, was something I had been indifferent to, when that wasn't the case. And I didn't tell you that there had, in fact, been an element of truth to it.

I was made to believe that it had been no big deal. That the situation I found myself in during that one party in the fall of my freshman year was normal. After all, hadn't it technically been my choice? Hadn't I made the decision to stay, instead of to leave? Hadn't I made the decision to drink, instead of to remain lucid? I had to have known better. But, don't worry, this kind of stuff happens all the time. It could have been much worse. Remember that, Stella. Remember that it could have been worse.

It's when the reminders start to fail you that you run into trouble. Your rewrites get messy, your cuts sloppy. You realize that you've been wandering the Labyrinth over and over again, searching for the Minotaur. Praying that you'll find it, and slay it, so that you can put an end to whatever it is that haunts you. But, however long it takes you, you come to the conclusion that there's no one else down there. It's just you.

And you've grown quite lonely, indeed.

So, no, I didn't just brush off that rumor that appeared to have graced each set of ears I interacted with. Because the reality hidden within the fiction had been something that haunted me.

Because I had only shared it with one other person.

I hadn't suspected him until a few more of the pieces had fallen into place. The society that still existed, that had always existed, made entirely of Legacy boys. Boys that could plagiarize and get off scot free. Boys that could run naked across the Main Quad each year without fail. Boys that could throw a party, after which three girls are taken to the hospital, and the authorities would simply turn a blind eye.

Speaking of Charlie's party, I told you that their greeting looked awkward. I said that he was always awkward around boys he didn't know. But I didn't tell you that what made it all so awkward was the way it seemed like they did know one another, but weren't supposed to.

So, here are two other things I didn't tell you:

I didn't tell you that I remembered where I'd seen that crest. The one on the teacup, and the wall of the tunnels. The crow perched within the wreath. It had been hanging on his wall, for me to see when he gave me my birthday present. I didn't tell you that, when I'd asked him about the tunnels that day in the library, he removed his glasses, inspected the lenses, and wiped them with a cloth. Instead I showed you Alice, the person I'd been wary of at the time. It goes to show just how much you can miss in a close-up, when you can no longer see the bigger picture.

I guess I thought that, by protecting him, I was protecting myself. I had trouble coming to terms with the fact that his allegiance to those boys, in all their twisted glory, outweighed his allegiance to me. I had trouble grappling with the humiliating realization that you don't know someone as well as you thought you did, especially when they know everything about you.

But here's to being vulnerable.

Alice was always vulnerable. She said what she meant and meant what she said. And she'd been right about a lot of things, things I doubted would ever be true. Like what she told me under the moon, when I asked her just who she thought I was going to fall in love with.

She said, "With you."

I still have the picture she took of me that night, and each time I look at it, I remember to keep proving her right. I owe her that much.

Now, if I'm going to really bring it home, there's one final scene I haven't shown you. One last chapter of this story. It's a difficult thing to write on paper, what really happened that night. But I can't rewrite it. I can't cut it. I have to show it to you for what it was.

Besides, I promised you a dead body, didn't I?

But first, another quick lesson in the art of omission: word choice.

I told you a dead body would be found in the tunnels beneath our school, but there's more to it.

I was the one who found it.

SCENE 43

––––

The scream sobered me.

I was suddenly jolted awake. The battery recharged and the system rebooted.

I peered around the corner to find an empty path leading back to the clearing. But I couldn't see down that far. I couldn't see any remnants of what might have happened.

I tried to remember who the scream sounded like it had belonged to. It was Alice's. Or was it Monica's? Shaw's? I mean, Rebecca's?

With all the focus I had placed on the sound, I realized I didn't pay attention to what came next. Whatever had preceded it or followed it. I hadn't listened for anything else.

The only way to know what had happened was to go back there.

I made my way down the right side of the tunnel, dragging my hand along the wall to keep my balance. I guided my mind toward focusing on the feeling of the coarse stone against my fingertips. I welcomed the slight discomfort as a distraction.

I heard something else as I got closer. Small noises, like the sound of breathing. The sound of wheezing. Someone was gasping for air.

I saw the clearing approaching, and pushed forward, not allowing myself to think about what I might find there. I saw someone sitting on the ground to the left. Rebecca, I realized. She was grasping at her neck, her chest rising and falling dramatically. When I squinted, I could see red, swollen marks there. Scratches. Her eyes were wide. With fear, maybe, or shock. She was looking up at something.

She was looking up at someone.

I can't explain why I sped up. I simply felt this desire to face them, whoever they were. I strode with purpose, preparing myself for the possibilities of what I was about to see.

The clearing was right ahead of me. I braced myself to turn the corner.

Lights. Camera. Action—

I jerked back the second I turned, the familiar feeling of fireworks igniting behind my eyelids overcoming me once more. I raised my arm to shield my face, thankful as the burning began to subside. My eyes cooled. I lowered my arm slowly.

I let out a sigh of relief when I blinked away the haze and saw that it was just Alice, who managed to catch me off guard yet again with her industrial size power lamp. I smiled, but she didn't return the gesture.

Her face was white as a ghost. If anything, she looked a little green. I noticed her teeth chattering silently. She looked at me with pleading eyes that said, *Help me, Stella.*

Then I heard the dripping. My first instinct was to look above me, to see if it was coming from the ceiling, like the last time we were down there. Running water, I'd thought I heard. But the sound wasn't running water. I knew that.

It was the sound of droplets falling one at a time, splattering against something. Something soft. Something that cushioned the fall.

Alice lowered her flashlight to the ground. As I followed the beam, I noticed that there was something dark trickling from it.

Zoom in.

Blood.

The flashlight was covered in blood, I realized. It was running all along the side, a trail even finding its way back to Alice's hand, painting her skin. I willed myself to glance down at what the drops of the crimson substance had been landing on.

It was a face.

Max Aldridge's face. His eyes were still open, but lifeless. The back of his head was bashed in, blood pooling in the crater that remained there. I forced myself to look away before I could no longer stomach the sight.

I focused instead on the beam of light that illuminated him, and the dust that danced within it, gravitating toward his skin. I decided to watch the particles float in search of refuge. His face was the ground upon which they landed like ash, Alice the raging fire that sent them to him.

Roll Credits.

CREDITS

——

It is now time to extend my sincerest thanks to the cast and crew. The cast being the ever-dynamic figments of my imagination (good work up there! you did it!), and the crew being every person without whom this book would not exist.

I think I'll start by thanking my professors. *The Dust That Danced* is, in a sense, an ode to my favorite classes at Notre Dame, and no matter how interesting the subject matter, a course always has as much potential to crash and burn as it does to inspire. I count myself lucky to have been inspired by many faculty members throughout my four years in college. Those who made homework fun and assignments rewarding. Those who made my family dread the mini-lectures and fun facts I might relay to them over the phone. Those who, above all, made me realize that one of the most fulfilling qualities you could have in life is the fierce desire to simply learn.

Whether or not any mention of your class made it into the final manuscript (I wanted each and every intellectual tidbit to contribute to the narrative—to foreshadow, to reveal— rather than to simply exist), I want to make sure the part you played did not go unnoticed. While preparing to return to school for one final semester, it crossed my mind that the thing I might miss most about college is all of you.

To my family, thank you for spending countless hours listening to my thoughts and my fears, and for being some of the earliest readers of the novel. To Emily, thank you for staying up late on FaceTime to listen to me work through my ideas. To Matthew, thank you for your unyielding determination to talk through time zones from across The Pond. To Mom and Dad, thank you for your stubborn refusal to do anything other than wholeheartedly believe in me.

To Dr. Karen Latham, thank you for dedicating your time and energy to provide such helpful feedback, and for remaining a supportive advisor of mine long after my high school days.

To my early readers and sounding boards, Anna Garatoni, Dessi Gomez, Grace Wang, Julia Gately, and Phil Lally, thank you for welcoming the responsibility with open arms. (And to Anna and Julia, thank you for welcoming the responsibility of my emotional fragility with open arms, as well. And for constantly reminding me that I should probably go to sleep.)

Thank you to Ilia Epifanov, my Developmental Editor, for putting up with the incoherent mess that is my thought process, and to Christy Mossburg, my Revisions Editor, for managing to keep me on track (a truly difficult thing to do, I must say).

Lastly, I can't forget to thank everyone who pre-ordered my book, my ebook, or contributed to my pre-sale in any way. Without you, *The Dust That Danced* would merely be a rough cut that never made it to the big screen.

Adam Brock
Alisha Sehgal
Ana and Darryl Antonacci
Angela and Dan Gimbel
Beth and Bob Enck
Beth Garatoni
Brenda Sharp
Brooke Ferrer
Caitlin O'Brien
Caroline Antonacci
Cerra Antonacci
Claire Cahill
Dessi Gomez
Elizabeth and Arnie
    Mascali
Elizabeth Pryor
Emma Ascolese
Emily Cavuto
Eric Koester
Ethan Brown
Gad Liwerant
Haley Newlin

Jack Mascali
James Sumantri
Jenna Gimbel
Jill and Michael Mundenar
Julia Gately
Lee and John Stamoulis
Mae Rose Dolan
Marie Cavuto
Mariya Pozdeyeva
MaryClare Hanley
Matthew Cavuto
Megan Crowley
Michael Shaich
Nancy and Ron Shaich
Nina Raman
Philip Lally
Robin Antonacci and John
    Cavuto
Rosemarie Andres and
    Frank Prendergast
Zev Burton

DIRECTOR'S STATEMENT

I strongly believe there is a point in every person's life when they realize that the thing they want most is to fall in love with being alive.

A sit by your window for twenty minutes to watch the snow fall, kind of love. A wake up in the morning with an urgency to experience what the world has to offer, kind of love.

Our lives are composed of scenes, the sequence of which will often follow no logical order. We move from one to the next, growing, evolving, experiencing that which we couldn't have possibly predicted, and we are left with the daunting task of trying to make sense of it all. So, what do we do? We rewrite, we edit, and we cut. We create a film that is far more comprehensible to us than the one that is playing—a film within our grasp, subject to our control.

But there are only so many revisions you can make before you forget what story it is that you are trying to tell.

Last year, I was given an assignment. I was to close my eyes, get comfortable in the director's chair, and watch the movie of my life. (It sounds whimsical but stay with me.) During the screening, I had various run-ins with younger selves and "inciting incidents" that came together to shape my story. I saw myself at three, twelve, eighteen, twenty-one, and throughout each of those moments, my job was simple: look at it for what it was.

"Simple," yes, *that's* the word.

When all was said and done and the reviews began to trickle in, the biggest critic in the room found herself walking away with the sense that there is much to be gained from facing your past head on. And she was so inspired by the realization that she decided to do something big.

She decided to write a book about it.

We often associate the phrase "growing up," with our childhood and adolescent years. We think of the coming of age movies where the protagonist overcomes some hurdle and ends up a better version of the person they once were, all set to continue into adulthood with their newfound perspective. Now, I can't speak for anyone reading this, but I know for a fact that I changed more each year of college than I ever did throughout the eighteen years that preceded it. I learned more about myself in the four years often dubbed "the best four years of your life" than from any of the obstacles that stood in my way on the road to get there. So, when it came to determining how to tell this particular story, I knew instantly that it was meant to be set in college.

I am of the firm opinion that the experiences of women in college cannot be communicated through statistics. The statistics that attempt to illustrate such experiences are not only obtained as the result of the rare willingness to share that which we often keep hidden, but are also rooted in the assumption that the things we go through can be concretely defined. However, they are not black and white. They do not fit neatly into certain categories.

Therefore, when crafting a story meant to detail the female collegiate experience, I realized I would need to leave certain areas up for interpretation. Because—spoiler alert—women are complex. And—you guessed it—so are the circumstances in which they may find themselves. Despite the elements or facets of emotion that we do share, I was not in the position to define what it means to be a woman in college. I merely aimed to breathe life into a narrative that gives credence to the notion that any battles we fight, no matter how "big" or "small," are worth recognizing.

One of the things I've loved most about my past four years as a film student is developing a better understanding of the world around me. The major has provided me with the means to grapple with questions of why we think and behave the way we do. It has offered me a lens through which to view history, science, love, and the ways in which the various components of the human experience manage to intersect. It has given me the opportunity to look at life through the eyes of another, and to learn more about myself as a result.

One of the areas of cinema that I find most fascinating, as you may have already guessed, is its relationship with psychoanalysis. The ways in which our psyches inform what is shown, what we see, and what we take away from a given story. The ways in which directors utilize a set of psychological tools, whether or not the decision is a conscious one. Within this sector, you'll find a term you may or may not have heard before: the male gaze. Whether or not you're familiar with its name, you are almost certainly familiar with what it looks like. You've seen it in the way the camera travels up a woman's body when a man watches her. You've seen it in the way time stops when she enters the room, the narrative unable to resume until he allows it to. You've seen it in the way she is assessed from a distance, studied in a manner that indicates that he can learn whatever he needs to know about her by simply looking.

Taking a step back, you'll find that most women operate under this gaze every day. We watch each other the way men watch us. We feed into the narratives constructed around one another, without pausing to question their validity. And when we fall victim to the gaze, we often look inward, and find fault within ourselves. I decided to utilize these cinematic elements of psychoanalysis, among others, to help inform our narrator's own psyche. A narrator who, for most of the book, is only suspicious of other women. A narrator whose arc is illustrated by her albeit subtle shift from the male to the female gaze. Constructing the internal mechanisms behind Stella's perspective was by far one of the most dynamic tasks I was faced with in the process of writing this book, and I enjoyed every second of it.

I also found joy in sprinkling each central character with a bit of myself, until I felt I'd told a story that is as real to me as it is to others. I was able to put all the time I've spent immersed in my own head to good use—the daydreams that have entertained me for years, the apologies I've had to offer my mother when she realizes once again that, even though I said "yes," the answer was, "no, I didn't hear what you said." I was able to be brave and accept that, if I was going to move people in the way that drove me toward storytelling in the first place, I could no longer remove myself from the stories I tell.

So, I created five central characters. All of them are me, and none of them are me. (And you're probably wondering, *wow, is she really that multidimensional?* To which the answer is, yes, I really am.) But I wanted the women who read this story to see themselves in our leading ladies as well. I wanted them to see themselves in Stella's tenacity, in Monica's wit, in Meg's kindness, in Josie's complexity. And I wanted them to see themselves in Alice's belief that, no matter how much time you spend lost in the Labyrinth, you can always find your way out. You can always fall in love again.

And for all the time they spend sleuthing, and discovering, and fighting their way toward the answers, they spend just as long learning, and laughing, and taking in the world around them.

They embody what I learned from that assignment I was given a year ago. They embody what Henry David Thoreau wrote, as quoted by Neil Perry in *Dead Poets Society*, "I went to the woods because I wanted to live deliberately. I wanted to live deep and suck all the marrow out of life… To put to rout all that was not life; and not, when I had come to die, discover that I had not lived."

I recommend you give it a shot, watching the movie of your life and looking at it for what it is. No rewrites, no edits, no cuts.

Because I believe that's all you can do—just watch the scenes unfold and find something truly cinematic about all of them. Just read what's in front of you and find poetry in every word.

After all, I'm certainly not the first person to fall in love with poetry.

Made in the USA
Middletown, DE
01 June 2021

40822276R00195